The Bold Stroke

a novel

by Barry Shannon

Copyright © 1999 by Barry Shannon

ISBN: 0-9666272-4-5

All persons, places and organizations in this book except those clearly in the public domain are fictitious, and any resemblance that may seem to exist to actual persons, places, events or organizations living, dead or defunct is purely coincidental. This is a work of fiction.

THE BOLD STROKE

Library of Congress Catalog Card Number: 99-65571

All rights reserved. No part of this book may be reproduced or transmitted in any form or by any means, electronic or mechanical, including photocopy, recording, or any information storage and retrieval system, without permission in writing from the author or his agent, except by a reviewer who may quote brief passages in a critical article or review to be printed in a magazine or newspaper, or electronically transmitted on radio or television.

TripleTree Publishing
PO Box 5684
Eugene, OR 97405

Cover art and book design by Alan M. Clark
Editorial services by Maggie Morgan Doran
Printed in the United States of America

St. Jones walked back to the plane, got inside and opened his flight bag. He put on his slightly used Second Chance vest and his .45 Colt 1911 shoulder rig. He covered the rig with a light nylon jacket from his bag. Then he pulled on the flight extender and snaked the tube down his left pants leg and velcroed the plastic bottle to his calf. Digging into the bag one more time, he came up with an ankle holster and attached it to the outside of his left ankle and inserted his Walther as a left-hand draw backup to his right-hand draw shoulder rig. He was running down his mental checklist of Mexican standoffs and Asian ambushes, when he saw the boys walking across the runway toward the plane.

Johnson opened the door and jumped into the right seat and turned on the SCR-16. "It's show time. Crank this puppy up and taxi into position. Jackson's on his way."

St. Jones started the engine and taxied to the centerline of the runway. They fastened their seat belts and sat idling, waiting for the signal to roll. The Reptile Brothers stood on the trail, just off the runway, and raised the net on Johnson's signal.

The Bold Stroke

a novel

by Barry Shannon

TripleTree Publishing
Eugene, Oregon

For those wasted along the way.

Somewhere in the Seventies...

BOLD

1

Revelations St. Jones was savoring the implications of the arrival of the black Lincoln limo at the curb downstairs. From his desk at the bay window, he had a view of the street below the older, Russian Hill apartment building and had watched the long, sleek car cruise by earlier. This time it had pulled to the curb and parked. He had been apprehensive all evening and was having trouble concentrating on the report he was writing and when the bell rang from the lobby entrance downstairs, it seemed inevitable, like the sound of one shoe dropping. He went to the intercom panel by the door and, salivating slightly, asked who it was.

"Delivery for St. Jones."

It was ten o'clock at night and he hadn't ordered out, and St. Jones was thinking that he had seen this movie not that long ago and he didn't like the way it turned out. Neither did the various monsters that lurked in his psychic swamp just beyond the light of the fire. But he overrode them, in clear violation of the Reasonable Man Doctrine, much like when jumping out of a perfectly good airplane, and pushed the button that buzzed the lock downstairs.

If the delivery man chose the 1920s vintage elevator there was an even chance he'd never make it, but if he took the stairs up three flights, then St. Jones had about two minutes to put on his vest. Pulling off his heavy, Irish wool sweater, he put on the Second Chance category III vest, velcroed the sides, and pulled his sweater back on. In the moment he had left, he walked to his desk and turned on the recording system.

This was something he'd learned to do early on in the business. Imagine his dismay upon learning that people will actually pay good money and then lie to a private investigator, and will occasionally even try to set you up in some way. A guy hired him once to find his missing wife and it turned out he had killed her and was using St. Jones to build his story. Tapes can be very useful in establishing innocence in such situations, as well as for later reference for missed details and nuances, and for possible voice stress analysis. And, taping freed him from taking notes so he could concentrate on the client, like in a poker game...the way they hold their cards, what they do with a cigarette or a drink, how they arrange their money. The interview, like the cards, is only a pretext for a much more subtle game.

St. Jones was tucking his Walther-PP into the appendix position under his sweater when the door buzzer sounded. In the movies, you can usually tell how you're doing by listening to the soundtrack, but other than Miles playing "Someday My Prince Will Come" on KJAZ, St. Jones didn't have a clue. He walked to the door and looked through the peephole and what he saw had the monsters checking for an open window. Even with the distorted image, St. Jones could tell he was huge, six and a half or seven feet tall, and wearing an Edwardian waistcoat, a bowler hat and Levis greasy enough to stand alone. When the giant bent down and leered at the peephole, St. Jones recognized the evil grin of the Angel Michael. The monsters peed on the rug.

To simply say that Michael was a Hell's Angel is like saying Idi Amin liked people. It just didn't quite cover it. Michael was right out of the Ancient Gallery, the guy with the black hood and the scimitar. He was one of the Turkey-makers, a small group of Angels who specialize in tying up loose ends and covering up mistakes.

St. Jones quickly explained to the weird zoo huddled damply at his feet that he was in good standing with the Angels and it was cool, and then he slid the dead bolt and opened the door, and kissed the Last Clear Chance Doctrine goodbye.

"To what do I owe the pleasure, Michael?" St. Jones asked, with as much confidence as he could manage. A glimpse of the sawed-off double-barreled 12-gauge hanging by a bungee cord under Michael's right arm wasn't helping.

""A" wants to see you." Michael was a man of few words. "He's waiting downstairs."

It was all starting to make sense now, and it was serious. "A" was the Angels' drug czar. Unlike the more visible members of the club, "A" wore tailored jackets and rode in the back of a limo when he was working. It was his office. He was a gentleman in a road warrior sort of a way and Michael was his driver. "A"'s status was such that no one said his name out loud more than once. Under most circumstances, to have them come for you meant you didn't have to worry about where you parked your car. But St. Jones had extensive dealings with them in the past and knew he was in good standing. Besides, what choice did he have?

"I'll get my jacket."

On their way downstairs, St. Jones thought back to his first encounter with the Angels. He wasn't a PI in those days. It was around 1970 and he was helping raise money to fund an event being staged to make the world a better place. Some serious rock and roll people thought it worthy and at that time in San Francisco, that meant something. Since Kesey's La Honda acid summit a few years earlier between the Angels, the Pranksters, and the Dead, the Angels had become political allies of the rock and roll scene.

It had been arranged for St. Jones to meet with T-Bone, one of "A"'s lieutenants, at the home of a rock band manager in Mill Valley. T-Bone was thick and bearded and bright and Jewish and St. Jones found him to be a very likeable and interesting guy, a criminal savant. While they were talking, "A" arrived.

"A" was charming in a day-tank sort of a way and dressed like a hip Montgomery Street executive, but his eyes followed you like a painting and when he laughed, St. Jones felt something cold grip his lower spine. He sensed the menace at an animal level and understood how "A" had risen to the position he held.

They did a few lines and talked about music and bikes and politics and the war. The Angels were very interested in the war and had volunteered as an irregular force before their political conversion. The Department of Defense declined the offer. Considering that it cost over one hundred thousand dollars per enemy kill, St. Jones thought the DOD made a mistake, until he remembered that was the whole idea.

As "A" was leaving, almost as an afterthought, he had handed St. Jones a gym bag with a kilo of cocaine in it and said T-Bone would be in touch. Just like that. Up to that time, St. Jones had bought a gram or two to party with and even a quarter ounce once in L.A. when he was deep-fucking a starlet at the Chateau, but he was overwhelmed by both the quantity and the trust of a very pleasant and extremely dangerous psychopath. One man's ceiling is another man's floor.

Predictably, St. Jones' career as a cocaine charity fundraiser had outlived the project he tried to save. But with his connection to the Angels, the money was just too easy and the entree' too seductive. His new charity had become the Church of the Hydrochloric Miracle and he had soon become a dope star. His clients were among the rock illuminati and the beautiful people on the "A" lists, straight and gay, and the only real winners were the superstar dope lawyers who kept them all on the street pumping money.

The coke whores and the star fuckers hadn't made it any easier to quit, but Halloween night, a guy he was supplying got into the product and went into an ego coma and ripped him off for a couple of kilos. Precept 16 clearly states that sooner or later everyone you know will go crazy on you. St. Jones had been on his way to send him to a better life when he had an epiphany...white powder and green paper are inanimate objects and fundamentally do not equal human life. What started as a revolutionary act, of sorts, had turned to karmic quicksand. It was time to quit. But he still had to see T-Bone the next Thursday night and he was down about fifty large. Trick or treat.

One of the rules of the Angels calls for the death penalty for any Angel who rips off a customer of the club in a dope deal. Consequently, they are the greatest guys in the world to do business with. They always do exactly what they say, and they expect the same.

Thursday night had come and St. Jones had the money, but this time he didn't take delivery of any product. He told T-Bone he was retiring. What he didn't tell him was he'd had to sell his Jag and his rug collection and his guns and cameras and all his toys and give up his house on Mount Tam to cover. It cost him everything he'd bought with the money he'd made and it put him on the street, and ultimately sent him to SE Asia, but it set him free from the dope opera he was living. He thought of it as his Method Karma period. As a legacy of his tour of the cocaine underground, St. Jones had a certain *cache'* with dope lawyers and the rock and roll criminal fringe. It was part of his stock in trade.

As he opened the door to the street St. Jones quickly scanned the block and stepped out into the cold San Francisco night, more curious than afraid. He wondered what "A" could possibly want with him. He wouldn't have to wait long to find out.

BOLD

2

Michael opened the door and with mock ceremony ushered St. Jones into the back of the limo and into the presence of "A".

"Long time no see, man." "A" was New York City Italian and aging well. He was as sleek as St. Jones remembered, wearing a finely made black leather coat of the kind fashionable among players in the seventies. "What's it been, seven or eight years?"

"Yeah, something like that. It's good to see you," St. Jones said, shaking "A"'s hand and settling back into the black leather upholstery. As anxious as he was to find out why this was happening, there was a kind of old world protocol to be observed and only after the formalities of hospitality would he find out what this was about.

The Lincoln began to roll through the fog down Russian Hill toward Alcatraz. Miles was still playing on KJAZ, giving a strange continuity to the scene. "A" poured from a bottle of Remy into a pair of snifters on the bar and handed one to St. Jones.

"Salud!" he toasted.

"Salud!"

"A" settled back into the upholstery with the sound of leather on leather. The limo turned left on Bay at the bottom of the hill and headed toward the Marina.

"For openers," "A" began, "when you cashed out back there a few years ago, I found out what happened, the burn and all. I heard you put yourself on the street to cover. That was very classy, not laying it off on T-Bone when you paid off. He sends his regards, by the way. Most guys wouldn't have done that. They'd have pissed and moaned and asked for more time."

"It wasn't your problem."

"Exactly! But most guys would have made it my problem."

"With all due respect, "A", doing business with you guys is like swimming in the deep end of the pool. Besides, like the man said in the song, you gotta be honest to live outside the law."

"That's what I've always liked about you, St. Jones. You break the law to do what you gotta do, but you're not bent, running against the wind, living against the law for the sake of it. But me, I would have blown the mothafucker away and I'd have taken his shit and turned his old lady out 'til it was square."

"I was on my way to do something a lot like that when I saw down that path all the way to the end and decided not to walk it. The asshole was trying to commit suicide anyway, using me for the gun. Guys don't do things like that unless they want to die. He just didn't have the guts to pull the trigger on himself and wanted to be punished.

Besides, when I first got into the game there weren't any guns. It was a gentlemen's business, not like it is now."

"Yeah, you're right, it's changed for sure," "A" sighed. "It keeps Michael real busy these days." The implications of that thought gave St. Jones chicken-skin.

They were driving along the Marina Green approaching the Presidio, the limo's tires slishing along the wet pavement. "A" took out a glass vial and dipped a small silver spoon into the white powder. He served himself and handed it to St. Jones. "Help yourself, man."

St. Jones took a hit and passed it back to "A". The coke was as smooth as the Remy. The monsters were curled up in a pile at St. Jones' feet. "A" was their kind of a guy. The limo passed under the Golden Gate Bridge beneath the toll booth approach and headed around the point toward Sea Cliff. "A" took another toot and handed the vial and spoon back to St. Jones. Recognizing the preliminary ritual to the main event, St. Jones took a good hit and passed it back.

"So your name came up yesterday, St. Jones." The monsters had their heads up, checking for an open wing vent. "A" reached into his inside coat pocket and came out with an envelope and handed it to St. Jones. "What can you tell me about this?"

"A" flipped a switch on the side console and a small airline-type overhead light came on. St. Jones lifted the flap and took out a single, small, typewritten piece of paper.

23, 15, 9, 124, 2, 11, 56, 23, 9, 78, 10, 9, 204, 34, 8, 44, 23, 1, 77, 22, 18, 190, 9, 9
CONTACT ST. JONES, S.F.   MAMA COCA

It looked like an encrypted fortune cookie, which in a way it was, and St. Jones thought he had seen the code before. He quickly totaled the number of numbers and when they divided evenly by three, he knew he was probably dealing with a book code. Each successive three number group was a page, line, and word number. It was the most secure of improvised codes. If you never used the same word reference twice, it was virtually as secure as the one-time pad, and unbreakable as long as the book used for encrypting was unknown.

"How did you get this, "A"?"

"It came in the latest shipment of motorcycle parts." That was how the coke was transported. "There were several of them scattered through the load, pressed into the bricks. There could be more that we missed. What does it mean? What are all those fucking numbers and who's Mama Coca?"

St. Jones felt the invisible hand and remembered whom he was dealing with. They were driving along the cliff facing the Golden Gate channel, an area where bodies were often dumped. It occurred to him that they probably drove that way out of habit.

"I hate to ask you about your business, "A", but where did this come from?"

"It's a righteous question under the circumstances. It came from Miami...Coconut Grove...Colombia before that. The usual route. I talked to the Grove today. They said they'd had other calls. Parts of the mother load went all over the country."

"Then the notes had to have been mixed into the batch at the lab in Colombia, right?"

"Had to have been. It's only distributed out of the

Grove. They don't cook it there."

They rode in silence through Sea Cliff while St. Jones searched his memory for a clue as to who Mama Coca could be. It seemed like something he should be able to easily recall, something right on the tip of his mind, but it was eluding him. He was beginning to fear the dreaded drain bamage. As the limo turned on Clement back toward town, "A" held out the spoon again. It was a signal that it was time for him to say something.

"Well "A", I think I recognize the code, but without the key it doesn't matter whether I'm right or not. Whoever Mama Coca is, she thinks I know the key, so maybe I do, but right now I can't come up with openers. But the thought of these notes with my name on them showing up all over the country in bags of cocaine scares the hell out of me. I'm legit now. It's not the kind of notoriety a guy in my business needs. I mean, if any of this load gets popped, I'm going to have a lot of guys with bad breath and suits to match wanting to talk to me in the worst way."

"Yeah, I see the problem. Well, that would explain the two guys."

"What two guys?" St. Jones' asshole clicked another notch tighter.

"When we first cruised by your place, there were these two guys parked down the hill in a gray LTD, watching your building through binoculars."

"I must be slipping. I didn't see any guys when we left."

"That's because they weren't there when we left, exactly." "A" was smiling that smile. "I didn't want them to see us together, so we parked around the corner and Michael paid them a visit."

"What did they look like?"

"A" pushed the switch on his console that operated the inch-thick bulletproof window between the front and back of the limo. "What did the guys look like, Michael?"

"Bad suits," he said over his shoulder. "They look like the same guy. Here's their stuff."

He tossed two wallets onto the bar. Tucked into one of them was a Federal type ID. St. Jones opened it and looked at the picture. Then he checked the driver's licenses in both wallets. Except for the different ties, they did look like the same guy.

"Know these geeks, St. Jones?"

"Yeah...it's the Narx Brothers. We have history. It's a long story. I'm almost afraid to ask what you did with them."

Michael and "A" were chuckling. "Tell him, Michael."

"I locked them in the trunk of their car handcuffed sixty-nine. They should be going steady by now." He turned around and leered at them.

Michael and "A" were cackling as the partition closed. St. Jones laughed for effect but he had mixed feelings. While he delighted in the situation, he also knew the Narx Brothers would never believe he didn't have something to do with it.

"The Narx Brothers, huh? You're full of surprises, St. Jones. Who are these assholes, anyway? This sounds like a good story."

"That's easy for you to say." It wasn't St. Jones' favorite memory. "A couple of years back, I'd been out on a long chase and I was severely burned out when I got back. The Marin Spin was killing me, so I went up north for a while to get away. I got a house in the country and opened a small office in town to keep my hand in, and took a few law courses at the local college.

"The Narx Brothers are identical twin brothers and both of them were local cops, but one of them got busted for selling drugs. The one that was still on the force continued to steal confiscated drugs and pass them to his brother to sell.

"I got involved in a dope defense case where Bro #2 was the arresting officer and Bro #1 sold my client the stuff. He swore it was the same guy. In the investigation, I tumbled onto their thing. When they learned of my involvement, they broke into my home and office, planted bugs and taps, sent wired bimbos around to try and get drugs from me, got into my bank account and followed me for months. And got nothing. So they went in front of a Grand Jury and lied like a rug.

"They busted me at five o'clock on a Friday afternoon, but I made bail in half an hour and they never got a chance to do the week-end jail house number that they'd planned. The DA was less than pleased when he had to drop the charges or have it all come out in court, so he did what most departments did with their garbage at the time and sent Bro #2, highly recommended, to the DEA. The Feds don't officially know about the evil twin, only that it suits their purpose to have an agent that seems to be able to be in two places at once. It's almost mythological. They're even Geminis.

"So now we have this Road Runner/Coyote thing going. Anvils are always falling on them and trains are coming out of painted tunnels and things like Michael are always happening to them. It's reassuring in a way because every time I begin to wonder if I'm on the right side, the Narx Brothers come along and prove it." St. Jones realized he was motor mouthing on the cocaine.

The limo was on Broadway, driving past Consulate Row, the black Lincoln blending into the neighborhood, about ten minutes away from Russian Hill.

"Jesus, St. Jones! You got snakes in your life. If I'd known that about the fuckers, I would've had Michael put them to sleep."

"Well, you know how it is, "A". Friends come and go, but enemies seem to accumulate." St. Jones quoted Precept 18.

"Fuckin' 'A' on that. I'm running out of places to bury them. I guess you heard about the farm."

St. Jones had heard. The police had uncovered more than twenty "mistakes" and were still digging.

"So it looks like you sort of got yourself for a client, St. Jones. What are you gonna do? Follow yourself around?"

"That's not that bad an idea. Everybody else seems to be doing it. I've wondered where I go sometimes. I'll probably tail myself down to the Grove, go see Bino and try to find out who Mama Coca is."

"I won't even ask how you know Bino."

"Oh, we have our own history, me and Bino, and it doesn't take a genius to figure out the connection." Bino was short for albino. He didn't have the eyes but his hair was white and his skin was the color of milk.

"Well, you're on your own down there. It's a territorial thing. You gotta duke your own self in."

"Understood."

They were on Taylor, in the saddle between Nob and Russian Hills, a couple of minutes away from St. Jones' corner.

"I appreciate you coming to see me personally with

this, "A". I'll let you know what I find out. Can I keep the IDs?"

"Michael will be disappointed, but he's got their guns and shit so he'll be okay behind the paper. This is their shit we've been snorting, you know. Some poor fucker probably fell for it."

"Maybe you oughta give me the keys to their car so they don't suffocate tonight."

"Fuck 'em...they're narcs. I should have Michael run their car off the end of a fucking pier. He'd like that a lot."

St. Jones paused long enough for "A" to think he was giving it serious consideration. He had a rep to maintain. "Maybe you could have Michael leave them in a dumpster with their heads tied together, shot through the hands."

"A" cracked up. "That's funny as hell, St. Jones. I gotta remember that. Wait 'til I tell Michael." St. Jones had a feeling guys who'd never play the violin again were going to start turning up in dumpsters.

They were a block up the hill from Green. "A" lowered the window to the front. "Pull over, Michael."

The limo eased to the curb. "I'm gonna let you out here. No telling who's watching your place by now. One for the road?" "A" held out the spoon. "Those fuckers have got better shit than we do. That's the part that burns my ass."

"It's a crime against nature." St. Jones took the toot. Michael had his own spoon out in front.

"Thanks again, "A"." St. Jones opened the door. "I'll be in touch."

"See ya, St. Jones. Watch the shadows."

He stepped out of the limo and closed the door and watched it glide down the hill leaving swirls of fog in its wake. St. Jones had a nose full of coke and a head full of strange ideas and decided to walk for a while, maybe go down to North Beach and have a drink. Walking down Taylor to Green, he turned the corner his building was on in time to see a wrecker towing away a gray LTD. The Narx Brothers had parked in a red zone, a very bad idea in North Beach.

If St. Jones hadn't been so loaded and enjoying the priceless irony of the moment so much, he might have noticed the blip on the screen sooner. He should have known something was wrong when the monsters took off, fast and low to the ground. The yellow Volkswagen was almost even with him before he recognized the silhouette of Lyla's Jewfro and it was way too late by then. With a thud of adrenaline, he felt his pulse pump in every part of his body as he saw the flash and heard the pop and then he was down on the pavement looking up at the street light, which was getting farther and farther away.

BOLD

3

The monsters were howling as they crashed through the underbrush looking for cover. St. Jones was slipping in and out of that dark tunnel behind the face of the clock and feeling very vulnerable lying on the sidewalk under a street light. The fastest way to a man's heart is, in fact, through his chest, as Precept 19 clearly states. Lyla was a good student, if nothing else. St. Jones' error was in disregarding Precept 14: "Never get in bed with anyone more fucked up than you are." St. Jones' problem was that he had a big dick and a high IQ and he knew how to use both of them well, though not necessarily at the same time. Simply stated, this was a case of lust gone awry.

St. Jones was a good-looking guy and women came easy to him. He was six foot two and one ninety-five and built like a swimmer. His shoulder length reddish blond hair and clear, very intense green eyes made him hard to forget, which was bad for the line of work he was in. It forced him to employ operatives, which he often did. But it was his eyes that made women crazy, and some believed he could read their thoughts. And when they believed that, he could, and Lola was one of them.

He met Lola at a party, at a time when he was scouting for someone to go undercover into a militant lesbian organization. She was beautiful and brilliant and "bi," and she knew the feminist rhetoric. She was six feet tall and weighed 125 and had an ass like a five hundred dollar mule, as an FBI agent from the deep South once observed. And St. Jones was an ass man.

He knew Lola had snakes in her head within minutes of meeting her, but she was like a book you can't put down. He had to read it to the end to find out how it came out. Having never actually encountered a multiple personality case before, St. Jones didn't fully understand what he had gotten himself into and by the time he discovered Lyla, he was strung out on the sex and couldn't cut it loose. The most interesting feature of Lola's madness was that the secondary personality of Lyla was not a result of some deep seated traumatic event or situation that she sought refuge from. It was more like Lola was a car sitting at the curb with the engine running and the door open and along came Lyla from points unknown and got in and drove away. St. Jones believed it was a case of possession, and, as they say, possession is nine tenths of the law.

Henry Miller observed that the more you fuck, the better you fuck, and St. Jones and Lola had gotten pretty good at it. They were on the road together for most of a year and the sex was incendiary and they were strung out like junkies, fixing three times a day wherever they were, and at night after dinner, they'd go out and pick up a girl together for dessert.

It kept going after they got back to San Francisco. Lola would encourage St. Jones to bring home other women. Sometimes she brought home other women. Sometimes they both did. And of course Lola was a *menage á trois* all by herself. Lola loved St. Jones, but unfortunately Lyla hated him, because she knew he knew who she was. And, there were other reasons.

Eventually Lyla dominated Lola and became increasingly violent toward St. Jones. This had become a bizarre feature of his life, like Clouseau and Kato, except for the hot sex and the live ammo. She had shot at him before, but this was the first time she had actually scored a hit and she put this one in the 10-ring. This was not a cry for help from Lola. This was Lyla. She'd been practicing and she meant to kill him.

The thought of her coming back for the *coup de grace* gave St. Jones the strength to pull himself up on the fender of a car and, still gasping for breath, lurch to the door of his building. Lyla would have shot him in the balls instead of the head. Lola loved his big dick but Lyla hated him for having it.

St. Jones keyed the door and was grateful to find the lobby empty. He still didn't have control of his breathing and was forced to take the 1920s vintage deathtrap of an elevator. But, like Camus said, a man dying of cancer never catches tuberculosis. When Death has found one way to you, It doesn't need another.

Out of the elevator, St. Jones still had a hundred feet of corridor to go. With any luck, if he ran into any of his neighbors, they would think he was up to his old tricks again, experimenting with the dose. When not otherwise occupied, in loving memory of Sherlock Holmes, St. Jones would alchemistically combine and recombine in various ratios, cocaine, cannabis, and cognac while carefully avoiding the deadly under-dose. It was an elusive thing that sometimes went awry.

St. Jones' luck held and he made it to his door. He crawled on his hands and knees to the bathroom and closed the door before turning on the light. Considering the events of the evening, there was no point in presenting a well-lighted target. After all, Sherlock was dead and St. Jones wasn't feeling that good himself.

Removing his jacket, he pulled off his sweater and unfastened the velcro on the sides of the vest and lifted it over his head. He wasn't bleeding but there was the beginning of a hell of a bruise directly on his solar plexus. The vest just became the best three hundred dollars he'd ever spent. Examining the impact point, he found the bullet, mushroomed almost flat, with two layers of Kevlar left. If he'd bought the cheaper vest, he would be dead. The base of the bullet was barely intact, and could have been a .380, 9mm, or a .38, .38 Special, a .38 Super or even a .357 magnum. They're all about the same diameter, but from the penetration of the vest and the way he hit the pavement, it had to have been the magnum.

Opening the medicine cabinet, he found some codeine tablets and took a few to get a jump on the pain he knew was coming. The monsters were beginning to straggle back to the edge of the firelight, whimpering. The next time they took off fast and low to the ground, he was going with them.

St. Jones put the vest back on and pulled his sweater over it. It was time to get out of there. Precept 9 is very clear on this: "There is no problem so large that it can't be run away from." When the going gets tough, the tough get going, and St. Jones was on his way.

Working by flashlight, he got his Halliburton flight case and the tennis bag he kept his work vest and equipment in, and quickly stuffed a small assortment of clothes into a leather shoulder bag. Crawling into his dark office, he noticed an LED blinking on one of the pretext line answering machines. Pretext lines are phone numbers used to support the legend of whatever case he was working. When not otherwise dedicated, these lines were answered by machines with messages recorded from the phone line of the voice of Ma Bell saying, "You have reached a number not in service at this time," etc. Only a very short list of people knew to listen past the recording and leave a message after the tone.

He rewound the tape and played back the message. "St. Jones, we've got a Code 53. Call me at home, ASAP."

He recognized the voice of Birmingham, senior partner in a law firm he was associated with. St. Jones was Minister of Intelligence and Tracking and did the investigative work for five attorneys as well as his own cases. A Code 53 was the Joker, the fifty-third card in the deck. It was company code for the slings and arrows of outrageous fortune. These were wild and crazy guys and a Code 53 covered a lot of territory.

St. Jones erased Birmingham's message and turned off the answering machines. No point in accumulating evidence. He had to assume that the Narx Brothers would hit the place like a meteor as soon as they were loose. He checked the VOX controlled room recording system. There were only the sounds of Michael's visit and St. Jones' return which he erased.

It was reasonable to assume that if the Narx Brothers had been sitting on his place, they had one of the Mama Coca notes, and if that was the case, they probably used it to go before a Federal Judge and get a Title III (U. S. Code). That meant that his phones were tapped, and they were reading his mail and going through his garbage and his bank accounts among other things. Not a pretty picture. But that was always a good assumption in his business and the reason St. Jones took rather elaborate precautions.

His telephone lines were terminated at the law office, and he used re-dialers to route his calls to and from the Russian Hill studio. While it hadn't been tested in court, his theory was that calls that physically passed through the premises of a law office enjoyed the same protection as calls that were made or answered there. It would take a 600-pound warrant covered with long, green, stringy hair to tap the phones or search the files of a law office. A judge issuing such a warrant would cause a mistrial in every criminal case the firm was working.

Of course, those precautions were useful only in keeping any phone conversation derived from a lawful tap from being used as evidence. In *el mundo real*, police and others, like St. Jones for instance, routinely tap the phones of people they're interested in and use the information they gather to set them up, rather than present as evidence. If they know when and where the deal's going down, they'll bring the probable cause.

However, the very existence of a tap provides a low-tech way to reveal its presence, even if it's an undetectable Ma Bell intra-system tap. Simply tell your associate over the phone in question to meet you at Union and Laguna at ten o'clock and bring the stuff. Then, arrive at 9:00 and see who else shows up. It works equally well on room bugs. And palace spies. It's called the "marked card" in spook trade-craft and predates the telephone by at least ten thousand years.

The firm's offices were in a large, three-story houseboat at Gate 5 on the Sausalito waterfront. Birmingham called it the Law Boat. It had a certain ambiance. St. Jones had an office there where he kept his files and met with certain types of clients. When he needed immunity on a delicate case, he had his client retain the law firm and they, in turn, would employ him and everything he developed was work product of an attorney and therefore privileged.

St. Jones locked up the files he had been working on and grabbed his Rolodex. Precept 40: Always take the Rolodex, yours or theirs. He put them in with his clothes and piled everything by the door and put on his flight jacket, proper attire for the occasion. He was giving the place the mental once over when he remembered the stash. He went to the bed and got the Bank of Maui currency pouch where he kept his recreational chemicals. Nervous as he was about holding, leaving it behind was unthinkable.

St. Jones grabbed his bags, locked up and took the stairs to the basement. Passing through the laundry room and past the furnace, he went out the back of the building and into the rear of another building where he rented a garage that opened onto the next street. He had adopted a disposable attitude about cars and rented them as needed, sometimes changing cars twice a day. He did keep a surveillance van, however, as well as a Harley for fun and occasional special situations.

After loading his gear into the van, St. Jones headed for Sausalito. He ran two routes on the way to make certain he wasn't being tailed. A route is a path worked out in advance that will expose a tail, like an overpass or a cul-de-sac or a dead end street. In his spare time, St. Jones would cruise the city looking for routes and escape routes. It was also one of the first things he did when working in a new town.

It was around 11:30 p.m. and traffic was light over the Golden Gate Bridge. He made the Sausalito exit in about twenty minutes and ran another route before parking a block up the hill from Sally Stanford's.

BOLD

4

St. Jones said hello to Luke Warm, Sally's bartender, got a Remy and stepped into the elegant, sit-down phone booth to call Birmingham. Admittedly, St. Jones had enough problems of his own, but this was no time to piss off his lawyer. There was a good chance he would need the firm's services before this was over, and this was a very good time to remind Birmingham how valuable St. Jones was to the firm and what an all-round, swell guy he was.

Birmingham answered on the first ring. Too eager. If they were playing poker, St. Jones would have folded. Birmingham told him to hang out at Sally's and said someone would be there soon. In spite of his own situation, St. Jones' curiosity was aroused.

Walking through the bar, he found a table by the fireplace. It was a cold night and he was still coming down from adrenaline, and the fire felt good. Sally's was very elegant. She had been a notorious madam across the bay in San Francisco in the thirties and forties. After her last house in the City was raided, she was sentenced to a convent. When she got out, she opened this place on the bay. It had the ambiance of the parlor of an old time Frisco whorehouse, but without the rooms upstairs.

St. Jones had chosen Sally's because he seldom went there, but as he scanned the room, the crowd was not as generic as he had hoped. Probably everyone there had the same idea. Bernie the attorney nodded as their eyes met. At another table was Perverto Obsceni, the porno king, with his latest companion and starlet, Gina Statutori. Noah Green, the smuggler, was in deep conversation with Andy Warhead, an arms and ordnance procurer, and Wet Willy, the contractor. Gregory Punk, the musician, was having a drink with Sid Seizure, the collector, and Joe Blow, the cocaine impresario, was sitting next to Mr. Natural of the Clear Light acid family, who was shimmering like a Christmas tree at the end of the bar.

People who are on the scene, players, use street names because a large part of everyday behavior is illegal. And even though people use a *nom de boulevard*, it's still bad form to call out anyone's name, or even recognize them without a sign. You never know what kind of grift they might be running. It's also a very bad idea to let anyone know where you live for any number of reasons, so people in the street world keep office hours at certain bars and can always be found there. It takes the social burden off of everyone.

The *grand dame* herself, in full sail, was ushering a party of four queens in cotillion drag into the dining room. Except for the Technicolor, Sally could have been Mother

Ginsling in old Shanghai.

The cocktail waitress was making her way toward St. Jones' table. "Well if it ain't Sherlock Shinola, the private dick." Her name was Nora Gomorrah, and she was privately famous for her Dance of the Seven Mucous Membranes. "What brings you in? Rounding up the usual suspects? Or are you just out privately dicking around?" Nora and St. Jones had history.

"I'm celebrating Charlie Chan's birthday and I just had to come to Chinatown and have a drink in his honor."

"Yeah, well in case you haven't noticed, this ain't Chinatown."

"I was misinformed."

Nora smiled, licked her fingertip and made a mark in the air in St. Jones' column on an invisible score card. He ordered coffee to back the Remy he was nursing. Watching Nora ooze through the tables like an oil slick reminded him that he was behind in his social life. The monsters were beginning to sniff under each other's tails.

He picked up the Chronicle from the antique table next to the sofa and turning to the classified section, located the lost pets column. It was a daily ritual. Someone had observed that the number of missing pets sharply increases the days preceding an earthquake. It was the most reliable precursor anyone had found to date. Totaling the pet ads for the day, St. Jones calculated a thirty percent rise over the recent average. "Travel is indicated," the I Ching would say.

He was watching Nora make her way to the waitress station when he noticed Winston, one of the partners in the firm, standing at the far end of the bar. He saw St. Jones and started toward the fireplace. They exchanged casual greetings in a poor imitation of a chance encounter, and Winston sat down as Nora arrived with St. Jones' coffee. Winston ordered a Remy and coffee and they watched Nora slipslide away. One of the monsters started humping his leg.

"So what's new in your life, Winston?" It was St. Jones' general purpose opening line but the question plunged Winston into a dark place and his breath caught on the exhale. His face looked like a diaper badly in need of a change.

"I've got a serious problem, St. Jones."

"Well, if I can be of any help to you at all, then you must be in deep shit. You don't look too good, you know. As your spiritual advisor, I suggest that you talk to me, Winston." St. Jones was also the company shaman.

"Well, earlier tonight I was having a little party with Screaming Mimi on the Playpen," he began, uneasily. The Playpen was a houseboat acquired in lieu of fee in a criminal defense case and was used by the partners and friends of the firm as a party pad. "We were drinking and snorting and took some Ludes and were rocking out on the water bed, when she suddenly jack-knifed up and her eyes got as big as golf balls and she screamed like a jungle animal and fell back, jerking and quivering. She almost bucked me right out of the saddle and onto the floor. I'd never fucked her before and I didn't know how she came, so I thought she'd just had one hell of an orgasm and that was why they called her Screaming Mimi, and it inspired me to greater heights and I'm humping away like a maniac. Because of the waterbed, I couldn't tell she wasn't moving. I didn't stop until I came. That's when I got a very creepy feeling and I discovered that she wasn't breathing." Winston was whispering at the end.

It was a good thing his back was to the room. The range of emotions that scrolled across Winston's face reminded St. Jones of Mick Jagger singing, a kaleidoscope of expressions.

"Did anyone see you with her?"

"No, I don't think so. I ran into her in the Bank of America parking lot across the street from the No Name Bar. I invited her to the Playpen for a drink and a couple of lines. It was after dark, about eight o'clock. She was just cruising."

"Did you wear a rubber?"

"Yes. She was into them and had an assortment of them in her bag."

Nora approached their table and placed a snifter and coffee in front of Winston. St. Jones handed her a twenty and told her to keep it.

"Thanks, St. Jones. You got class, baby. You're still the one, you know."

"We'll always have Paris."

They watched her as she made her way to another table. Some of the monsters followed.

"So what did Capt. Schtupin have in mind regarding this...problem?" St. Jones referred to Birmingham by his office title.

"He said he would regard it as a personal favor and consider you for a partnership if you would make the...problem...go away." Heavy words from a senior partner.

They were playing poker now, what lawyers call client management. It was a foregone conclusion that St. Jones would take care of the...problem. He even had an inspired idea of what to do with Screaming Mimi's vacant body, but he had to maximize his advantage. After all, these men were lawyers, and when was the last time your lawyer called you in the middle of the night?

"There's a *quid pro quo* involved here, Winston. I'm probably the only guy in town that's had a more bizarre night than you."

St. Jones reached into the inside pocket of his flight jacket and retrieved the envelope "A" had given him, and handed it to Winston. He opened it and took out the numerical fortune cookie and read it.

"Is this a joke? Where did this come from?"

"The Angels. These are turning up all over North America in bags of cocaine."

"Well, remember Precept 5. 'If you don't like the fortune, don't eat the cookie'."

"That's easy for you to say. There's more. The Narx Brothers were outside my place tonight."

"What did they want?"

"They were surveilling me. They probably have one of these notes, and got a Title III with it. Michael Motorcycle locked them in the trunk of their car and they were towed away." St. Jones smiled in spite of himself.

"Oh, shit." The significance of the situation wasn't lost on Winston. He knew the history.

"It gets worse." St. Jones paused for effect. "As I was watching them tow away the Narx Brothers, Lyla drove by and shot me."

Winston choked on his coffee. "Are you okay? Do you need to see a doctor?"

St. Jones was touched until he remembered Winston probably had an injury suit in mind.

"I was wearing a vest. It didn't penetrate, but it hit me so hard my houseplants died. I've got a hell of a stomach ache, and my head doesn't feel that good, either." St. Jones began searching his pockets for the bottle. "I'm really gonna hurt tomorrow."

"You're going to have to do something about her, you know."

"Yeah, I know," St. Jones acknowledged. Shun Zen, his philosophy of profound avoidance, was no longer working. Lyla had crossed into *terra incognito* tonight. It was time for Shun Fu, the dynamic form of the philosophy.

"I don't suppose I could get you to take Lyla out and maybe hone your technique a little. Is that something they teach in law school?"

"That's a cold shot, St. Jones. Serves you right that this is the one job ChuChu can't handle for you."

Alas, he was right. ChuChu was St. Jones' enforcer. He was five-two and maybe 103, half Sicilian and half Japanese, and the hottest little queen St. Jones had ever seen, and we're talking Frisco before the plague. He got the name because he liked to pull a train and was known to do a dozen guys at a time. When St. Jones put ChuChu on somebody's case, they were in serious trouble. ChuChu would begin showing up everywhere in their life, treating them with intimate familiarity. And when they denied knowing him, it only made it worse. This would accomplish things that the threat of violence never could. Unfortunately, it only worked on men. Women adored ChuChu. And Lyla would probably find a way to do him.

Confession must be good for the soul. Winston was looking a little better, like someone had changed his Huggie. "I see what you mean about your own situation. As your attorney, I would advise you to get out of town."

"Travel to the Southeast is indicated. You and the I Ching and Precept 9 are all in accord on this." St. Jones left out the lost pets column. "For openers, I'll probably fly down to the Grove and try to find out who Mama Coca is."

"I thought of something that might help you." Winston's encyclopedic mind was beginning to function again. "About ten years ago you had a book, a rare book published around the turn of the century. It was about the Incas and cocaine. 'The Divine Drug of the Incas,' or something like that. There was an illustration in the front of the book of a goddess figure. I think her name was Mama Coca. I borrowed it from you for a few weeks. Remember?"

A flash bulb popped in St. Jones' head and he remembered. He knew who Mama Coca was. Her name was Nickie and she had been his High Priestess in the Church of the Hydrochloric Miracle. She had the fire down below and they had made an attempt at the record together during the Great Blizzard of Seventy, as survivors referred to the cocaine inundation of the Bay Area in that year.

Nickie had the fire up above, too, and had been a graduate student in molecular biology at Berkeley. St. Jones had given her the book as a birthday present because she liked it so much. Among other things, it contained a chapter on field expedient methods for refining cocaine with little more than what one would find around an 1890s farm household.

He hadn't seen her since the early seventies, before he went to Southeast Asia. She had driven from San Francisco to Austin to get married, along with the best man, but by the time they got to Texas she kissed off the groom and married the best man instead. After an intense discussion and much parable swapping, the previous groom became the new best man. Before the service she gave St. Jones a blow-job for old times' sake, and then he gave the bride away. She was a very horny girl. The last he knew of her, she was living with both of them in south Texas, smuggling weed. He'd seen fire and he'd seen rain, and he always thought he'd see her again.

Meanwhile, he had several more immediate problems to deal with. He could have kissed Winston, but he didn't want to waste his *quid pro quo*. After all, this man was a lawyer.

"Winston, I need you to do something for me. Not on the order of what I'm going to do for you, of course, but very important none the less. I need you to find a copy of that book, in that edition. It may take a little work. It was published in England around 1900. When you find it, I want you to decipher that fortune cookie. Do you remember the book code?"

"Page, line, and word number?"

"Right. Break it into three number groups. But it has to be the right edition. Same as the one I loaned you, because that's the one she's got, and it won't work if it's off by a line. I'll call you in a few days. Brief Birmingham on my situation and tell him I'm going to be out of town for a week or two. I don't have any court appearances on my calendar for the rest of the month. Tell him the...problem...will be taken care of. I'm actually glad you called me about this." St. Jones was warming up to the idea. It wasn't every day that an opportunity like this came along. "And I hope I don't need to call in your marker, but if I do, remember the gratitude you're feeling at this moment. I'm going to want to see megawatt juice. I'm talking 100-foot sparks."

"Anything you say, St. Jones. Just one question. I guess it's the lawyer in me, but why are you glad I called you about this?"

"Now Winston, as a lawyer you should know better than to ask a question like that. The Mullah said, 'Only children and fools expect to find cause and effect in the same tale'." St. Jones quoted the Sufi Saint and the seventh Precept of the Order of the Bold Stroke, the Sly Pass, and the Ace in the Hole. "Besides, who else would you call?"

BOLD

5

Driving up the Sausalito hillside, St. Jones took the narrow, winding streets through the residential area to the other end of town, running a route in the process. He needed to do a little recon to see if his idea of what to do with Screaming Mimi's earthly remains was possible. Cruising through the Gate 6 parking lot, he saw what he was looking for and headed back toward the middle of town, avoiding Bridgeway, the main drag. The Fourth Amendment is optional there after dark.

Sausalito was a ship building town during WWII and the waterfront was lined for miles with maritime construction ways that were accessed by six main gates. Most of the great paddle-wheel ferries that ran on the bay before the bridges were built came to their final resting place here. For many years after WWII the waterfront, with its many meandering piers and hundreds of acres of debris a half-mile wide and five miles long, had been a free-for-all with space available for anyone bold enough to take it. It became one of the great bohemian scenes of all time, much to the chagrin of the rich folks who lived on the hillside.

Pulling into the Gate 3 lot, St. Jones parked the van and walked out almost to the end of the meandering, unlighted, three-hundred-foot pier. Carefully negotiating the steep, slippery gangplank, St. Jones stepped onto the deck of a thirty-five-foot power cruiser with the classic lines of a 1930s bay and coastal runner, and stood in the clear. People who live on boats instantly recognize the motion of boarding, even when they're asleep. The cabin was dark, but in a few seconds the hatch slid open a foot and he could just make out Randy, standing naked in the opening, pointing a large pistol at him.

"Is that a gun in your hand, or are you just glad to see me?" St. Jones whispered loudly.

"Hey, man...come in out of the cold and let's burn one," Randy said, dropping the Colt .45 hammer to half-cocked and stepping back into the darkness. He lit a candle on the table and disappeared into the forward cabin, returning in a moment with jeans and sweatshirt on. After lighting the burners on the stove to warm up the cabin, he sat down at the other side of the galley leaf table and started rolling a joint from a 35mm aluminum film can of cleaned weed.

"Not that I ain't glad to see you, but it's a little late for a social call." Lighting the joint, he took a long hit and passed it to St. Jones. "So it must be...'The Work'," Randy said archly.

St. Jones took a long hit and passed it back. "Are you up for one?"

"Sure, man. It's too late to turn back now." Randy had

been St. Jones' accomplice in more dark deeds than either of them cared to recall, and therefore never would. "What's the gig?"

"It's a sanitation job, removing a body from the scene."

"How fresh?"

"A few hours."

"How much?"

"A yard and some immense satisfaction."

"There better be a lot of satisfaction at that price."

"Oh, there is, there is. And the Frankie comes out of me for waking you up. Are you in?"

"Of course." Randy took a long hit and passed it. "But tell me about that satisfaction thing again. I must've missed something."

"Okay...well, this is one of those 'good news-bad news' things. The bad news is that the vacant body was previously inhabited by Screaming Mimi. She got too high and stroked out in the middle of a party. She probably died coming."

"Bummer. I told her she had to stop doing that. She had a weak blood vessel in her head. But, if you gotta go, I guess that's the way. Especially for her. She was born to use and hoped to die, you know. They didn't call her Screaming Mimi for nothing." Randy paused and took a reflective hit from the joint. "Shit, man, this is a privilege, being part of her honor guard. Forget the C-note. But unless I missed something, I still don't see all this satisfaction you're talking about."

Randy had dumped some coke on a plate and was chopping it into lines with a Buck knife. He passed St. Jones the plate and the rolled-up hundred dollar check he kept on the table.

"That's the 'good news' part. Remember Stone, the asshole that off'd Annie last year?" St. Jones picked up the check and did the lines and remembered the gruesome details. Annie was going to leave Stone and he shot her in the back of the head as she walked out the door. He rolled her up in a rug and was on his way to dump the body when he got stopped by the cops. They were rookies and got excited and blew the search and under the "Tainted Fruit Doctrine," Stone walked.

"Ah-haaah." Randy instantly comprehended. "Oh, I'm so glad you came to me with this. I like this a lot. Mimi would like this a lot. She was really pissed that Stone got away with snuffing Annie."

"Yeah. I thought she'd like it, too. I was thinking we could use your outboard and go down to Gate 1 and get Mimi and then run up to Waldo Point and move her to the trunk of Stone's car. It's in the Gate 6 lot. I've already checked. While we're on the water there's no chance of getting stopped by the cops."

"Sounds like your basic, bulletproof plan to me." Randy passed the plate back. St. Jones heart was revving like a Harley in first gear. He thought there was probably something weird in the coke, but he needed the energy and did the lines.

"How are you going to get into his car without fucking it up and leaving marks and giving him an out?"

"One of the advantages of being a PI is the mailing lists I got on when I got my license." St. Jones reached into one of the pockets of his magic WWII Navy flight jacket and produced a ring of keys. "Repo keys. Stone drives a T-Bird and one of these keys will open it."

"You should have been a genius, St. Jones."

"That's what my Mama said. It was her second choice, right after Saint."

"Wait a minute. You mean you're really Saint Jones instead of St. Jones?"

"Yeah, but don't call me Saint. Besides, I don't think the Roman Church has a St. Jones. If they do, he must be the patron saint of dopers and grifters. I'm just glad I didn't wind up Genius Jones."

"What is your first name, anyway? In all the years I've known you, it's always just been St. Jones."

"Yeah, well, there's a reason for that. My mama was a very religious woman and was much taken by the Book of Revelations of St. John. So that's what she called me...Revelations Saint Jones. Try living through a thousand roll calls with that."

"So, that's why you became a PI."

"What? You think I became my name?"

"Most of us do. Take me, for instance."

"Yeah, I see what you mean. Why am I telling you all this, anyway? It's that damned Incan truth powder again. You're working for them, aren't you? Since I saw you last, you were bitten by a lawyer and now you're one of them."

"Don't worry, your secret's safe with me."

"Oh God, that's what they always say." St. Jones made the sign of the Cross with his index fingers and held it toward Randy. "Are there pods in the bilge?"

Randy pushed the film can and papers across the table and got up. "Roll a couple for the ride while I get ready."

"You got any WD40?"

"Yeah, sure. Living on a boat, I buy it by the case. Why?"

"Bring along a can."

BOLD

6

"Our timing is good," Randy said over the sound of the motor as they cleared the end of the pier in the outboard. "The tide is still coming into the bay. It'll be high in about an hour. The gangplanks will be almost level and we won't have to fight the Farallon Express." That was Randy's name for the eight-knot current that runs in and out of the bay with the tide. The Farallons are five solid granite islands that lie twenty-six miles off shore from the Golden Gate. You can see them on a clear day. Randy had lived on boats on the bay for twenty years and knew his stuff. "A lot of problems have disappeared when the tide goes out of the bay."

They turned to starboard and ran parallel to the shoreline a few hundred feet from the ends of the piers. It was about forty-five degrees and the water was about the same and they were moving through occasional swirls of fog.

"Fire up one of those joints," Randy said. "We've got

about a fifteen minute ride."

St. Jones lit a joint and passed it. The motor was droning in his ears and the coke was buzzing in his brain as he struggled to keep his mind on the job at hand, but the events of the night kept creeping in.

First, there was Mama Coca. Nickie was a very bright girl. She would have understood the repercussions of a note like that, how much it would heat up his life. The fact that the notes were in the coke rocks and that she was a chemist suggested that she was at the lab and probably cooked the batch. And if "A" was right about the origin of the load, and he probably was, then she was somewhere in Colombia. And if the load passed through Coconut Grove, then Nickie probably did, too. Occam's Razor: The simplest explanation consistent with all of the facts is almost always the correct one. Precept 46.

Having worked and partied in the Grove from time to time, St. Jones knew some of the more prominent dope cognoscenti. It would be plausible enough for him to drop into town, depending of course on who knew about the notes.

He also realized that it would be a splendid idea not to be in the Bay Area when the sun came up. Nothing would convince the Narx Brothers that he wasn't responsible for what happened to them. They would be driven by Checkered Demons to seek terrible, savage revenge. These guys were not above killing St. Jones by furtive gesture.

"He made a furtive gesture, your Honor. We had no choice. We believed he was reaching for a weapon."

Even though the Narx Brothers were fuck-up artists, no matter how many mistakes they made, St. Jones couldn't make any. That's the thing about cops. They're connected to the system through an invisible blue thread that gives them vast resources and awesome power. They're sanctioned. It's in their eyes. They've always got their high beams on. Very few men can keep themselves separate from that kind of power and there's a psychosis receptor just waiting for it. The threat of losing that blue thread is the real reason so many of them eat their guns in the end.

And then there was Lyla. She was a quick study and had learned every move she or Lola saw St. Jones make or even heard about while they were together. Now she was using it all against him. In the beginning it was only vicious pranks. She would somehow slip out when Lola wasn't watching and cancel his credit cards and utilities and cable and telephone and have his mail transferred to Guam. Lyla gave great phone. When she became bolder, she called up clients and demanded money and put the word out that St. Jones had been busted and had rolled over and was working for the cops. That's like hearing that your surgeon is a cannibal. Very bad for business. Next came the blunt instrument phase, followed closely by knives. Fortunately, when he was younger, St. Jones had spent several years studying martial arts and could deal with that, at least while he was awake. But then she escalated to cars and tried to run him down at Columbus and Green and Stockton one night. He never learned how to block a car. He must have been absent the night they taught that.

The guns came when Lyla was in complete control. No matter how many years of study and practice one might have in the martial arts, any idiot with no prior experience can kill you from across the room in a heartbeat. And angry women never miss. It's uncanny. Ask any homicide cop. Sam Colt's great equalizer. The trouble is that some people are more equal than others, and some gun fag can kill a Saint on a whim and a twitch. The decline of the species began when we devised weapons that could kill beyond arms reach. Unlike other species, the weak began to survive and it's been downhill ever since. Precept 32: "Don't cull us, we'll cull you." The cry of the cerebratonic ectomorph.

The sensation of the boat making a slow turn brought St. Jones back into the moment. They were approaching Gate 1 pier. He looked at Randy and nodded his head to starboard, indicating the side of the pier where the Playpen was moored. As they approached the houseboat, he pointed to it.

There were several other outboards moving on the water. It was bar closing time, and the hardcore waterfront characters avoided police encounters by using boats instead of cars. It was in St. Jones and Randy's favor that people were used to hearing traffic on the bay at that hour. And seeing strange things. Randy killed the motor and they coasted up to the Playpen. St. Jones stepped over the railing and onto the deck, securing the bow-line to a cleat. Randy followed with the stern line.

Like most of the newer houseboats around the bay, the Playpen had a ferro-cement hull and more or less conventional house construction with nautical trimmings and touches of California wood butchery. There were several lights on inside and they paused and looked through the deck windows for a moment. Nothing was moving or out of place. St. Jones did a head count of the monsters and they were all present and calm, so he unlocked the door and stepped inside. He had his own key to the Playpen.

It was warm and smelled like pot and Bill Evans was playing softly on the stereo. Randy looked around while St. Jones went into one of the bedrooms, the one with the waterbed. There was a dim, red-tinted lamp glowing on a table beside the bed and he could see Mimi, lying on her back staring at the ceiling with a look of surprise on her face, her dark hair splayed across the pillow. He pulled back the covers, exposing her naked body lying with her arms open and her legs spread. A large wet spot spread around her from her bladder letting go. The monsters whimpered softly, and slunk away. He nudged her jaw muscle with his knuckle. The room was warm and rigor was beginning to set in.

Randy came through the door. "Just as I remember her."

"She'll be missed," St. Jones said, concealing his own sense of loss. He too, knew the scream of the wild Mimi. "We better try to get her clothes on. She's starting to stiffen up. But wait, don't touch her yet."

Going into the kitchen, St. Jones looked under the sink and found some small plastic garbage bags and peeling off four, returned to the bedroom. "Put these on your hands while you're touching her skin." He handed Randy two bags. They managed to get her jeans and sweater on her and stuff her hair up under her watch cap. Randy put on one sock and boot while St. Jones put on the other. They struggled her pea coat onto her and stepped back and admired their work. She looked just like a guy. Only one thing missing.

St. Jones reached into the inside pocket of his flight jacket and came out with a pair of Groucho glasses and put them on Mimi. He never left home without them.

They're an instant, non-threatening disguise that everyone accepts without question. The trick to street camouflage is the sooner they think they know who or what you are, the sooner they quit looking at you and thinking about you. It's a sleight of mind trick.

"Let's get back on the water while there's still traffic out there," St. Jones said. They got on each side and lifted her until her arms hung over their shoulders. After negotiating the bedroom door, they walked her through the living room area to the door leading to the deck. They walked her outside like a drunk and St. Jones held her up while Randy stepped into the boat. Picking Mimi up, St. Jones handed her to Randy like a child asleep.

"You got that WD40?"

Randy reached into his coat pocket and tossed the can to St. Jones. "What's this for?"

"Prints." He went back into the houseboat and began spraying anywhere that they or Mimi or Winston might have touched; the lamps, the stereo, the fridge, the toilet flush lever, everything. WD40 instantly obliterated fingerprints. One of the many uses not listed on the label.

Taking a final look around, St. Jones stripped the sheets and mattress pad off the bed and brought them along, locking the door and spraying the handle. Casting off the lines, he stepped into the boat as Randy cranked the motor. He was spraying the railing as Randy added a little power and they eased into the darkness of the bay.

They turned to port at the end of the pier and began making their way toward Waldo Point. It was a four or five mile ride and would take most of an hour.

BOLD

7

St. Jones had taken some strange boat rides, but this one was almost mythical, like the boatman on the Styx River Ferry. Sitting in the bow of the boat, facing astern, Mimi's arms hung over his legs and her head was in his lap, her empty eyes searching the dark sky.

Remembering the joint in his pocket, he lit it, and after dragging deeply, passed it to Randy. St. Jones slipped into the memory of the first time he saw a stiff in the wild, outside of a funeral home. He had instantly, instinctively thrown up at the sight of a couple of overripe corpses. After a few days in the sun they had turned black and swelled up to the point of splitting the seams of their clothing, and smelled like some ultra sweet spice grown so insanely strong that it burned into the brain itself and was unforgettable for the duration of your time on earth. The living body automatically reacts to the sight of its own form in that state with total revulsion, seeing its own ultimate fate.

He had seen that light go out many times and wondered where it went. Was Mimi watching from some ethereal portal, or do we really only go around once and she discorporated into a shower of psychic sparks? Are we exchange students from another dimension and periodically get our sign changed and are reassigned to another backdrop of historical scenery and karmic circumstance, or do we only go around once and every second is fatal? The thought of eternal life or even a long one was something St. Jones had never allowed himself and he considered the desire for it to be a consciousness feedback trap. He thought that light at the end of the tunnel was probably an artifact of deep brain oxygen deprivation. As crude as these meat suits are, he thought, they're still one's best bet for being alive, and the world was the only place he knew for sure where he could get a good steak and a screw. If there is eternal life, he'd take it right here. St. Jones so loved this world that he'd stay until the oceans flowed through his veins and the four winds filled his lungs and the light of the sun shone through his eyes and the drama of the world played itself out in the theater of his mind.

St. Jones was of that generation that had from earliest childhood lived with the certain knowledge that every second could be the last, that any moment of any day that blinding white flash could come and the wind would blow away the ashes after the rain put out the fire. He never thought he would live to be twelve. Then he never believed he could possibly make eighteen. Living to be thirty was incomprehensible and natural causes were never even on the table. The Bomb was the ultimate Tyrannosaurus Rex in the swamp of existentialism. It forced him to live everyday like it was his last and to make no long-range plans. Take a generation of young people who grew up like that and throw in birth control pills and LSD and a mindless meat grinder of a pointless foreign war and you've got yourself the sixties, when those who weren't busy being born were busy dying.

"Five minute warning." Randy's voice snapped St. Jones back to the moment. "Where do you want to tie up?"

"How about at the end of the dock? It's a long walk, but we'll have more options if something goes wrong."

"I got a pal up at the Pink Palace that has a boat about half way down the dock," Randy said. The Pink Palace is the Marin County jail. It was designed by Frank Lloyd Wright. There are parts of Marin County so exclusive that even the police have an unlisted number, and if you don't know it, you don't belong there. But the Sausalito waterfront wasn't one of them. "How about we tie up there?"

"I like it."

Turning to starboard, they ran parallel to the shore, cruising along the dock until Randy cut the power. They glided to the stern deck of a houseboat very similar to the Playpen, and tied up. After getting Mimi on deck, they walked her along the narrow passage between the bulkhead and the railing to the bow of the boat. Negotiating the gangplank with her between them was an aerial circus in the dark and any or all of them could have gone into the water, but they made it somehow, and started up the dock toward the parking lot. Two guys supporting a third guy between them was a common sight on the waterfront at that hour.

They turned right when they reached the end of the

dock and headed through the parking lot to Stone's car. This was the most vulnerable part of the scenario and had to be carried off with good theater, but St. Jones felt immune. They were on a mission from God, like Jake and Elwood. If the cops had another shot at Stone, they'd do it differently, and Mimi was going to give them that chance. This was covered under Precept 13: Getting even is the best revenge.

Such was the nature of The Work. If there is a God, he must be a very busy fellow, and St. Jones believed in generating as little paperwork for Him as possible. The Work was anonymous, third-party, *pro bono* revenge, case load permitting. He felt that if you truly want to leave the world a better place than you found it, then don't walk past evil and leave it for Him to deal with. St. Jones believed in dealing with matters of the living while they're alive. That's the problem he had with the Christians. They seemed to think if they kept their eyes closed during the movie, they'd get their money back when it was over.

Luck was with them. Stone's car was parked next to a step-van, providing cover from the light. When the first key St. Jones tried worked the trunk lock, he knew the Golden Light was shining on them. They lifted Mimi into the trunk and laid her out sideways. She just fit.

"Go to a better life, baby, if there is one." St. Jones removed the Groucho glasses and closed the trunk lid.

"Amen." Randy crossed himself.

St. Jones began looking in the grass next to the parking spot. "See if you can find a beer can or a booze bottle. Let's make it easy for the cops. We'll put hair around it for them."

"Here's one." Randy reached under a bush and came

up with an empty Southern Comfort pint bottle. "What's this for?"

"Probable cause." He unlocked the passenger door and sprayed the bottle with WD-40 and tossed it on the floor behind the seat. "When they see the bottle, they'll have probable cause to search the trunk." Picking up a rock from the curb, he smashed the left taillight. "And that will give them probable cause to stop the car."

"That's truly insidious, St. Jones, a fucking work of art."

After he sprayed the trunk lid and door handle, they crossed the parking lot and walked back to the houseboat where they had tied up. They were motoring away onto the bay before either of them spoke.

"God, I love this feeling."

"I told you there'd be immense satisfaction. The Work is very rewarding. That's why you do these jobs with me. Satisfaction guaranteed."

"Yeah, well, you get extra points in your credibility log. There's something extremely satisfying about this one. It's even better than wasting the guy. I'd give almost anything to see the look on his face when he opens the trunk for the cops and sees a fucking body in there. 'Deja vu, motherfucker.' It's perfect."

"It's like the Eighth Precept says, 'You can't fool the cards by changing places at the table'."

"Not as long as we're around."

They passed the fifteen-minute ride back to Randy's boat in silence, each with his own thoughts of the night's deed. By the time they tied up and went below, St. Jones had a pain in his head to rival the one in his stomach. It was around three a.m. and the drugs and the adrenaline of the last five hours had taken their toll. Randy read the signs and dumped some coke on the plate and started chopping lines.

"You look like you could use some of this." He slid the plate across the narrow table to St. Jones.

"Like you said earlier, it's too late to turn back now, but what I really need is some sleep." He bent over and snorted the lines.

"Go crash in the foc's'le bunk. Janet Planet's asleep in there, but she'd be real glad to see you. She still talks about you."

St. Jones' heart wound up tight in second and shifted into third. "That's a deeply tempting offer, but in my condition she'd probably fuck me to death. It's going around, you know. Then you'd have to go out and do this all over again."

"Naaa, I'd just put you on the Farallon Express and you'd be out the Golden Gate faster than you could run. The bay is like a big toilet that flushes twice a day and whatever's on the water that ain't tied up is out of here." He poured some brandy into a couple of coffee cups.

St. Jones was searching his jacket pockets for the codeine bottle. Each time the pills wore off, he was greeted with a new level of pain. He found the bottle and swallowed a couple of pills with the brandy and considered the possibility of internal injuries.

"What's that? Anything good? You're not holding out on me, are you?"

"Naaa, I wouldn't hold out on you, man. I've got a toothache." He kept quiet about the real pain. Randy had already chewed St. Jones' ass out about Lyla. No point in getting another lecture.

"Well, here's to Mimi." Randy raised his cup. "May she scream in paradise."

"To Mimi." St. Jones raised his cup and remembered the night the police showed up at his door after receiving calls from the neighbors of bloody murder. He had come so hard, he had rammed Mimi's head through the vertical bars of his brass bed, and he had to pour a bottle of Wesson oil on her head to get her free.

Randy had been rolling a joint while they talked. "Here's one for the road."

St. Jones took the joint and stood up. He fished in his pocket and came up with a wadded up hundred-dollar bill and tossed it on the table. "May the forces of evil become confused on the way to your door." St. Jones slipped through the hatch and into the very stoned night.

He walked up the pier to the parking lot and unlocked the van. Searching through the collection of magnetic signs behind the seat, he selected "Palladini's Fresh Fish and Sea Food," and placed them on the sides and the back of the van. He never missed a chance to add to his collection of magnetic signs. Or business cards. He went to trade shows just to collect them.

St. Jones headed back up the Sausalito hillside, avoiding the cops at either end of town that waited to pounce on the unwary like junkyard dogs. Turning north on 101, he began the hour drive to Sebastopol, where he kept the plane. There was no traffic and it was like having his own personal freeway, like some gigantic theme park ride. He lit the joint Randy had given him and turned KJAZ up loud and ignored the strange little hitchhiker he kept passing every few miles. He made only one stop, at a pay phone in Novato, to leave a message on the answering machine of Inspector Falcone of SFPD homicide from the "Grease Man."

Arriving at the old WWII bomber strip east of Sebastopol, St. Jones drove up to the hangar and, opening the door, pulled the van inside next to the wing of the Cessna. After securing the hangar door, he climbed into the back of the van. He managed to get his shoes off and crawled into the bunk and set an alarm by the pillow for six a.m., about two hours away, and cut the strings to the puppet.

BOLD

8

When the alarm went off, St. Jones didn't know what it was, or where he was, or what time it was, if any. It became the seed of a dream that his chemically singed and exhausted mind grew into a hideous flower. When he rolled onto his side to escape the chain saw the alarm had become in his dream, he awoke in a nightmare of pain. Struggling to a sitting position, he turned on a light and fumbled through his jacket with hands that couldn't grip, searching for the codeine bottle. He poured out four and washed them down with a bottle of Calistoga water he found in the fridge.

St. Jones' brain was deep-fried. He knew he was in no condition to plan a three thousand mile flight in the conventional way, but he thought he could fly okay. It's like falling off a bicycle. It's something you never forget how to do. He would just have to do it in stages. First priority was to get airborne and get the hell out of northern California. He would navigate as he went along.

As far as he knew, the Narx Brothers weren't aware of this place, but they did know about the plane, and so did Lyla. Lola had flown with him once on a cross-country hot pursuit. Since then, he had moved the plane from Gnoss Field in Marin to Sebastopol in adjacent Sonoma County. It wouldn't take a genius to figure it out.

The Cessna was St. Jones' ace in the hole. It allowed him to stay outside the system. Admittedly, it couldn't keep up with a 747, but it could fly directly to anywhere, anytime. Still, he had to stay out of the FAA computer, or the Narx Brothers could locate his last stop with a phone call to Oklahoma City. He could try to make it to Miami by sneaking through the system using uncontrolled airports, but he decided to change the "N" numbers on the aircraft's wing and fuselage and hide in plain sight, the aviation equivalent of switching license plates.

One of St. Jones' various spin-off hustles had been the Aircraft Recovery Bureau, which consisted of a Washington, D.C. mail drop and answering service and a very official looking picture ID that highly resembled Treasury Department credentials. At the time, planes were being stolen with great frequency and used to smuggle weed out of Mexico. Running ads in the classified sections of various flying magazines, the official sounding name and the D.C. address attracted more business than he expected, and he spent a lot of time south of the border negotiating for, or if necessary, stealing back aircraft. Since most of the growers were *Federale* protected, usually by their uncles and cousins and brothers, after a while there was a bounty on St. Jones and it became dangerous for him to show his face in Mexico.

Struggling out of the back of the van and into a standing position in the dark freezing hangar, St. Jones turned on a light and opened up the Cessna. The Turbo-210 was the last plane he recovered, and he stole it fair and square. It got a little shot up in the process. Because the pilot carried only a .38, the Mexicans thought he was a pussy and they killed him for the plane. Mexicans carry big guns and are very impressed that way. Carrying anything smaller than a .45 is considered going off half-cocked south of the border. St. Jones carried a MAC-10 on that run. *Mucho cojones.* They were duly impressed.

When St. Jones attempted to deliver the aircraft and collect his fee, he discovered the guy who hired him had been indicted for conspiracy to smuggle. The alleged smuggler's attorney had trouble maintaining sphincter control when he learned about the plane. It was the missing link in the conspiracy formula he had been dreading. The attorney was overcome with gratitude when St. Jones suggested that he sign off the plane to the Aircraft Recovery Bureau for services rendered. While he kept the ARB alive on paper to keep his ID good, St. Jones quit running the ads and stayed the hell out of Mexico. It was a nice place to visit, but he didn't want to die there.

The T-210 was not a stock aircraft. The two back rows of seats had been removed in cargo configuration and the plane had been STOL (Short Take-Off & Landing) modified by the time St. Jones acquired it. He added additional tanks in the wings and long-range ferry tanks constructed to fit in the floor area where the rear two rows of seats had been mounted. The tops of the new tanks formed a level surface about two feet higher than the original floor level, and he had naugahyde covered foam pads made to conceal the tanks. It turned the area into a double bed and made it look a little less like a long-range smuggling rig. Side curtains completed the image.

The plane also came with a full Collins IFR panel and high frequency SSB communications, weather radar, and a few other goodies. It was a hot setup that could take-off and land on less than a thousand feet of dirt and fly more than two thousand miles at well over 200 mph in virtually any weather short of a hurricane.

St. Jones also added a slick, or hiding place, large enough to conceal a payload of twelve cubic feet as part of the ferry tanks' construction, a tank within a tank. In it he kept a few weapons and some survival gear, some cash, extra ID packages, and a few spray cans of paint that matched the aircraft, and an assortment of pre-cut stencils of "N" numbers of other 210s that he'd made note of at various airports. It was the sort of thing that you had to plan ahead for.

Opening up the slick, St. Jones put the Narx Brothers IDs with the others and got out the paint and stencils. After wiping down the number areas with acetone to remove the wax, he sprayed a matching base coat of fast drying paint over the old numbers. While it dried, he made coffee and foraged around for food. He found some Hoffman Bars that he bought by the case and kept in the van for extended surveillances, and had a breakfast of sorts. Hoffman Bars are complete meals in a candy bar form, with four or five hundred calories and fifteen grams of protein and all the carbs, fat, and vitamins and minerals you need to stay alive. People have lived on them for months at a time. It wasn't exactly steak and eggs, but it did put some life back into the beast.

St. Jones chose a stencil with numbers from a cannibalized Cessna 210 he'd seen at Garberville a few weeks earlier. Its engine had been removed, and St. Jones thought it unlikely that it was back on the line. Taping the stencil to the bottom of the wing, he squatted on the concrete and sprayed. After another cup of coffee, he peeled the stencil off and did the same with the fuselage numbers. He rigged a clip-on heat lamp to a ladder to dry the paint faster and loaded his gear into the cockpit along with a case of Hoffman Bars and a case of Calistoga water from the van. He finished off the job with a quick coat of aviation wax that would completely mask his work.

The windsock at the runway intersection hung limp, giving St. Jones the option of take-off direction. He turned on the ignition and ran the starting fuel pump for about thirty seconds and cranked the big turbo-charged engine to life. Taxiing to the west end of the east/west runway, he did a run-up and checked the controls and set the altimeter and gyros and dialed in the communications and navigation frequencies from memory. Pushing the throttle forward, the sounds and smells of the throbbing aircraft cleared his mind of everything and, a few seconds and less than a thousand feet later, he was airborne. No matter how many times he took off, it never failed to exhilarate him. Understanding the physics of flight in no way diminished the miracle of actually leaving the ground.

Highway 101 was passing below as the Cessna climbed through 3,000 feet headed VFR (Visual Flight Rules) for Mt. Diablo, the eastern boundary of the Bay Area, flying into the rising sun. St. Jones felt relieved now that he was airborne. Unless the Narx Brothers were willing to resort to surface-to-air missiles, he was temporarily out of their reach. And he was hopeful this journey to the southeast would lead him to Nickie. St. Jones' watch read 7:03 a.m. and a quick calculation of 3,000 miles at 200 mph told him he had about fifteen hours of flying time and three time zones to Miami. He could make it with one fuel stop in Texas but the thought of flying nonstop for eight hours made him cringe. He had a pain in his head to match the one in his stomach, and the monsters weren't feeling that good themselves.

St. Jones leveled off at 7,500 feet, passing just north of Mt. Diablo. He dialed in the Fresno VOR (VHF Omni-Ranging) frequency and tracked straight in on the 295 degree radial as the terrain of the long, flat, San Joaquin Valley scrolled by like a Japanese panel painting.

The altitude and the drone of the engine were working with the short sleep and his indulgences of the night before and St. Jones caught himself slipping into a pre-sleep trance. After alpha-jerking a few times, he decided it was time to get out the stash and see what kind of chemical magic he could conjure. Retrieving the Bank of Maui currency pouch from his shoulder bag, he began an inventory of the pharmacy. He didn't want anything too strong or psychedelic because it got weird enough flying alone, so he decided on Dexedrine, the trucker's little helper, as being the right tool for the job. Opening a Calistoga to wash them down, he swallowed three 5-mg hearts and ate another Hoffman Bar while he still had an appetite.

St. Jones dialed in KGO on the ADF (Automatic Direction Finder), and began arguing with the talk radio callers to keep from slipping into the alpha zone until the Dexies kicked in.

BOLD

9

In St. Jones' defense, he was properly trained and always observed the "Twelve Hours from Bottle to Throttle Rule," and never used anything stronger than coffee when flying. His downfall came when he took a civilian contract job flying in Southeast Asia in the early seventies. He was over thirty and long out of the military, but he was flat broke and winter was coming and it seemed like a good idea at the time. He had never heard of Air America. His new colleagues were guys who didn't think they were flying at all unless they were going Mach 2, upside down, with their hair on fire and a Thai stick clinched in their teeth. There, St. Jones was initiated into the ancient and arcane practice of Adrenalini Yoga.

There are few drugs as powerful as adrenaline. It's an acquired taste. Cocaine and methamphetamine are mere shadows of the real thing. On adrenaline, a little old lady in a wheel chair can jump up and lift a truck off her cat. A man can jump eight feet straight up in the air, properly terrorized. But unlike most drugs, we manufacture this one internally. And instead of using some sort of paraphernalia to ingest it, we produce situations of extreme fear, or somehow get going so fast that we exceed the mind's ability to participate and, Shazam, the internal geeze. Suddenly, like Doestoyevsky's idiot on the gallows, you have all the time in the world. "Now" dilates and you can slice a second into a thousand moments of perception. Mach Zen. Velocity Narcosis. If Lao Tsu had a Harley, he would've been dead before lunch. On the approach of a violent high Sierra thunderstorm, John Muir would climb to the top of the tallest tree and lash himself to it, just for the ride. Definitely an adept.

Unfortunately, there's an insidious side effect. It wears off. Therefore, like most powerful drugs, adrenaline is highly addictive. Life between adrenaline rushes becomes tedious, at best. Excessive use undoubtedly shortens your life, but it's unclear whether it comes off the end or out of the middle.

Adrenaline was the specialty of the house at the Purple Porpoise Bar in Longchen, Laos, one hundred kilometers north of Vien Tien. Most of the off-the-book, black operations that were too weird for the John Wayne Hotel at Tan Son Nhut were run out of Longchen. This was the place that Nixon lied about. One of them, anyway. The Purple Porpoise was like the spaceport bar in Star Wars, except it was frequented by every spook, contract pilot, and clandestine operative in Southeast Asia. Probably even some ETs. St. Jones had always been suspicious about a few of them.

It was a war zone and somebody got shot almost every

night, usually accidentally. Everyone was armed to the teeth, and as the nights wore on and the liquor flowed like blood on the sand and the room filled with the pungent fragrance of the world's strongest weed, judgement became scarce, even rare. One night, St. Jones watched a guy put one round in the magazine and play Russian Roulette with a P-35 automatic.

At the Purple Porpoise, St. Jones learned that when you enter a room, if you can't spot the mark in sixty seconds or less, leave immediately. It's you. He also learned that if you get too careful you can lose your luck, and that the game's not over until you run out of balls. Those clots of wisdom, for indeed he bled for each of them, would later become Precepts One, Two, and Three of the Order of the Bold Stroke, the Sly Pass, and the Ace in the Hole.

The VOR flipped to "FROM" and St. Jones looked down to see Fresno passing a mile and a half below. His watch read 8:05 a.m. as he dialed in Bakersfield on the second VOR. St. Jones was feeling better and realized that the Dexies were shaking hands with the codeine. St. Jones calculated that he would be in Santa Fe around noon and the thought of lunch at La Fonda filled his mind. He salivated, and that was the one true sign of a good plan.

Since the beginning of combat, men have been surprised to discover they got an erection in the heat of battle. They say the fear of imminent death triggers the reproductive instinct. After a particularly close shave in Burma, St. Jones had experienced the phenomenon first hand, only it wouldn't go away. Observing that life was far too short under the best of circumstances, and since his contract was up anyway, he decided to stop and smell the hormones.

While hanging out at Longchen, he had stumbled onto a top-secret project. As it was explained to him by the mysterious Dr. Echs of the OIC one stormy afternoon in the Purple Porpoise, somewhere on earth, probably in the Orient, was a woman with a tongue in her cunt. Growing there, not passing through or left behind, *flagrante delicto*. The theory was that because of the number of blowjobs women have performed since the origin of the species, in spite of the many virtues of the vagina as a lust receptacle, through natural selection women would eventually grow tongues in their cunts. And, just as a few Cro Magnons began to appear among the Neanderthals, it was possible, even probable, that even as they spoke, such women existed. Furthermore, since the Orient was the sighting place of the fabled slanted pussy, this was obviously the place to begin the search. There was even the remote possibility of finding both, maybe even together in the same woman. The war was finally starting to make sense. This one, and the one before, and the one before that. This was something worth fighting for. His duty was clear. It was a dirty job, but somebody had to do it, and St. Jones was well equipped for the mission.

Like Darwin in the Galapagos, St. Jones began his search in Bangkok. He'd always had a theory about the name. He made a heroic attempt to inspect every AN/SBFU (Army Nomenclature/Small Brown Fucking Unit) on Pat Pong Road. After failing to turn up anything significant, he followed persistent rumors of sightings to Saigon, where he conducted a thorough house-to-house search of Tu Do. War zones can be fun places, but the writing was on the wall, and the ceiling, but mostly soaking into the floor, and it said: one should not be where one does not belong. The Fourth Precept. Since St. Jones was in the enviable position of being a civilian, actually a nephew of his Uncle Sam, once removed, he decided to let Saigons be Saigons.

In relentless pursuit of his research, St. Jones followed fresh rumors of sightings to Hong Kong, where he conducted a door-to-door search of Wan Chai. His early optimism faded when he realized the sheer numbers he was up against, and he settled into a routine of systematic elimination. This was obviously going to take some time.

Hong Kong was an exciting place in the early seventies with all the side action from the war, plus its role as *de facto* capital of Asia due to the British banking laws. Every Burmese opium king, Laotion war lord, and Vietnamese general, as well as American, Chinese, or other who knew which way the wind blew, did their banking and their banging in Hong Kong.

St. Jones discovered that by hanging out in certain places, a guy with his skills could make significant money flying charters of opportunity. If brunch in the lobby of the Peninsula didn't yield the mission *du jour*, then late afternoon cocktails in the bar at the Empress certainly would. It was like Terry and the Pirates, flying a mystery man to Chang Mai or a duffle bag to Vien Tien. As an Australian colleague put it so succinctly one night in the Wanch (Wan Chai), "Smuggling is a bleedin' white man's privilege." Even in Hong Kong, two Wongs don't make a white.

His research continued unabated until he came down with a social disease, and on doctor's orders St. Jones arranged for a convalescence. He took a ninety-day contract flying photo-recon for the Christians In Action (CIA) on Mindinao, in the southern Philippines. Twice a day he would take off out of a remote, womanless jungle camp and fly designated, predictable, parallel stepping patterns at an uncomfortable altitude, tactically speaking, while an imaging pod mounted on one wing mapped the jungle in the visible and infrared spectra. On the other wing, a synchronized pod scanned for the faint local oscillator frequency of radios tuned to Armed Forces Radio playing irresistible American rock and roll. Anyone who listened to those particular stations became bombing targets.

One beautiful spring morning three days before his thirty-fifth birthday, small-arms ground fire punctured the wing tanks of the Helio Courier he was flying. Very bad for mileage.

He had managed to land the plane intact in the upper layer of the dense triple canopy jungle by using the bucking horse maneuver, but before he could get out of the craft it slipped through the vines and settled another fifty feet into the middle canopy. This left him about sixty feet off the ground and about twenty above the bottom layer of branches that were interwoven with vines. He used to play in trees like that when he was a kid in the bayous. They were like big circus nets and you could bounce on them like they were trampolines.

Standing orders were to destroy the plane and the contents, and pilots had been issued Willie Peters (white phosphorous grenades) for that purpose. They were incendiary devices that burned so hot the aluminum aircraft body would ignite and once burning, it was impossible to extinguish. St. Jones' problem had been the four-second fuse. Once he pulled the pin and released the spoon, his work was cut out for him. But the head start he had on the opposition had been slipping away fast, so he pulled the pin like a good ranger and dropped it on the floor of the cockpit. It could never be said he wasn't a good field man.

St. Jones had done a flop dive out the door and scrambled almost to the ground when the brilliant flash lit up the jungle and showers of white fire blew everywhere. He hit the ground running and he didn't stop for an hour. He knew there had to be guys on his trail, guys that were born in that bad-assed jungle. He was worth something to them if they could catch him alive, and he had just told them exactly where he was.

St. Jones wound up taking a hundred-mile hike along the Zamboangan Peninsula. It was like a nature walk through the Book of Revelations. He spent ten days thinking every second was going to be his last, chanting the, "If only, I'll never" prayer, known to adventurers throughout time. "Dear God, if only you'll get me out of this one, I'll never, ever do this again." Later known as Precept 24.

St. Jones' survival kit had consisted of a canteen, a .45 Colt 1911A with one extra magazine and a Randall model 12 survival knife, its hollow handle filled with penicillin, Benzadrine, codeine, and Halizone. His method of survival was to begin taking the penicillin, the Bennies, and the codeine immediately and disregarding pain, hunger, and fatigue, keep moving whenever possible, and remain alert when he couldn't. Except for water, which he treated with the Halizone, and what little fruit he could recognize, he lived on speed and pain killers for ten days.

He learned that among the many curious features of the human mind is the need to dream. Man continues to sleep at night because of an organic memory of his cold-blooded origin before he developed thermiostasis, the ability to maintain a body temperature independent of his environment. When the temperature dropped, so did he. However, man doesn't really need to sleep but continues to because he needs to dream, and after he's been awake long enough, usually three or four days, he begin dreaming awake. His unconscious mind rear-projects his dreams onto the scenery of his waking reality, and he experiences them as one, without any differentiation between the two. It was in this state that St. Jones had first noticed the monsters. At first they were just fleeting shadows in the periphery of his vision, but as the days and nights crept by, they became more solid and he could make out their shapes, and eventually their faces. They were ugly little fuckers, but they were somehow his.

One morning St. Jones had been waiting in a tree for enough light to move, and not too sure what was real and what wasn't, when the monsters came running, frantically gesturing in the direction from which he had come the day before. And that's when he saw the Moro (warrior tribe) guerilla, moving silently with his eyes to the ground, obviously tracking St. Jones' spoor. Because of snakes, St. Jones had had his Colt in his hand since he first hit the ground seven days earlier, and he silently took very careful two-handed aim and waited. The Moro had his weapon unslung and knew his prey was near and St. Jones knew he would only get one chance before the AK-47 defoliated the tree he was in and him along with it. The Moro stopped almost directly under him and when he began to raise his eyes, his weapon was already moving and in the last possible instant, St. Jones squeezed the trigger. The big Colt jumped and the man sat down hard, his shoulders hunched forward, quivering, and then he fell backwards, blowing pink froth and gurgling and went limp, and St. Jones knew he would be seeing that face in his dreams. He hated killing. Any man who enjoyed it was corrupt in his soul. But if there was a God that gave him life, then it was St. Jones' number one duty to let no man take it from him. That was Commandment Zero, and came before the other ten.

St. Jones had known it was only the point-man he had killed, and when the monsters took off running through the jungle, he followed them. They seemed to know where they were going. St. Jones had run like naked prey and hadn't stopped until after dark. He had been utterly lost, but he kept following the monsters and three days later they led him into camp. He was never the same after that, and the monsters never went very far away. The world had changed, too. Saigon had fallen. The last dollar had been made and the party was over. St. Jones reluctantly abandoned his quest for the golden nookie and repatriated to the land of pink nipples and the all night generator.

Sooner than he expected, the VOR flipped again and St. Jones was over Bakersfield at 7,500 feet. He looked up the Kingman VOR in the AIM (Airman's Information Manual) and dialed in the frequency. It wasn't too solid so he climbed to 11,500 feet for better reception and maybe a smoother ride over the mountains ahead. It was a CAVU (Clear And Visibility Unlimited) day and he was feeling pretty good, all things considered.

BOLD

10

After returning to San Francisco, St. Jones had fallen in with another bad crowd, lawyers this time. They were mostly guys he had known when they were students at Boalt Hall, the latest generation of young scions of the early San Francisco robber-baron families. In the old days they had faithfully worshipped at the Church of the Hydrochloric Miracle. Now they were bright young attorneys legacied to the top firms in San Francisco. It was from them that he learned the first law on money: find out where it's changing hands and get in the middle. Precept 26. Now that he was back, it wasn't long before he was looking into this matter and that on their behalf, finding one guy and another. Without realizing it, he had become a private investigator.

Since he was doing the work anyway, St. Jones eventually applied for a license, which is not a simple matter in California. He had to prove by affidavit that he had performed four thousand compensated hours of investigative work under someone else's license, or some equivalent experience such as police work or journalism. After he'd been photographed and fingerprinted and passed the FBI vetting, the state allowed him to take the written exam, which ran about four hours and read like a mini bar exam. When he passed and paid the licensing fee and posted a bond with the state, they issued him a license. As he owned more than the shirt on his back, he also took out a million dollars insurance on top of that.

For a permit to carry a gun, he had to complete a week-long course consisting of eighteen hours in the classroom studying the use and the consequences of deadly force and six hours on the range qualifying with whatever weapons he planned to carry. He learned that if he shot someone with a type of gun he hadn't qualified with, he could be sued for negligence. After receiving his FQC (Firearms Qualification Card), the local police chief or sheriff issued a concealed weapon permit at their discretion.

The entire process took about three years if he worked every day. If he'd been into power, it would have been much easier to become a cop. Or go to another state. Many states require only a business license.

The investigative business had been good to St. Jones. Except for a few Hal Lipset proteges, who were the new breed investigators, the field was full of ex-cops of one kind or another, and he found that most people responded to him infinitely better than they did to someone with a cop mentality. Coupled with the fact that his friends were mostly lawyers, musicians, and dealers, this made it a business that fit St. Jones' lifestyle. His business was all referral, and he stayed as busy as he wanted without ever having to open himself up to fate with a listing in the yellow pages. The clients liked that, too, being introduced by someone they knew.

St. Jones discovered he had a natural talent for finding people and, for a while, specialized in tracking. It's a fun game, man-hunting, he thought. Over time and out of general necessity, his electronics background emerged and he became a wire-man, because that's where the business was. But finally, he found his true calling, the thing that brought it all together. The Sting.

The Order of the Bold Stroke, the Sly Pass, and the Ace in the Hole was born at a cast party in LA after his first successful, big time sting. The client was a woman who had been swindled out of a half a million dollars by a Fucking Asshole, which is a technical term taught in police academies and criminal investigation and evidence courses everywhere.

A couple of LAPD alumni surveilled the FA with St. Jones for three weeks, three shifts a day, and then he holed up in a hotel room in Burbank for a week, listening to tapes of bugs and wire taps and reading surveillance reports. He'd even had the FA's handwriting analyzed and his astrological chart done.

St. Jones had a theory of personality structure, influenced by Gurdjieff, Wilhelm Reich, Charles Groddeck, and others too numerous to mention. Endless hours of drug driven conversations with various experts and madmen, his own LSD experiences spent crawling through the primordial ooze in the labyrinths of his own unconscious, and years of casual and professional people-watching, led St. Jones to certain conclusions. Among them, that most everyone, at a very early age, seems to feel that something is wrong with them, that they are flawed in some way and inferior to others. This happens to the eenie-weenie, to use Alan Watts' term, with the onset of the socialization process, usually at the beginning of school. The first compensating mechanism is created by the child to deal with the "chief flaw," as Gurdjieff called it. Gurdjieff said that man makes himself up as he goes along. Over time an immense construction of delicate psychological scaffolding is erected upon the chief flaw. By observing the apparent strengths of an individual, it is possible to deduce the location of the weakness for which he compensates. That is where the lever, or the charge, is placed, to manipulate or destroy that personality. It is the blind spot, and it's the thing that personality can never see that always gets it. Precept 59.

St. Jones had used all of his surveillance reports and various expert analyses to fill several hundred 3x5 index cards with individual facts, and covered the floor of his hotel room, arranging and rearranging them, looking for the magic pattern. In spook trade-craft, it's called mosaic work. He would fall asleep with hundreds of little pieces of this guy's life in his head. One night, he woke up about 4:00 a.m. with the Muse of Karma whispering quite clearly in his ear, and by dawn he had written a morality play, a psychodrama in one act.

The formula was based on the dynamics of a three-act play. The first act was the client's situation when he or she first came to him. The third act was how the client wanted things to be. Act two, the only act to be performed, was transitional drama. What it took to get there.

That afternoon St. Jones had gone to an actor friend in Hollywood. He laid out the story over hot brisket sandwiches at Cantor's Deli on Fairfax and gave him the script to read. A true thespian, the actor fell in love with the idea of theater superimposed on real life. By the time the bars closed that night they had cast the play and went into rehearsal the next afternoon.

For the cast, who were working actors for the most part, it was a new dimension in theater, more interesting and exciting than anything they had done before. Some of the roles they played came from productions in progress, complete with wardrobe.

One of St. Jones' ex-cops had duked his way into the FA's office to get the layout, and they had decided on a conference room at the One Wilshire address for the performance. They did a rough mock-up of the room, and even cast an actor who physically resembled the F.A. for rehearsals.

The script ran eight minutes, and when the day of the performance came, it went off flawlessly. None of them ever thought it would be so easy to take a half a million dollars off a guy without a gun or even a physical threat. That day, Central Shafting was born.

The "TO/FROM" display on the VOR began to flutter and St. Jones looked down to see Kingman, AZ. His watch read 10:05 a.m. and he was over halfway to Santa Fe with about six hundred miles down and five hundred to go. 12:30 p.m. was looking like a fair ETA, or 1:30 p.m. local time, since he had just crossed into the Mountain Time Zone. He looked up the Flagstaff VOR frequency in the AIM and dialed it into the second VOR.

A girlfriend of one of the cast members was night

manager at one of the more exclusive Beverly Hills hotels, and she arranged for a private dining room and an excellent menu for the Central Shafting cast party. St. Jones had done the job for twenty-five percent of the recovery and made six figure money, and decided that five grand for a party would be a suitable bonus. In addition to dinner, he had authorized the acquisition of two ounces of the best weed and two ounces of the finest blow that they could find in LA on short notice. The waiters were part-time stunt men or part-time waiters, depending on how things were going at the time, and were trusted friends of the cast. When St. Jones came down from his room in the hotel, he gave both bags to them to be served as courses along with the food and the wines.

There were about twenty of them, counting cast and crew and girlfriends, and it was a very elegant dinner, the men wearing tuxedos and the women foxed out Hollywood splendid. This was the Oscars presentation for sub rosa theater and they were feeling magnificent about their success and new found power and the fresh money in their pockets. The many toasts, jokes, and recountings of the "show" exhilarated everyone. It was a Mission Impossible scenario they had pulled off as well as Mayhew Associates, upon whom the series was based, could have.

After dessert was finished and the cocaine was being served on crystal platters already chopped and laid out in designs like Indian sand paintings, and concentric wheels of rolled joints on round silver serving dishes were passed around, the group began calling, "Author! Author!" It was the one thing St. Jones hadn't anticipated, and he hadn't prepared a word, but when he stood up and began to speak, the muse of the Purple Porpoise was whispering in his ear, like Jimmy Reed's wife with the words of the song.

St. Jones was soaring on the coke and the buds and the fine wine and cognac, and he became eloquent. He began by saying that every success he had witnessed ultimately came down to one of three things: a bold stroke, a sly pass, or an ace in the hole. Or a combination of the above. In full rant, he proposed the formation of a secret society based on these principles: The Order of the Bold Stroke, the Sly Pass, and the Ace in the Hole.

He had articulated a thought in the group mind and everyone leapt to their feet and cheered and clinked glasses all around. Realizing that he was onto something, he asked one of the waiters to bring in a chalk board on a tripod, the kind found in hotel conference rooms, and wrote down the first three precepts of survival learned at the Purple Porpoise and the fourth observed in Saigon. The next few hours were filled with hilarity as everyone suggested precepts. By the end of the evening they had a working list.

Since that night, Central Shafting has performed its special theater whenever justice required and there was something about the concept of the Order that was highly contagious. Over time, the Precepts became known among a certain circle of cognoscenti as a credo of enlightened self-interest.

The VOR/DME read twelve miles to Flagstaff with a mile flipping off the display every fifteen seconds and it was time to make a decision about where to land. Santa Fe was three hundred miles and change, and not that bad of an idea, even though it wasn't on a straight-line course to Miami.

The major problem with Santa Fe was that it was a nexus of many realms. You never knew who you might run into there. St. Jones had noticed that the more you travel the more you begin to see the same people everywhere you go. Not just their local equivalents. That, too. But actually the same people he had seen in other places along the trail of the late, late West. Santa Fe was a station on that trail, but it did offer anonymity of a sort. Because there were so many bizarre characters in Santa Fe, St. Jones would go unnoticed. Except by the paranoid and those who knew him, and of course, that was the problem.

But Santa Fe was an uncontrolled airport, and he had taken off without rigging his flight extender and had to piss so bad his teeth ached, and being spotted in Santa Fe wasn't really that bad of a diversion. He could manage to be seen around town and maybe lure the Narx Brothers into searching northern New Mexico for a week or so. Meanwhile, he would be gone with the dawn. Dialing up the Gallup VOR, he began mentally reviewing the menu at La Fonda. The monsters liked the idea a lot.

BOLD

11

After the crisp, dry air of the un-pressurized plane, St. Jones felt like he was walking on the bottom of a heated swimming pool in the hot, humid, south Florida weather. He slept until noon at the hotel, ate a leisurely breakfast in his room, and read the Miami Herald through to pull up to local speed. Around four o'clock, he took a taxi to within a few blocks of Bino's place on the border between Coconut Grove and Coral Gables and walked the rest of the way.

By the time he covered the distance, St. Jones' clothes were stuck to him like he'd taken a swim. He made a mental note to clean his piece, and dry out the suede Bianchi clip-on inside holster before it rusted from his sweat. He had to remember to dust it with baby powder every day, one of the tricks of carrying a concealed weapon in the tropics. Otherwise, it tends to stick, and you can find yourself in a Three Stooges movie. Or Two Stooges.

Bino's place was an old, walled, Spanish style compound that was miles out in the country when it was first built in the twenties, and town had gradually grown around it. The wall fronting the street was encrusted with seashells and the gate's arch was inlaid with large pink conch shells, their flared sides forming an uneven mother of pearl facade. The back of the property bordered on one of the many canals that ran miles inland from the ocean. It was the kind of place that had real pink flamingos.

St. Jones put on his Groucho glasses when he got within a block of the place. As he walked through the open gate and started up the long, curving drive, he wished he could have called ahead, but there was a reasonable chance that he would have been announcing his arrival to the same federal task force that was probably photographing him that very moment. As the main house came into view, he stayed to the middle of the driveway, trying to be as conspicuous as possible. People in south Florida have a lot of firepower laying around, and have good reason to be paranoid even before they get into the powder.

The arched, Spanish style, double front door was wide open, and St. Jones could hear guitar music coming from inside. As he took the two steps up onto the veranda, he pocketed the Groucho glasses and called out, "Hello...hello."

The music stopped, and several minutes later Slow Eddie appeared in the door. He was a local musician and part of Bino's salon. Slow Eddie played the sound track for the Bino Show, like a down-in-front Paul Schaffer.

"Hey, man. Ain't seen you in a while," he said, slow as molasses.

"Hi, Eddie. Is Bino in?"

A smile crept slowly up his face. "Yeah, you could say that." He turned and walked back into the house like he was doing Tai Chi. St. Jones went into slo-mo and followed him into a huge room that took up most of the downstairs of the sprawling, two-story place. It reminded him of the bar set in Key Largo. Four ceiling fans turned slowly, stirring the thick, tropical air like gumbo.

Eddie nodded his head toward the far corner of the room, and sat down in a wicker chair. He picked up his guitar and began playing again. St. Jones' eyes followed the nod to a triangular shaped stage fitted into the far corner of the room, where there was a piano, marimbas, a set of drums, some amplifiers and mikes, and a variety of percussion instruments, including a full set of congas. A deeply tanned, naked woman was arched backwards with her ass on the middle drum and her long, blond hair pooled on the floor on the other side. Bino was standing between her legs, stroking in time to Eddie's guitar. He was in alright, just like Eddie said. It was always startling to see Bino, his long white hair falling down on his milky white shoulders. Bino was the whitest man St. Jones had ever seen.

"Hey, St. Jones," Bino said, without stopping. "I thought I might be seeing you. Say hello to Girl."

"Hello, Girl."

"Hi, St. Jones," the upside down face said with a lascivious frown, a smile, properly seen.

"Grab yourself a brew. You know where the fridge is. I'll catch you in a minute," Bino said, without missing a stroke. "There's some blow over there by Eddie and some smoke on the bar. Help yourself."

St. Jones went behind the bar, got a very cold beer, and thought about how much he missed southern hospitality. Walking back around the bar, he sat down in a wicker chair next to Eddie. St. Jones made a couple of lines from the pile of powder under a shot glass on the mirrored Coca-Cola tray, while Eddie played a free-form Bolero-like accompaniment to Bino and Girl. St. Jones did the lines and drank the cold beer and watched them fuck, while the monsters humped his legs. In the South they know how to make you feel right at home.

Before long, Girl began sounding as though she was working up to the biggest sneeze of her life and then burst into insane giggling as Bino beat wildly on the drums on either side of her and Eddie hit a crescendo on the guitar. St. Jones applauded and shouted "Bravo! Bravo!", but didn't stand up.

Bino put his hand on his stomach, bowed at the waist several times in different directions, and stepped back. Placing her hands on the floor by her hair, Girl lifted her legs over the drums into a handstand, and then flipped to a standing position. She was drop dead beautiful. St. Jones' eyes flared, and the monsters were on her like paint.

"Girl's an acrobat," Bino said, as he casually sauntered to the bar. Even his pubes were white.

"She plays a hell of a conga drum, too," St. Jones added.

Girl smiled and walked over to his chair and sat down on his lap, putting her arm around his neck. The monsters were in a frenzy from the smell of fresh sex. She wiggled her ass against him and laughed. "Is that a gun in your pocket or are you just glad to see me?"

"Tough choice."

Bino and Eddie laughed. St. Jones was known to always be armed, and horny.

"Well, I better get up before something goes off." Girl stood up and stretched. "I'm going to go take a swim. Are you going to be around for a while?" She gave St. Jones a look humid with meaning.

St. Jones returned the look. "I may never leave." He watched her walk away. What a creature. She was everything Barbie was reaching for but couldn't quite pull off. And, she was anatomically correct, and then some. It was good that nobody else could see the monsters.

St. Jones looked down at his lap and laughed. "I've got come all over my pants, and it isn't even mine. How lucky can a guy get? This is even better than that dog you used to have that pissed on people's legs when they said 'Nixon'."

Bino and Eddie laughed. Bino walked back from behind the bar, picked up a bar towel and the coke tray, and sat down opposite Slow Eddie and St. Jones. "That's okay, man. You're next." He tossed St. Jones the towel. "I can tell by the way she looked at you. There was Voodoo in the air. I could feel it."

St. Jones wiped his pants off and looked at Slow Eddie. Eddie had a special talent. He was a human lie detector, and he kept everybody honest just by being around. If somebody said something that strained the limits of credulity, all eyes turned to Eddie. He looked up from his guitar and slowly nodded. Things were looking up.

"I've been expecting you since yesterday." Bino made some lines on the mirrored tray with a playing card, the Joker from a deck of Bicycles.

"How'd you know I was coming? Been reading the chicken guts again?" Bino dabbled in Voodoo and Santa Ria.

"Oh, you know, Sunday's on the phone to Monday, and Tuesday's on the phone to me." Bino smiled enigmatically and bent over the tray and snorted a couple of long, thin lines. "Actually, "A" called and said you'd probably be showing up." He handed the tray to St. Jones. "I told him it was cool, that you and I went way back. He said you had an ace rating with the boys."

"Yeah, me and "A" go back, too."

"So what's this Mama Coca shit, anyway?" Bino came right to the point. "And what do all those fucking numbers mean?"

St. Jones bent over the tray and snorted. "Mama Coca is an old friend of mine. Her name's Nickie. As for the numbers, they're code and I've got somebody working on that. Meanwhile, I'm waiting, and coming to see you is the only other move I had. Since the notes were in the rocks, I figure she must be in Colombia. I was hoping you might be able to help me with that part. Do they know about the notes?"

"I don't think so. The only way to communicate with the lab is by radio and the guys who do the transport have that equipment. They're here in the Grove, and I can contact them, but I haven't. After I heard from "A", I thought I'd wait and talk to you. I knew you'd be showing soon."

"Is there any talk here in the Grove?"

"Nada. Everything that comes through here goes out of state. We found one note in the kilo we broke open for the house, but that's the only one I know about in south Florida."

"Can we keep it that way?"

"Sure, man. Whatever you say. I owe you big-time for that scene down south, a while back. Just don't get me killed. I may owe you my life, but I have absolutely no intention of paying you back."

St. Jones had extracted Bino from a dope deal gone bad in the "you no send, me no come" country in the mountains of Jamaica. St. Jones wasn't going to bring it up unless he had to.

"I think I can help you with this," Bino continued, "but you mustn't piss off the Colombians. Those fuckers are crazy. They've done for body-bags what Calvin Klein did for jeans. Even the Cubans and the Dagos are afraid of them."

"I think that's probably why Nickie sent the notes. She's very bright and wouldn't have done this, if it wasn't that serious." St. Jones hoped he was right.

"Well, I hope it turns out to be worth it. People live or die down here on a whole lot less. And that goes for the people around them, too. The freeways here have diamond lanes for cars with two or more bodies in the trunk."

Slow Eddie and St. Jones laughed and Eddie stopped playing and picked up the tray.

"Did you bring your plane?" Bino asked.

"Yeah. I've got it outside of town."

"Good. I'm going to introduce you to the transport boys. They're always looking for pilots. We'll invite some people over for a party and I'll duke you in. You're on your own after that."

Girl came back into the room still naked except for a towel wrapped around her wet hair. She walked behind the bar and got a couple of cold beers from the fridge and, holding them to her breasts, danced up and down. When she took the bottles away, her nipples were the size of unfired .45 rounds. "Anybody need a beer?"

"I'll have one of those," St. Jones said, a beat too quickly.

"Yeah, baby, bring us some beers," Bino said, smiling at St. Jones. "And get on the phone and call up some people. We're gonna have a party. Call the guys at the VFW, too." Bino stood up. "Make yourself at home, St. Jones. Take off your shirt and relax. I'm gonna take a shower and get dressed and we'll go get something to eat before people start showing up." Bino walked naked from the room and up the stairs to the second floor. He was so white he made Casper look ethnic.

Girl picked up the dope box on the bar and brought St. Jones his beer and sat down in the chair Bino had vacated and started rolling. Eddie began playing again, humming in his basso profundo voice. St. Jones stood and unbuttoned his Hawaiian silkie floral print shirt and hung it over the back of his chair. His bruise had spread to the size of a pancake and his piece was visible above the top of his Levis.

"Wow, you weren't kidding, were you," she said, staring at his gun and then his stomach. "How did you get a bruise like that?"

"The hard way."

"That's what I thought. You're just another cocaine cowboy."

"No, not true. I'm from Vague magazine. I'm here doing an article on the Bermuda Triangle. They say you can really lose yourself there."

Girl laughed and passed him the joint. "Then why do you carry a gun?"

St. Jones took a long hit and handed it back to her. "Actually, I run a past-life collection agency. I find people who owed you money in a previous life and I collect it for you, for a percentage, of course. Hindus and Buddhists are a piece of cake. Christians are the worst. That's how I got the bruise. From a Protestant. He hurled a Bible at me with such force that it would have killed me, if it hadn't hit my lucky bullet."

Slow Eddie liked that one a lot, laughing out loud along with Girl. He stopped playing his guitar and took a hit from the joint. Girl was looking at St. Jones with a mixture of humor, curiosity, and lust. "I think you're some kind of secret agent."

"Nothing gets by you, does it? What gave me away? You're right, of course. I'm from the OIC. Does the name Pavlov ring a bell?"

"What the hell is the OIC?" she said, beginning to crack.

"Oh, I see," St. Jones said, archly, drawing it out like Bela Lugosi.

Girl almost peed, laughing. "Whatever it is that you do, you're a funny guy." She stood up, unwrapping the towel from her head. Her damp hair fell around her shoulders and her nipples sprang to attention. "I've gotta make some calls and go get ready." She bent down and kissed him lightly on the lips.

"You look ready to me, baby." St. Jones reached out and tweaked her bullets.

"You make me wet," she whispered, and turned and walked across the room and up the stairs, leading a parade of skulking monsters.

St. Jones laughed at the irony and savored her exit to the last frame. "What a piece of work," he said, turning to Eddie. "Every now and then the gene pool comes up with a royal flush."

Eddie hit a minor chord and held it. "'If it wasn't for women's unique anatomy, they'd be hunted for bounty,'" he slowly said, quoting Shopenauer.

"That was easy for him to say. He was queer."

"Just the same, I wouldn't want one of those things between my legs." Eddie continued his search for the missing chord. "It's hard enough to find the path, and even harder to stay on it. Just think what it would be like to wake up one morning with all that unearned power. And so young, too. It's a wonder they're not all crazy."

St. Jones reflected on that for a minute. Like still water, Slow Eddie ran deep. The only thing really slow about him was the way he talked and the way he moved. St. Jones had seen oysters move faster. But when Eddie played his guitar, his hands sometimes blurred, and his mind was often waiting for you at the next off-ramp.

"You ever been in love, St. Jones?"

"I don't know, man. Maybe, maybe not. I wanted to so bad once, I may have made a mock-up of love, and went for that, instead."

"Went for the menu, instead of the meal?"

"Yeah, something like that. But the Goddess keeps moving. First, She's looking at me through one woman's eyes, and as soon as I get close, She moves on to another. And, of course, so do I. Chasing the Goddess has been a way of life for me. The kind of women I meet these days are mostly coke whores and star-fuckers, or they're starring in their own movie. In my life, they'd be an extra, at best."

Eddie hit a minor chord on his guitar, held it, and began to sing.

> Life is full of corners
> There's one everywhere you turn
> Around some you find true love
> And others you get burned
> And wind up learning lessons
> That you didn't want to learn
> And with a reputation
> That you know you didn't earn
> I taught myself to be a user
> I taught myself to be a boozer
> But I learned to be a loser from you.

Eddie's love song was interrupted by Bino coming down the stairs. "Ready to go eat?" He hit the bottom step and sauntered toward Slow Eddie and St. Jones. "That's the secret to these parties, you know. It's like running. Load up heavy on carbs before it starts, because it might be a while before you're hungry again. These things take endurance. They're not for lightweights. We used to have them catered, but nobody ate anything, and they turned into food fights and we had to hose the place down." Bino was motor mouthing. He had obviously taken a hit for the road. "You staying at the hotel, St. Jones? We'll eat there."

"Yeah. That reminds me, Bino...can you fix me up with some blow? I didn't bring anything with me. Coal to Newcastle, you know."

"Sure, man. When you come back tonight, I'll have something made up for you."

The red AC Cobra's big Ford engine rumbled as they rolled slowly around the circular drive and out the gate onto the street. What good is having it if you can't flaunt it? Bino looked over at St. Jones and saw the Groucho glasses. "You crazy fucker. Have you still got those things? I'll never forget when you walked into that room in Jamaica with those fucking things on, and the Rastas burst out laughing. Up to that moment, I was a goner. That was sheer fucking genius, St. Jones."

BOLD

12

This time, St. Jones took a taxi to the gate. It was around nine o'clock and the temperature had plunged to about ninety and he didn't want to sweat out his clothes again before he got to the party. He put on his Groucho glasses and stepped out of the air-conditioned taxi, and the heat was on him like a full house on a busted flush. As he stepped under the arch and through the gate, a large shadow loomed in front of him.

"Good evening, sir. May I have your name to check against the guest list?" The apparition spoke with a politeness unnatural to his type.

"Good evening. The name is St. Jones."

"Mr. St. Jones is at the gate." The shadow was apparently speaking into a walkie-talkie, and he must have been wearing an ear-piece because St. Jones didn't hear the reply.

"Please proceed to the main house, Mr. St. Jones," he

said, almost immediately. "You're expected. Enjoy the party." The shadow dissolved back into the darkness. Spooky. St. Jones made a mental note to compliment Bino on his security. The circular drive was lined with up-scale cars that spilled out onto the street for blocks. As he approached the house, the music was getting louder and it was great, sort of an Afro-Cuban, rock 'n roll, reggae, jazz thing.

As he started up the steps to the front door, he pocketed the Groucho glasses. As if on cue, Girl emerged from the crowd that reached to the entrance. She was wearing a piece of floral print material wrapped around her waist Polynesian style, with a red flower over her left ear, and she was topless.

"Love your outfit."

"They call me the hostess with the mostess," she said, shimmying her shoulders. She took his hand and, standing on her toes, kissed him on the lips.

"I'll bet they do." He tweaked her nipples.

"Come on inside and let's get you a drink and go find Bino. There are some people here he wants you to meet." Girl took his hand and led him through the door. They made their way through the milling and dancing people to the bar, where there were four large cut glass punch bowls arranged along its length. The two on the left were filled with tropical punch with pieces of various fruits and large chunks of ice floating like icebergs. In the first bowl, the punch was green, and in the second bowl it was red. The third bowl was half filled with at least a kilo of cocaine with a variety of implements stuck into the opalescent powder. The fourth bowl was similarly filled with cleaned pot, Colombian gold by the look of it.

Girl led him to bowl number three, picked up a plastic implement and shoveling up a mound of powder, held it toward him. St. Jones leaned forward, holding a finger to one side of his nose and snorted. They repeated the ritual on the other side, and then she served herself.

"You roll a joint, and I'll get some punch," she shouted over the thundering music. "Red or green?"

"What's the difference?"

"Just like a traffic light."

"In that case, I'll take the green."

"My kind of guy."

St. Jones moved down the bar to the right and, picking up a pack of Blanco Y Negro papers, rolled a couple of cigarette-sized joints. By the time he finished, Girl was standing next to him with two plastic cups of green punch. She motioned with her head toward the stairs.

They wove their way through the dancing people to the foot of the stairs and started up to the second floor. As they reached the top, St. Jones touched Girl's arm and motioned for them to sit on the steps. He reached into his shirt pocket for one of the joints he had rolled, and lit it. "Let's sit here and smoke this. The boys can wait a few more minutes."

They sat and smoked and watched the scene downstairs. There were about a hundred and fifty people, sleek people in a tropical way, with lots of silkies and Bikini dresses and straight noses and long blond hair. And great bodies. The kind you find in the tropics, where people wear scant clothing, and can't wait to get out of it.

St. Jones spoke first. "What's a girl like you doing in a place like this, anyway?"

"Everybody's gotta be somewhere. Besides, where else

would a girl like me be?"

St. Jones thought about that for a minute, remembering the beautiful women he'd known and the special blues they all had. He handed her the joint and remembered what Slow Eddie said.

Girl took a long hit and held it. "Maybe it's not whether you win or lose, but where you play the game."

That was a precept if St. Jones ever heard one. He field commissioned Precept 99. She handed him the joint and exhaled slowly, looking into his eyes. Because of all her goodies, somehow he just hadn't gotten around to her eyes until then. The clear light of intelligence was shining there, and he realized that she was more than some Dopec bimbo with a great body and good on the congas. She was a victim of her type. Her eyes were also searching his, and he thought he saw a similar flicker of recognition.

"There you guys are." Bino walked up behind them. "I heard you were here and I was coming to find you."

"I stopped to survey the scene." St. Jones and Girl stood up. "Great party, great hostess, great music. That's what I like about the South."

"Yeah, there's some good players here tonight. Marley's around somewhere. He's gonna sit in later." Bino took a hit off the joint and passed it. "Hey, those guys I told you about are here. Let's go meet them and then we can take the rest of the day off and join the party."

"I'm going to go mingle." Girl took a couple of steps down the stairs, turned, and looked back at St. Jones with Voodoo in her eyes. "I'll see you after a while."

They watched her descend the stairs and disappear into the sea of blond below.

"What an extraordinary creature, Bino. Where did you

find her?"

"She's something, ain't she. She was Miss Florida a few years back. Her and her old man were staying here last year. He looked a lot like you, come to think of it. One day, he went out on a Cigarette to pick up a load from a mother ship a hundred miles out and never came back. People thought he split with the shit, and was living high down south somewhere. I had to protect her from his partners. They thought she knew where he was. She had a tough time. It was a lose/lose situation for her. If he had split, she lost. If he was dead, she lost. Later, we found out that he'd been jacked up for the load and fed to the snappers in the Glades. She's been here ever since."

"Like a rolling stone."

"With no direction home." Bino finished the line. "Good to see you again, St. Jones. It'll be fun hangin' out for a couple of days. Girl will like that, too. Don't let that scene this afternoon throw you. There's nothing going on with me and Girl. It's the just the coke. Sometimes we get so high there ain't nothing left to do but fuck. You know how it is. Who knows? Maybe you're the one. Hey, worse things could happen to a guy."

They started walking along the upstairs main corridor. "Wait here a second. Let me get you that blow you wanted." Bino unlocked the door to his office and stepped inside. He returned a half a minute later with a foil wrapped bag. "Here's a half-ounce. It's in a blister bag. I've been using these for insulation. Besides body temperature, the fucking room temperature down here is high enough most of the time to melt this shit, if it's any good."

"What do I owe you?" St. Jones bent down and tucked the bag in his right sock.

"Hey, it's on the house. I don't see you that often. Besides, I'm giving it away downstairs. At ten thousand dollars a kilo, that's about a hundred and fifty dollars you've got there. Buy me dinner before you leave and we'll call it even."

"You're on." St. Jones knew it could cost him twice that much. Bino liked to order the menu.

They continued walking along the upstairs corridor. "These guys you're gonna meet, I told them about you and they liked what they heard. If this meeting goes okay, they'll probably offer you a job, and that will take you to the source. That's the best I can do for you. But watch your ass. These boys are the Black Tuna. They're like the Angels only they're military instead of bikers."

Black Tuna was a group of Vietnam combat vets who had gone into the security and transport business in the Southeast U.S. They were Dopec Rangers, well equipped and very high tech, with a lot of firepower and a willingness to use it.

At the end of the hall, they turned right into a long room containing the largest, most elaborate slot car track St. Jones had ever seen, with a thirty-foot straight-away and all the usual racing course features.

Two cars, a red one and a black one, were close on each other coming through the turns, hitting the straight-away in a dead heat. They accelerated with lightning speed, but when they should have started letting up to make the left turn at the end, neither one would back off first, and they both flew off the end of the table and slammed into the wall. St. Jones made a note and turned his attention to the two guys at the controls.

If this were the movies, these guys would be Jerry Reed

and Gary Busey in their thirties. Bino and St. Jones walked to the far end of the room where the boys were standing at the controls, sizing each other up as they closed the distance. St. Jones liked these guys on sight. They looked like him. Not just physically. There was something else. It was the mutual recognition of types. St. Jones remembered a test some Ph.D. had devised where the subject was shown a group of photographs and asked which one he would sit next to on a train. It turned out that people always chose their own kind, even though there were no significant visual clues. Manic-depressives picked manic-depressives, schizophrenics picked schizophrenics, pederasts picked pederasts.

Bino made the introductions. "Johnson, Jackson, say hello to St. Jones."

"Hi, guys." St. Jones shook hands with them. He could tell by their grips, they were rangers. "I like the way you finessed that last turn." Everybody laughed and relaxed. Bino produced a glass vial from his shirt pocket and dumped out about half a gram of coke on the end of the giant slot table, and began making lines with a Buck knife.

"So, Bino says you're a pilot. What have you flown, St. Jones?" asked Johnson, the one that looked like Busey, while Jackson bent down and snorted a couple of lines through a rolled up hundred.

"I'm checked out in most light and medium twins and B-18s and C-47 series heavy twins and Mitchells. Also Cessna Citations and Lears in jet class, and Bell 47s through 500s, and most military choppers."

"How much time you got?" Jackson asked, while Johnson took his place at the table.

"Around 10,000 hours fixed-wing...maybe 3,500

hours rotary-wing."

"Bino says you own a plane."

"Yeah, I've got a Turbo 210 STOL with ferry tanks and an IFR panel," St. Jones answered, taking the rolled up hundred-dollar bill from Bino. He bent down and did a couple of lines off the table. On the way down, he saw them nod and smile at Bino. So far, so good.

"Bino mentioned that you flew in Asia," Johnson said. "Were you in Nam, or what?"

"I flew out of Laos to just about everywhere." St. Jones reached into his shirt pocket and found the second joint and lit it with a paper match from a book on the table. "I was on a civilian contract flying unarmed aircraft that technically didn't exist, 'in country.' After that, I flew out of Hong Kong for a while. Contract stuff."

"Ever get shot at?" Jackson asked.

"In the air and on the ground." St. Jones' stomach twitched. "I had one shot out from under me once and had to walk home."

"How far?" Johnson asked, passing the joint to St. Jones.

"I took a hundred mile nature walk along the Zamboangan Peninsula. The guys in camp went nuts when I walked in a week and a half later. Turned out, nobody had ever made it back before. If you went down out there, you were VSF...Very Severely Fucked. Pilots were considered disposable. They didn't even look for you. They hoped to hell you were dead, for everybody's sake. They just sent out for another one."

Johnson bent over the table and did a couple of lines. "We don't do this when we work, only when we play. Is that a problem?"

"Not for me. I only snort socially, and in bed. But never when I work, and seldom when I'm alone. That's where the line is."

"How's your Spanish?" Jackson asked.

"Adequate."

"Ever fly down south?" Johnson asked.

"I've flown in Mexico a lot, and the Caribbean, and to various parts of South America."

"What about Colombia?" asked Jackson.

"Cartagena. Bogota. Also over Colombia to get to points south."

There was a break in the questions and St. Jones used the lull to bend down and do a couple of lines, giving them a chance to signal each other. He took his time. It was a closing technique.

"Let's have lunch tomorrow, St. Jones," Johnson said. "We can talk more, then. Meet us at the VFW about two o'clock."

"You're on." St. Jones recognized the dismissal signal and extended his hand to Johnson. "Now, if you gentlemen will excuse me, I passed through a great party downstairs that I barely said hello to." He shook hands with Jackson and patted Bino on the back and made his exit, leaving them to talk.

BOLD

13

St. Jones stood at the top of the stairs, scanning the crowd for Girl. This was no easy task, as most of the people there, men and women, had long blond hair. The monsters wanted to go back to the bar and go bowling, and on the theory that if you were kind to your monsters they would be kind to you, St. Jones headed downstairs.

There were more people now and the band was cooking and moving through the crowd was more difficult. This was a very stoned crowd, and a kind of purple haze floated over the room. That observation had St. Jones speculating about the punch. By the time he reached the bar, he decided to find a beer and pass on the red and the green. He found an ice-cold San Miguel in the fridge and decided that life was good, if fleeting. The monsters reminded him that you only go around once, so he helped himself to a couple of liberal hits of gusto from bowl number three. With very little prompting, he moved on to bowl number four, rolling a cigarillo sized joint. He lit it and watched the Bacchanalian frenzy on the other side of the bar and considered the possibility that it might be later than it seemed.

The room was hot and very high and St. Jones began to see more and more topless blondes, further complicating his search. He was grappling with this latest development, when he felt a hand on his goodies. He had one foot propped up on a case of beer under the bar, and when he looked down he saw fingers moving. Praying he would find a woman connected to the hand, he turned his head to the right and coughed twice.

"I estimate you at about a ten," the incredibly skinny blonde woman said.

"Uncanny." He turned to face her, dislodging her hand. "Are you from the Bureau of Standards, or what?"

"I was talking about your BDD quotient." She was stick figure thin, almost an x-ray of herself and very reptilian. He could tell by her eyes that she had reached escape velocity.

"I know I'm gonna regret this, but what's a BDD quotient?"

"Brains, dick, and dollars," she smirked. "It's your IQ times the length of your dick in centimeters divided by the money in your pocket, U.S."

Remembering that he was carrying about five hundred dollars, St. Jones ran the formula in his head. "Amazing. That must have taken a lot of research. You must be a...ahh..." He groped for the right word.

"I'm a nurse."

"Of course. And you learned that at the hospital?"

"Yeah. That, and why doctors wear rubber gloves."

"So they won't leave finger prints?"

"Oooo, you must be a doctor."

"I've played a little doctor."

"I bet you have," she said, eyeing his crotch. "You're a doctor if I've ever seen one, and every doctor needs a nurse." She caressed the bulge in his jeans with her skeleton like fingers, and sat down on the case of beer under the bar, and when he felt his fly being unbuttoned, St. Jones didn't resist. After all, she was a woman of science.

While the monsters were gathered under the bar observing the procedure, St. Jones remembered that "D" stood for dollars, and removed his wallet from his hip pocket and put it in his shirt. He propped his elbows on the bar, and looked up to discover he was standing directly in front of bowl number three. They say it'll kill you, but they don't say when, and if there was ever an experiment designed to resolve that question, this was it. Piling a mound of cocaine on one of the implements, St. Jones snorted deeply. He was in the process of doing it again, when Girl appeared out of the crowd.

"Hi, sailor. Buy me a drink?" She had a curious look in her eye.

He dipped the implement into the powder and held it out to her. She snorted the coke, and while he was dipping into the bowl again, he could feel her eyes studying him. He held out the implement, trying to distract her, but women are sexually psychic and he knew it was only a matter of seconds before Girl would bust him. Not that it mattered after their introduction that afternoon. It was more a matter of style. No guy wants to get caught with his dick in his hand, so to speak. But as luck would have it, that's when the shooting started.

It's difficult to describe all that happened next. Under

the bar, the x-ray nurse forgot all about where she was and what she was doing and tried to leap to her feet, with predictable results. Precept 41 observed that in a crisis you will not rise to your expectations, but fall to your level of training. St. Jones reverted to training and dropped to the floor and drew his weapon with one hand and tried to stuff his dick into his pants with the other. The monsters were half way to the Bahamas and the nurse was out cold under the bar, as he crouched low, his pistol in one hand and his dick in the other, an inspiration to real men everywhere.

St. Jones was a graduate of the Colonel Jeff Cooper School of Serious Social Work, and had been trained to a color-coded threat identification and response system. Condition Green was pastoral serenity. Condition Yellow meant there was a disturbance in the force, as yet unidentified. Condition Orange indicated a clearly identified danger. Condition Red was reflex response, double tap to the center mass (two rounds through the heart). This system was taught in endless, maximum stress, live-fire drills until he actually began to see the colors in his peripheral vision. It was a conditioned ESP phenomenon.

St. Jones was flashing bright yellow as he cautiously bobbed his head up and down over the edge of the bar. The shooting was still going on, but he couldn't figure out where it was coming from. The scene in the room was pandemonium, with the blond leaping the blond, trying to crawl into the cracks in the floor, and more guns drawn than St. Jones had seen outside of a Peckinpah movie. Everybody in the room had a piece.

Precept 21 stated that interiors were traps, and St. Jones wanted out of there. This was south Florida, and for all he knew, there was a fire team of Colombian *cocaleros* sealing off the house for a massacre. They did things like that. St. Jones painfully jammed his dick into his jeans and crept around the end of the bar to where he had last seen Girl. He grabbed her hand and pulled her up and crouching low, ran across the backs of the cursing crowd toward the door. As they came to the entrance he stopped, and ducking down, bobbed his head quickly in and out the door and studied the photo his mind had taken. He raised up a couple of feet and did it again, just to confirm the source of the gunfire. It was a very thin, older Cuban wearing a wide brimmed Panama hat and pleated white slacks that came up almost to his armpits, in the style of old Havana. St. Jones had seen him earlier at the bar and remembered him because of the inch long fingernail on the little finger of his left hand that he used to scoop cocaine.

The Cuban was standing in front of a black Cadillac convertible, firing a Browning Hi-Power 14 shot 9mm into the well perforated hood and cursing in Spanish. Finally, the slide locked open on the last round of what must have been his third magazine and in the roaring silence that followed, he turned and looked at St. Jones and Girl.

"*Buenos noches, mi amigo.*" St. Jones managed a smile. "*Que pasa?*"

"It was self defense, *señor*," the Cuban said, in heavily accented English. His eyes had lost vertical hold. "It was going to kill me."

St. Jones instantly saw the perfect logic of the Cuban's thinking, and lowered the hammer on his Walther. St. Jones thought it commendable, and very Cuban. He slipped his weapon back into the inside holster under his shirt.

"*Es verdad, señor,*" the Cuban mumbled, saliva running from the corner of his mouth. *"Es verdad."*

The Cuban melted into a puddle at the front of the car while St. Jones and Girl stood there, throbbing with adrenaline. Now that the firing had stopped, people were beginning to look through the windows and come out the door. The apparition from the front gate came running up the drive with the silhouette of a MAC 10 in his hand. As he approached, St. Jones pointed in the direction of the Cuban with one hand and kept the other hand in clear view. St. Jones had observed that danger seldom came from within the gestalt he was working in. It more often came from being at the wrong place at the right time.

"What the hell happened?" the shadow asked, skidding to a stop.

"The Cuban killed his car before it could kill him and he's napping now," St. Jones said, keeping it brief.

The shadow unclipped a walkie-talkie from his belt and described the situation to someone, presumably in the house. He referred to Armando, who must have been the Cuban. St. Jones and Girl couldn't hear the other side of the conversation, but the shadow sounded worried. He listened for a few more seconds, and then turned to Girl. "The cops are coming. The bar is being taken care of. Take Mr. St. Jones to the blue room. I'll give you thirty seconds head start and then I'm going to make the announcement to the pretty people. Go, go, go."

Girl grabbed St. Jones' hand and swiftly led him back into the house, through the confusion to a door next to the stairway that led to the kitchen. She walked straight to the refrigerator, dragging him by one hand, and took a magnetic carrot from the door, the kind used to post notes. Turning to the wall opposite the fridge, she held the magnet to a calendar on the second Tuesday of the month and there was a click and a section of the wall swung open. She replaced the magnet on the fridge and led him through the opening.

Girl pushed the wall closed behind them, and led St. Jones down a steep, narrow, metal stairway, and along a lighted corridor for about fifty feet to another door that opened as they approached. The door was inch thick solid steel plate, and as he stepped through it, he understood why they called it the blue room. The walls and ceiling were sky blue with a cobalt blue carpet. There were two couches that looked like they made into beds, and a large low table that held the four magic bowls from the bar upstairs. Against the wall was a video security console with six monitors, a small VHF two-way radio base station, a scanner and a phone. There was also another door.

A guy was sitting at the console watching the scene upstairs. He turned and smiled slyly at St. Jones. They could see Bino's security man making his way through the chaos to the bandstand and hear the confusion in stereo. A professional-grade audio tape recorder with ten and a half inch reels was taking it all down. The second monitor was focused on the bar where the bowls had been and St. Jones understood why the guy was smiling. He could see the nurse, still out cold behind the bar. Another monitor showed the area in front of the house where Armando lay sleeping. Now he understood how Girl's timing had been so good, both times. A fourth monitor displayed the street in front of the gate. The next showed the corridor they had come through to reach the blue room, and they could see Bino and Slow Eddie approaching the steel door. The last monitor had a view of a street St. Jones didn't recognize. The guy at the console pushed a button under the table and the door clicked open and Bino and Slow Eddie entered the blue room.

"Ladies and gentlemen, could I have your attention, please?" the security man said through the lead vocal mike at center stage. "Due to the unfortunate incident that just occurred, we are about to be visited by the police. There is no time to leave, so I would suggest as a precaution, doing up anything that you might have on you in the way of recreational substances of marginal legality, not that we condone such behavior." The crowd laughed. "We'll take care of the police as best we can and the party will resume when they leave." Stash started coming out all over the room.

Their attention was drawn to the fourth monitor as police cars began arriving at the gate to the compound.

St. Jones articulated the only important question. "Is there another way out of here?"

"Yeah, through the bathroom." Bino nodded to the other door St. Jones had noticed earlier. "But it would take a LAWS rocket to get through that steel door and there are Claymores plastered into the walls of the corridor and two of my lawyers are in the crowd upstairs."

"I'm sure you're right, but I've had enough excitement for one night," St. Jones said. "I'm still wiped out from the last few days and I want to be fresh for my meeting tomorrow."

"Show him the way out, baby," Bino said to Girl, and then turned to St. Jones. "Good luck tomorrow. Come back over after your meeting. We'll still be at it. These things go on for days, 'til all the bowls are empty."

Girl led St. Jones into the bathroom and closed the

door. She stepped into the shower, picked up a bar of soap from the dish, and held it to one of the tiles and the back wall of the shower clicked open into a dimly lit corridor. They stepped through the opening and pushed the tiled wall closed behind them. They were in a passageway that appeared to be an old underground storm-drain. A plywood floor had been added and lighting was strung along one side. After going several hundred feet along the damp tunnel, and making several turns, they came to the end, where a steep stairway went up to a door. He followed Girl up the stairs through the door and found himself in a walk-in closet. They made their way through the hanging clothes and she slid open the closet door and they stepped into a bedroom.

"Where are we?" St. Jones asked.

"In a safe house on the next street over. Slick, huh?"

"I'm impressed. This is as slick as I've ever seen. Which way out of here?"

"Not so fast." Girl said, taking his hand. "You know, I watched you on video with that bitch under the bar. I guess that makes us even. I know how it looked this afternoon, but what can I say? Your timing was lousy. But I wore this flower over my left ear for you, and I just can't let you leave without telling you that."

"Come back to the hotel with me."

"I thought you'd never ask."

"Is there a phone? I'll call a taxi."

"There's a car in the garage."

Half an hour later they were in St. Jones' room at the Coconut Grove Hotel.

"How about a drink?" St. Jones took off his silkie and tossed it on a chair.

"Vodka rocks would be nice." Girl smiled. "But first, I need to use your bathroom."

While Girl was in the bathroom, St. Jones poured himself a JD from two airline bottles and made Girl's drink. He sat down on one of the barstools and took a deep sip from his glass and retrieved the half-ounce of coke from his right sock. Taking off his shoes and socks, he took the drinks to the bedside table and crawled up onto the bed. St. Jones preferred the bed for hanging out. Especially in hotels. It was the closest thing to home. He made a pile of pillows and leaned back as the door opened and Girl walked out of the bathroom naked, smiling slyly as she crossed the room. She crawled up on the bed and sat opposite him, cross-legged, and leaned over and kissed him on the lips. He handed her the drink and reached behind him and got the bag.

When she saw the coke, she laughed and shimmied her shoulders. "Hoooo boy, are we in trouble." She rubbed her hand softly against the bulge in his jeans. "Why don't you get out of those pants and hand me that picture on the wall and something to work with."

He handed her the picture off the wall, a photograph actually, of either a sunrise over the Atlantic or a sunset over the Gulf of Mexico, and got a straw and a hotel business card from the bar. He took off his jeans and tossed them on the chair with his shirt and walked to the bed, already swelling in anticipation.

"Ooooo baby, look at that. I just knew you had a big dick. I could tell by the way you look at women." She reached out and grasped it like she was shaking hands.

"How big does this thing get, anyway?" She laughed and her eyes flashed. "All this cock and all that coke. Oooo, baby, are we gonna have fun tonight."

St. Jones crawled up on the bed and picked up the phone and called the desk, leaving a noon wake-up call. After that, it was a slow fade to pink.

BOLD

14

When the phone rang at noon, St. Jones awoke tangled up in dreams of the night before. He had dreamed one of the great classics. He was out walking one day when a tiger began to chase him. When he came to the edge of a cliff, he climbed over and hung from a root to escape the tiger. When he looked down, he saw another tiger waiting for him below. While pondering his situation he observed two mice, a white one and a black one, chewing on the root above. Just then, he noticed a strawberry growing wild on the side of the cliff. He picked it and ate it, and it tasted very, very good.

St. Jones sat up and the room spun and a Checkered Demon began kicking his head like a Chinese gong. St. Jones staggered to the bathroom and dry heaved over the toilet a couple of times. Remembering Girl, he lurched back into the room but she was gone.

St. Jones called room service and ordered two coffees

and a danish. Stumbling back to the bathroom, he dry heaved again, reminding himself of his deeply bruised stomach. Rather than risk standing up, he crawled on his hands and knees into the shower and turned the cold water on full blast. He barely felt it, but after a while the cold needles began to penetrate his nerve endings. Standing up on his hind legs, he added hot water and began washing himself. He discovered he had a tender dick and had flashbacks of hot, frenzied, drug-crazed sex. He turned off the water and stepped out of the shower and, looking at his watch, remembered why he ordered the wake-up call: lunch at the VFW with Johnson and Jackson at two o'clock.

There was a knock at the door. St. Jones wrapped a towel around himself and gave the room a quick scan, hanging the picture back on the wall. He went to the door, and peeling back the tape from the peephole, saw that it was room service. St. Jones always taped the peephole in any hotel room he used because hotel security, police, and others, have a device that, when held to the peephole from the outside, allows a full view of the room. There's also a "C" mount camera attachment. St. Jones had one. He opened the door and the middle-aged Cuban wished him a *buenos dias* and put the tray on the table and lingered while St. Jones found his jeans and dug a five out of the pocket. The Cuban was pleased. "Please ask for Jesus, señor." St. Jones hoped it wouldn't come to that.

He drank the first cup straight down without stopping, and realized it was going to take more than consumer grade chemistry to pull off the meeting. Rummaging around in his leather carry on bag for the medical kit, St. Jones mildly panicked until he found it. He decided on the combination that he had used to make the flight: T-3's and Dexedrine.

He swallowed two of each with coffee and took a couple of bites of danish and almost barfed it all up. He rolled a joint from a film can of cleaned weed that he kept in the kit for medicinal purposes. After a few hits the nausea began to subside, and he tried some more pastry. He was making a slow but steady recovery.

He opened the drapes covering the floor-to-ceiling, wall-to-wall window facing the Atlantic, and was almost knocked down by the brutal wall of light. This must have been how Dracula felt when he didn't beat the dawn. St. Jones left the drape open because, unlike Dracula, he had to go out into that photon hell.

He sat at the table, smoked another joint, and finished the danish and the second carafe of coffee. As the various substances began to take effect, he checked his pulse and was pleasantly surprised to find one. When his watch chirped one o'clock, St. Jones decided it was time to get dressed, and stood up from the table with only mild nausea and manageable pain. He decided on shorts and a tank top for his foray into the afternoon inferno.

After dressing, St. Jones got out the tennis balls he kept in his bag and began playing two handed, two ball, handball against the walls and floor and ceiling of the room. It was a game for one he had developed from years on the road and countless days and nights of boredom in hotel rooms. It helped pass the time and calm his mind and it kept his reflexes tuned.

By one-thirty, he was feeling almost human and decided to walk the four blocks to the VFW. He put his piece and various contraband in the slick he had made when he first checked into the room. Concealing items in a hotel room was a very important aspect of trade craft. This time he had removed a six inch section from the top edge of the closet door with the saw on his Swiss Army knife and lowered his things into the door on a piece of string, tying it off on a thumb tack stuck into the top edge of the door. Housekeeping would be coming in and he gave the room the once over before leaving. It occurred to him that he should take a back-up room when he returned from the meeting.

When he stepped out of the lobby and onto the street, St. Jones wondered if WWIII had broken out while he was in the elevator and he had walked into a nuclear fireball. His mirrored aviator's shades were no match for the onslaught of light. He needed welding goggles. His clothes were soaked by the time he reached the corner, and after he walked four blocks he was numb. St. Jones thanked St. Jude for codeine. He reached the VFW easily five pounds lighter, his Adidas sloshing from the sweat that had rolled down his legs and collected there.

St. Jones pushed open the door at five minutes 'til two o'clock and was enveloped in industrial strength air conditioning and darkness. He stopped in his tracks, completely blind. He took off his shades and waited for his eyes to adjust. As he began to be able to see shapes and outlines, he saw arms waving at a booth across the room. He carefully made his way through the tables. Only when he got within a few feet did he recognize the boys for sure. There was a third guy with them he hadn't seen before.

"Hi guys. This is more like it." St. Jones sat down on the ice cold naugahyde next to the stranger and shivered involuntarily.

"We donated the money for the air-conditioning with the agreement they would keep it cold and dark in here,"

Johnson said.

"Well, they covered their end of the deal."

"Say hello to Jefferson," Johnson said. They shook hands all around. St. Jones still couldn't see well enough to make out his features. "Jefferson is our Minister of Security. It's SOP for every FNG (Fucking New Guy) to be cleared by him. That's one of the reasons we've had so few problems."

"How about something to drink?" Jackson asked.

"I'd really like some iced tea. I'm a couple of quarts low from the walk over here." After the drinking and snorting and fucking and sweating of the night before, St. Jones was dehydrated.

"Hey, Lightning," Johnson called out to the bartender. "Bring us two pitchers of ice tea and four specials."

"Is it really dark in here, or is the end near?" St. Jones asked.

"See, I told you he was a funny guy," Johnson said to Jefferson.

"Jefferson's a funny guy, too. He used to throw guys out of helicopters to see if they were lying."

"Could they fly if they were telling the truth?"

Everyone laughed.

"Most of the time I used the polygraph," Jefferson said. "And that's what I use now. All FNG's have to be polygraphed. So after lunch, before we start talking about business, I'd like for you to come into the office and we'll see if paleface speaks with forked tongue."

"Just so long as you don't offer to fly me back to the hotel."

They laughed. Jefferson was smart and knew his business, and was probably an alumnus of the Phoenix project.

He told St. Jones this before lunch so he would have to think about it and dwell on any areas of guilt he might have, thereby intensifying his reaction. But not sooner, so St. Jones would have no chance to condition himself or take a masking drug. On the other hand, he was already a walking drug store.

St. Jones followed their eyes to Lightning approaching their booth. He put a tray on the nearest table and served their plates. The fried fish and potatoes and salad actually looked good. Lightning had a wild, stark look in his eyes. Not the well known thousand-yard stare, but something else. His hair seemed to be standing on end. Not really, but somehow giving that impression. He placed two half-gallon sized pitchers of iced tea on the table and walked back to the bar. St. Jones curiosity won out.

"I can't help asking. How'd Lightning get his name?"

"It's a war story," Johnson began. "Korea. Lightning, although he wasn't called that then, was in the armored corps and was a sergeant in a tank crew at the Inchon landing. It was a three-man crew, with a college boy captain and a black corporal. It was the first day of the landing and they were rolling along with the hatch open and the captain was standing up with his head out looking around, when a mortar round landed directly on top of the turret. The blast took the captain's head clean off at the shoulders, and when the headless body dropped down inside, it began to run. When the black corporal saw that, he went stark raving berserk and began trying to outrun the captain. The inside of a tank is a very small place, and at that moment Lightning came to the realization that he wasn't cut out for that shit, and leapt eight feet straight up in the air and came down running.

"There's old boys here at the VFW that were there that day, and they say he was as busy as a dog with two dicks, running this way and that, dodging fire from infantry and snipers and tanks. Every gook for a mile and a half around was shooting at him.

"During all the confusion of battle, no one had noticed the weather. A squall was moving in off the sea. Lightning was being driven up a hill by a pattern of fire and when he reached the top, he was trapped, silhouetted against the sky from every direction with no place to hide. And that's when it happened. KABOOM! A bolt of lightning struck him. Everybody just froze, on both sides. Nobody had ever seen anything like it before. Everybody stopped firing. They all thought he was toast. It saved his life.

"He was still shooting sparks when the medics picked him up. They say it was a good thing the chopper pilot knew the terrain, because every instrument on the panel went south. But other than being scorched, there wasn't a mark on him, but his combat days were over. The Army, in its infinite wisdom, gave him a purple heart and a bronze star and shipped him home by way of Letterman Hospital. When he came back home, the VFW hired him and he's been here ever since. The way I figure it, he's the luckiest man in the world."

"Wow. What a story," St. Jones said. "I'll be thinking about that one for a while. I wonder what went through his mind when the lightning struck. After being shot at by everybody on Earth, to be fired upon by God, Himself, and then to discover that it was a gift."

They ate in silence, each pondering the mysteries of fate, chance and destiny. Even through the drugs, the meal was good, the fish caught that morning. St. Jones could feel himself gaining strength. One by one, the monsters were slinking back.

"That was a hell of a party last night." St. Jones was trying to keep it light.

"You mean, *is* a hell of a party. It's still going on," Jackson replied.

"How long do they usually last?"

"Around five or six days, if you're talking about original cast performances where most of the people at the end were there at the beginning," Jackson answered. "But there have been some SDR... Sex, Drugs, and Rock 'n Roll... revivals that lasted for weeks."

"We just missed you in the blue room last night," Johnson said. "You'd just left when we got there. That turned into a hell of a party its own self."

"Yeah, Marley was there," Jackson said. "He said he knew you from Frisco the first time he was there. Between him and Bino, you've got pretty good bona fides."

"You gotta be honest to live outside the law." St. Jones quoted the Dylan Imperative and the Twenty-ninth Precept. All he had to do now was ace the polygraph.

BOLD

15

The lie detector is an interesting device. It doesn't really detect lies. It measures stress. The body reflects in various ways the stress the mind feels. In the old days this principle was applied by tying a cord around the neck of the subject, tightly enough to all but cut off the flow of blood to the brain. Then, if the subject lied upon questioning, the physiological reaction of the body would cause an increase in blood pressure and a subsequent slight increase in the size of the neck with predictable and fatal results. If you're lyin', you're dyin.'

There is one field expedient way of beating the polygraph, and that is to think of something stressful with every question, including the control questions, thereby cloaking the ones that mattered. But since St. Jones had no intention of ripping them off or setting them up, he decided to just relax and wing it. Besides, his mission was righteous. He was on a knight's quest to rescue a damsel fair from the lair of the evil dragon. He decided to hold that righteousness in the wings of his mind to offset any guilt he might harbor about his lack of candor.

St. Jones was dealing with a Twentieth Century Torquemada, the evil genius of the Spanish Inquisition. Torquemada found that the fear of torture was vastly more effective than torture, itself. Therefore, he would place his real target in the cell nearest to the torture chamber, so that others being tortured would be dragged past him on the way to and back from interrogation. By the time the true subject was brought into the chamber, they were singing like Little Richard on Angel crank. The guy that Jefferson didn't throw out of the chopper was the real target. That's why Jefferson told St. Jones about the polygraph before lunch. He wanted him to think about it, like the opposing team calling time out before a field goal attempt.

He didn't see Lightning until he was practically standing next to him, but St. Jones could feel his charge crackling in the darkness as he approached. Lightning cleared the table and served Cafe Saigon. No Folgers crystals here. Four French filter presses and a bowl of Eagle brand sweetened, condensed milk.

Everyone observed the ritual of pushing the handle down, pressing the filter and coffee through the water to the bottom. Pouring their coffee into cups, they stirred in the thick, sweet milk.

"I hear you're a private dick, St. Jones," Jefferson said, taking him by surprise. Jefferson had obviously been doing his homework.

"That's true," St. Jones said, taking a sip of coffee.

"How'd you get into that line of work? Most PIs that I

know are ex-cops."

"Most of the ones I know are ex-cops, too. That's why I've managed to be successful at it. In San Francisco, there are a lot of people who need help who can't call the cops, and who feel very uncomfortable dealing with guys with cop mentalities. Dealers who have been ripped off. Gays who have been extorted. Vampires. Underground people with all sorts of problems who can't do business in the daylight. That's about half my work. The rest is trial prep. I have a relationship with a law firm. I work mostly dope defense cases, but not entirely. It depends on the lifestyle of the client. The DA has the cops and his own investigators working to put my clients in jail. Defense attorneys have guys like me to try and keep them out. I find it very satisfying work and I'm good at it. I've kept a lot of good guys out of the joint. It's a nice feeling to run into a guy on the street and have him thank you for his life. That happens to me fairly often and it's not something that I apologize for."

Jefferson seemed satisfied with St. Jones' answer, and Johnson and Jackson nodded their approval. Everyone took a sip of coffee and Johnson and Jackson laid out, letting Jefferson solo.

"So, why are you interested in joining the company, St. Jones?" he asked. "Seems like you've already got your plate full."

"Well, it's a target of opportunity for me. Having entreé to you guys is something I would be foolish not to exploit. This would allow me to finance several projects of mine, not to mention my lifestyle. And then, there's retirement. I never thought I'd live long enough for that to be a consideration, but since I've lived this long, anything is possible."

"Ever work for the cops, St. Jones?" Jefferson asked sharply.

The monsters all started to howl at once and St. Jones couldn't understand a snarl they were making but he got the idea. The booth was wired for sound and he was being recorded for voice stress analysis, or maybe even analyzed real-time by someone he couldn't see. This was the test, itself. He had used the PSE (psychological stress evaluator). It had been developed by the CIA and tested in Vietnam, just like Jefferson.

The device works on the principle that there is normally present in the human voice a sub-audible microtremor that is suppressed when we lie. Its range is in the order of ten cycles per second and it is, in fact, the brain's alpha rhythm appearing as a sub-carrier in the voice. The PSE/VSA works by detecting and measuring that vibration. Its advantage over a conventional polygraph is that it can be used without the subject's knowledge, and it can also be used on tapes and recorded material. The Dektor, which was the standard machine in use in the 1970s, had a three digit display and anything that read over sixty-five was considered suspect.

"I've worked with the cops on cases involving stolen children, and missing persons, and I've worked with the FBI and various DAs, too," St. Jones answered. "There are some situations where you have no choice but to work with the cops. That's the environment the game is played in. It's like computers and IBM. But work for the cops? Absolutely not. I don't like cops and they don't like me. They're my adversaries, personally, professionally, and philosophically.

"There's two kinds of people in the world and they're

like red corpuscles and white corpuscles. The red corpuscles are carriers of energy and nourishment and vitality...life, to the body. Poets, artists, lovers, and in general, people who come good, in the Reichian sense. The white corpuscles scavenge the body and fight infection and empty the wastebaskets. When there gets to be too many of them, it's called leukemia. Their equivalents in society pick up the garbage and put out the fires and keep water in the pipes and control predators, and when they get out of control it's called fascism. Their world view is one of good guys versus bad guys, with a large number of very inconvenient citizens in the way. We need them so we don't have to do that shit ourselves, but it's the nature of their type that they think they are the reason for society, instead of the other way around."

"I never heard it put quite so well, St. Jones," Jefferson said, after a pause. "You should've been a lawyer."

"That would've made your job a lot easier. You don't need a box to tell when a lawyer's lying."

"Yeah, how's that?" Jefferson asked suspiciously.

"Their lips are moving."

Jefferson held back, but Johnson and Jackson laughed.

St. Jones decided it was time to call. "Do you think I went over sixty-five during my rant, Jefferson?" St. Jones laid down his hand, revealing his knowledge of the PSE.

"It appears that I have a worthy adversary," Jefferson said, smiling.

"So did he or didn't he go over sixty-five, Jefferson?" Johnson asked, chuckling. "I think we can drop the game at this point."

"He never went over fifty," Jefferson replied. He took an ear-piece from his opposite ear and put it in his shirt pocket where he carried the receiver connecting him to the office.

"I gotta hand it to you guys," St. Jones said with genuine admiration. "This is a hot set-up and I'm very impressed. My comfort level just went up knowing that everyone in the company has been run."

"What tipped you off?" Jefferson asked.

"No one thing. It just all started adding up. I've used the Dektor myself. I would have tumbled to it sooner if you had used any control questions, but you didn't."

"We did that last night at the party," Jackson said. "We recorded you and Jefferson analyzed the tape to establish your base line."

"If you hadn't passed that part, you wouldn't have gotten this far," Jefferson said. "And if you had come through that door today with a wire or a tape recorder, you would have tripped a sensor and we would have been gone before your eyes got used to the dark."

Black Tuna was a very sophisticated outfit and St. Jones was impressed.

"You're the only guy that ever figured it out," Jefferson said. "It's too bad you're a fly-boy. I could use you in security. If you ever get tired of the friendly skies, let me know."

"Let's cut to the quarter mile final here," Johnson began. "I think we're all in agreement that you would be an asset to the company and we'd like to have you work with us. We pay two-fifty large per run. You can work as much as you want. Most of the boys fly twice a month. We have an excellent outfit and a very good system and we're better equipped and more qualified and definitely more motivated than the opposition. We have good intelligence on them, and closely monitor their radio traffic. There's a whole group that does nothing but that. We support each mission the same way we did in combat, with ground teams and communications and intelligence and rescue if necessary. We guarantee bail and legal fees in a worst case scenario. That hardly ever happens, though. Everybody is the best at what they do. We only recruit exceptional people, and we try hard to keep them happy. Most of our boys have been with us for years and we've had very few casualties. We run things along military lines and everyone is very well paid. It's the best of both worlds. We even have an investment and retirement program, if you're interested. Off shore, very conservative, very safe."

St. Jones thought briefly about revising his career goals, but remembered why the money was so good. The career was so short, and the retirement so long. And confining.

"How soon do you want to start?" asked Johnson.

"Well, I'm here now."

"Where are you staying?"

"At the hotel."

"Meet us here tomorrow morning at ten for breakfast. After that, we can go for a ride in your plane."

"You're on. I like the food and the ambiance here, not to mention the service."

"Yeah, we try to maintain a high standard here," Jefferson said. "It's like a Bachelor Officers Quarters . Members and guests only. This is the most secure place in town."

"I'd like to try dinner here some night," St. Jones said, draining his coffee cup.

"You'll get a membership card tomorrow. Come as often as you like. This is the clubhouse. We hang out here." Johnson got a vial out of his shirt pocket and took a couple of hits from a small silver spoon and passed it over the table to St. Jones. He did likewise and passed it to Jefferson. It was a ritual signaling the end of business. St. Jones had passed the test. "We were thinking about going back to the party. Wanna come along?"

"I was thinking about going back to the hotel and crashing until dark. I'm going to have to revert to Dracula mode to survive this heat. But I'll probably be over after dark."

"Can we drop you at the hotel?" Jefferson asked.

"That's very funny Jefferson, but I think I'll walk."

They all laughed. St. Jones stood up and shook hands and made his exit. Stepping from the ice cave into the South Florida afternoon inferno was a shock to mind and body. St. Jones thought about Camus on that white-hot Algerian beach all the way back to the hotel. By the time he got there he was surly enough to kill an Arab, too.

When St. Jones walked into the lobby, there was a desk clerk on duty he hadn't seen before, and he took the opportunity to rent a second room across the hall from his original room under a *nom de voyage*. This would give him surveillance of the first room in case it was blown. He went up and moved his stuff to the new room and went to work on the closet door with the saw on his knife, making a new slick. That done, he got naked and crawled between the cool sheets and slept straight through until the next morning.

BOLD

16

St. Jones' second visit to the VFW wasn't quite as dark as the first. It was only Johnson and Jackson this time and they had an excellent breakfast of Hangtown Fry. After a final round of Cafe Saigon, they exited the club by way of the office door and left in a white Mercedes, making their way out of town west on the Tamiami Trail, the old highway from Tampa to Miami through the Everglades. A few miles out of town they turned south off the highway into the airport where St. Jones had landed three days earlier.

They parked in the oyster shell lot and walked onto the concrete tarmac to where the T-210 was tied down. The place was deserted except for a couple of guys over by the main hangar working on a B-18. St. Jones checked the security system through the cockpit window to see if the plane had been touched or entered, then unlocked the door and did a very careful walk-around inspection, paying particular attention for tracking transmitters. They were deep behind enemy lines in terms of the Feds.

"Nice set-up, St. Jones." Johnson was looking around inside the plane. "You've even got a bed in here. You could put this puppy on auto-pilot and climb in the back and play hide the salami. What's under there, tanks?"

"Yeah. I had the cushions and the curtains made so it wouldn't look quite so obvious. One of you guys gets to ride back there."

The windsock at mid-field was hanging limp. Taxiing to the east end of the runway, St. Jones declared his intentions on 122.8mhz Unicom and took off to the west.

"Climb to 500 feet and set VOR-1 on Miami and VOR-2 on Fort Myers," Jackson said. "Fly east about forty miles until we intersect Radial 220 on VOR-1 and then drop to 300 feet. We'll be turning south into the Everglades following a small river. As you make the turn, drop to fifty feet. We'll be below the tree line and under the radar by then."

A few minutes later they crossed Radial 219 and St. Jones saw the river. He throttled back and held the nose high to burn off speed and banked into a 30-degree left turn, dropping below the tops of the cypress trees and leveling out over the river at 120 mph. Alligators rippled the calm surface as they slipped into the water at the sound of their approach.

"Okay, the turns are going to come fast," Jackson said. "As the river forks we are going to take first the right fork, then left, right, left, right, left, left, right, right. That's nine turns. Memorize that order, forward and backward. When you come out of that last turn get set up for final approach with thirty degrees of flaps and gear down at thirty feet over the water. Dump all the speed you can on final. Be ready to flare right away and brake the instant we touch down. There's 1500 feet of runway and no place to go if you fuck up. Not even up. We'll be landing under camouflage netting strung fifty feet over the runway. Got it?"

St. Jones nodded and kept his eyes on the trees, which were less than fifty feet off each wing tip. No room for error at that speed. He throttled back a little more. The first turn came up fast.

"Which nav-com can I use for communications?" Jackson asked.

"Use number two."

Jackson dialed 131.2mhz into the Collins on the right. Around a turn in the river the next fork was on them instantly. St. Jones veered to the left, banking steeply into the turn. He tasted metal and the monsters began whimpering. Adrenaline is an acquired taste.

"You got a minute before the next one, but after that it's one after the other. Be ready." Jackson said.

St. Jones began adding flaps, ten degrees at a time, cutting back power and pushing the yoke forward to fight the lift. By the time he hit the next turn, he had it down to 90 mph and it was a good thing because the turns came fast, just like the man said. They had two turns to go when Jackson began keying the radio mike on and off in some pattern St. Jones couldn't decipher. Jackson never spoke but a few seconds later he was answered with a series of clicks. As low as they were, the ten-watt transmitter wouldn't carry very far.

They made their last turn and leveled out over a relatively straight and fairly wide stretch of river about five hundred feet long. At the end he could see two lights about fifty feet apart marking the threshold. St. Jones hit the landing gear switch and pulled back on the yoke to compensate for the extra drag. Throttling back to 1500 rpm, he got down to about ten feet over the water, his hand on the throttle in case he had to abort the approach with full power and climb out over the tree tops.

"Beautiful," Jackson said. "Hold her steady on the lights. Start flaring now."

St. Jones pulled the power all the way out and pulled back on the yoke and the stall horn was blowing as they cleared the bank and went under the netting. The T-210 settled onto the metal grate runway and he stood on the brakes and held the yoke all the way back, watching the solid wall of jungle at the end of the runway grow larger. He was light and could have taken it a lot easier. The plane slowed to a roll with about a third of the runway to spare.

"There are turn-outs close to the end," Jackson said. "Nice flying."

St. Jones taxied almost to the end where there were turn-out areas to each side, large enough to turn a plane around in and park. As he ran through the shut down sequence, two guys came out of the undergrowth and approached the plane and were waiting when St. Jones and the boys stepped down.

Johnson, who had ridden in the back during the flight, made the introduction. "St. Jones, meet the Reptile Brothers, Billy and Joe Bob."

"If we'd a known y'all was comin', we'd a baked a snake," Joe Bob said.

They shook hands all around and started walking across the runway toward the thicket where the brothers had come from. It was eerie under the netting, a giant green tunnel as high as a hangar roof and overgrown with foliage. As they crossed the runway, Joe Bob keyed a walkie-talkie and the camouflaged netting lowered into place over the opening at the end of the runway.

After following a trail a hundred feet or so into the thicket, they came to a clearing also covered at treetop level with overgrown camouflage netting. He could faintly hear a generator running somewhere. In the clearing was a cabin built on stilts, about ten feet off the ground. The stilts had snake barriers on them. There was an interesting array of antennae on the roof. Billy pulled a rope that brought down a ladder hinged to the deck that ran all the way around the structure. As they climbed the ladder, St. Jones' eyes were attracted to the walls. From a distance it appeared to be tiger-stripe camouflage, but as he got closer he could see they were covered with hundreds of snake skins.

Billy pulled up the ladder and they went through the screened door into a room about twenty feet square. Along one wall were three racks of two bunks each that would sleep six. In the center of the room was a long table and in one corner was a kitchen with a stove and refrigerator. In the other corner was a table covered with communications equipment. On a video monitor was a view of the waterway by which they had approached. There was even a color TV. Curled up in a chair, a huge black cat with luminous green eyes followed St. Jones' every movement.

"Y'all got any coffee made?" Johnson asked.

"We got some left from this morning that'll eat a spoon. Hang on and I'll make some fresh," Joe Bob said, walking to the sink and putting a pot of water on the stove. "What's new in Gomorrah?"

"There's a Super Bowl party going on at Bino's place,"

Jackson said, sitting down at the table. "It started a couple of days ago, and it's still going strong."

"Oh shit, Joe Bob. Just think about it," Billy said.

"Oh shit, Billy. I can see it. God Almighty. All that pussy in one place. It's a wonder the house don't catch fire."

"Sounds like y'all been out here too long," Jackson said.

"You can say that again. Joe Bob's startin' to look better all the time. With that long black hair, sometimes, from certain angles, he looks just like Cher."

"Yeah? Well, you know why Billy crossed the road?" Joe Bob asked. "His dick was stuck in the chicken."

"Talkin' to him is like beating your head against a dead horse," Billy said to the rest of them. The Reptile Brothers were a funny act.

The coffee was ready and Joe Bob set out five cups and poured. St. Jones could tell by the aroma that the coffee had come from the VFW. Joe Bob put a bowl of Eagle Brand on the table and sat down with the rest of them.

"So you're the FNG," Billy said. "Where you from, St. Jones?"

"Frisco."

"Uh oh. Looks like you came to the right place," Joe Bob smirked. "Is it true, what they say? That over half the people in Frisco are...single?"

"There's even tri-sexuals there, Joe Bob," St. Jones said.

"Tri-sexuals? How do they do that?" Billy looked puzzled. St. Jones watched his face as he ran the permutations.

"St. Jones used to fly for Air America," Johnson said. "We brought him out here today to show him the set-up," Johnson explained. "He's going to be making his cherry run in the next few days."

"Well, have we got a deal for you, St. Jones," Joe Bob said, grinning. "Practically all you gotta do is lie back and enjoy it."

"On my back or on my stomach?" St. Jones smirked.

They cracked up. "That's funny as hell," Billy said. "I'm gonna carve that over the door. That's what it comes down to, all right. Them's words to live by."

Johnson got up from the table and went to a footlocker against the wall under the radio table. Before opening it, he carefully slipped a knotted cord from a slot in the edge of the lid.

"We keep all maps and frequency lists and code pads and stuff like that in the box," Johnson explained. "That cord that I unhooked is tied to the pin ring of a willie peter. You don't want to forget that."

Johnson brought a map to the table and unfolded it. It was an aeronautical planning chart for the Gulf of Mexico and Caribbean. St. Jones understood why they kept it in the burn box. Their position was marked on the map along with various air routes to Colombia.

BOLD

17

"So here's the deal, St. Jones," Johnson began. "We didn't just throw a dart at the map and come out here and build this place. We sort of inherited it. This was one of the training camps of the 5506th Brigade for the invasion of Cuba. Some of the charter members of our outfit were involved in that, among other things. If these walls could talk we'd have to kill 'em. We get the use of this place as a payoff on an old debt. We're pretty much sanctioned as long as we don't draw attention to ourselves.

"Whether by design or accident, there's a gap in the radar coverage here. There's a six-mile-wide pie-shaped area that's blind below 3000 feet to both civilian and military radar. We checked it out by flying a pattern over here with our transponder on standby. They don't seem concerned about it. I guess the way they figure it, there ain't nothin' but a bunch of alligators out here, and gators very seldom get up over a thousand feet even on a good day.

"So, that's the history of this place. The way we do the magic trick is, one of our planes takes off from a civilian field somewhere around Miami on a flight plan that takes it over this place at 3000 feet. On a radio cue from that plane, you begin your take-off run and as he comes over, you intercept his course and get above him as close as you can and stick with him right on up to altitude. Your plane is perfect for this because it has a high wing. Remember, the beard plane is on a legit flight plan to South America and he's going up high, not down on the deck where they're looking for bogies. He'll have his transponder on and you'll have yours on stand-by, so when you hit radar coverage, he's gonna light up real bright on the radar screen and they're not gonna see you at all, as long as you stay close to him. The higher you climb and the farther away from the coast you get, the more room you'll have to move."

"How do we communicate?"

"Good question," Jackson answered. "Billy, get an SCR-16 out of the box."

Billy retrieved a radio transceiver about the size of a CB radio from the burn box and brought it to the table.

"Are you familiar with this type of radio?" Jackson asked.

"I've used them before."

The SCR-16 is a scanning transceiver. It changes frequency sixteen times a second in a predetermined order over a fairly wide chunk of spectrum. Without the frequencies, of which there are thousands of possibilities, and the order of transition, not only is the communication secure, the signal duration on each frequency is only a few thousandths of a second and not long enough to get an RDF

(Radio Direction Finding) fix on. On any given frequency it sounds like a burst of static.

"We use these to communicate air to air, and air to ground at either end out to a hundred miles or so depending on altitude. We also have HF/SSB at both ends and can communicate from point to point as well as air to ground anywhere along the route. Do you have an extra VHF antenna port?"

"I can disconnect something."

"When we get to the other end in Colombia, it's pretty much the same routine in reverse, except it's even easier because of the mountains. The radar coverage is very marginal down there. At a predetermined point, you'll break off and land at the lab. It has a very interesting landing strip. You fly up a canyon that would be certain death if it weren't for the runway. No room for Chandells and no missed approaches. And it's short, the first 300 feet is close to level and then at midfield it slopes upward gradually to about twenty degrees for another 300 feet. Your plane is perfect for this strip. And when you take off, it's like flying off a fucking ski jump. It's a rush. You're gonna love it."

St. Jones flashed back to the slot car race at Bino's place, when they both blew right off the end of the table.

"You'll spend the night at the finca... the country home. They'll load and refuel your plane, and the next morning the beard plane will come back over on a flight plan from Bogota to Miami. You'll pull right up on top and fly the route back, dropping off here as the other plane goes over on its way to land in Miami. The crew here will unload your plane and then you fly out of here clean and back to the strip where you had it parked, or anywhere else you like. So, just like Joe Bob said, practically all you gotta do is lie back and enjoy it. On your back, if you do it right."

"Sounds like your basic, bulletproof set-up," St. Jones said. "Just two questions. How do I find the lab and how do they know who I am?"

"Because I'm going with you on this first run," Johnson said. "And Jackson will fly the beard plane."

St. Jones found this latest development discouraging. Getting Nickie out of Colombia was going to be difficult enough without having a passenger along, particularly one of the boys.

Johnson drained his coffee cup, pushed back from the table, and stood up. Jackson took the cue and St. Jones followed.

"I hate to drink and run," Johnson said, "but I've got a three o'clock dentist appointment in town."

"Well, it's been a real slice seein' y'all," Joe Bob drawled. "I hope we're not here when y'all come back, but if we are, we'll show you the obstacle course."

"Yeah, the boys have restored the original obstacle course. A few years back this place was a full blown training camp."

"We've got a lot of time on our hands out here and that's how we stay in shape and keep from going crazy at the same time," Billy said. "Since we can't have no babes or drugs out here, we gotta do something."

"That's why you boys get paid the big money," Johnson said. "When you're in town you can get as fucked up as you like, but out here, rules is rules."

"Who holds the course record these days?" asked Jackson.

"Tell him, Joe Bob," Billy smirked.

"Billy holds the new record for all crews," Joe Bob said, grudgingly. "I timed him myself. Nine fifty-six. He broke the ten-minute barrier."

"These are the boys that will come to rescue you, if it ever comes that," Johnson said. It was left unsaid that they would also be the ones to come to get you if it ever came to that.

Billy folded the map and picked up the radio and replaced them in the burn box, resetting the trigger cord.

"We'll install the radio when you come back," Johnson said. "We only deploy them when we're operational and we change sequence and frequency codes daily from a one-time pad. Without that, these things are just very expensive, mil-spec paper weights."

Joe Bob went out the door first and lowered down the ladder. As they walked the trail back to the plane, the weirdness of the deep Everglades settled in on St. Jones. There was an eerie beauty to it, but an average man wouldn't last an hour out there. He thought of the Spaniards that walked from the tip of Florida all the way to Texas and beyond in the sixteenth century. Tough dudes. As if to underscore the point, a water moccasin three feet long and as thick as St. Jones' forearm slithered across the path in front of him. That brought the day sharply into focus. He watched where he stepped more closely.

With the snake still fresh in his mind, St. Jones checked the landing gear wells and control surfaces closely. He remembered stories of gears and controls being jammed by snakes and incidents of guys screwing it in the ground after being bitten by snakes that came on board in cargo. Hell of a way to go.

"We'll try to round up a crew to relieve you in the next

few days," Johnson said. "When were you suppose to rotate, anyway?"

"Uh...oooh," Billy said. "The terrible truth comes out. You tell him Joe Bob. You started this shit."

"The end of this week," Joe Bob confessed, slyly.

"You fuckers. I ought'a leave you out here an extra week for that bullshit," Johnson said.

"We're sorry, Captain. Time passes real slow out here." Joe Bob and Billy hung their heads in mock contrition. The Reptile Brothers were funny. They developed the style to pass the long stretches of time in that God-forsaken place, without the company of women or the solace of drugs.

St. Jones climbed into the plane and began to run through the checklist while the boys talked. When he cranked the engine, Johnson and Jackson got on board and the Reptile Brothers stood clear. Joe Bob took the walkie-talkie off his belt and keyed in the code that activated the electric jeep winch that raised the camo netting over the end of the runway and gave St. Jones the all-clear sign. He acknowledged the signal and taxied into position. Pushing the throttle forward, he stood on the right rudder to compensate for the "P" factor and kept it lined up on the narrow runway. No mistakes allowed. It was an eerie visual sensation running underneath the overgrown netting. As they gained speed, the patterns caused a strobing effect that was disorienting. They reached VR (Velocity Rotation: flying speed) several hundred feet before they were clear of the netting, and St. Jones held the yoke forward to keep the plane from coming off the deck too soon. Toward the end, he had to take his mind off the strobing and lock onto the end of the runway, easing back on the yoke at the last possible instant. The magic worked again.

St. Jones held it about forty feet over the water and throttled back and began setting up the first turn, which was coming up fast. After that, it was like running a downhill slalom, one turn after another, until they were straight and level fifty feet over the water with two turns to go.

"You can sign your name with this fucker, can't you?" Jackson asked, as they all breathed out slowly.

"That's the advantage in flying one aircraft a lot," St. Jones replied. "It becomes an extension of your body and you can cut out the middle man. It's a very Zen thing, like archery, except that you're the arrow."

"I bet the chicks eat that J. L. Seagull shit up," Jackson laughed.

They hit the last two turns and climbed out to 500 feet, banking thirty degrees into a turn to the east, a quarter mile south of the highway. A half hour later, they were on the ground. St. Jones walked over to the hangar and made arrangements for the fuel truck to top off his tanks, then jumped into the Mercedes air-conditioning and headed back to Coconut Grove, just ahead of a line of thundershowers that rose up over the Everglades every afternoon like clockwork.

"So, sometime in the next few days we'll be in touch," Johnson began. "We'll leave a message at the hotel for you to call your travel agent. And just in case you didn't know, most of the staff at the hotel are federal or state agents or informants of one kind or another. Half the dope deals in south Florida go down there. Go to a pay phone at least six blocks from the hotel and dial JOHNSON, and wait for a second dial tone and then dial JACKSON. Someone will answer 'J & J Travel'. We've got to give you a company name. Any ideas?"

"Yeah," Jackson said. "He's from Frisco. He could be Mr. Bay. Or Bridges. That's it, Ray Bridges."

"Okay, identify yourself as Ray Bridges. You'll be on a secure line and can talk freely after that point. They'll give you your orders and you'll be operational. You and me will be hooking up at some point. Could you get to the beach house without any help?"

"Is that what you call that place, the beach house," St. Jones replied. "Yeah, sure. No problem, except for the radio code you keyed in. You'll have to give me that."

"Nothin' gets by you, does it?" Johnson said. "I like that. The code goes like this. First the frequency. The first day of the month you use 130.1mhz and the second use 130.2mhz and so on up to 133.1mhz for the thirty-first. The code is the day of the week. Monday is one tap on the mic switch and Tuesday is two taps, up to seven taps for Sunday. Send odd numbered groups in the A.M., and even number groups in the P.M. So if it's Friday afternoon on the twenty-third of the month, the frequency would be 132.3mhz and you send five taps, two times. You'll be answered back in kind. When they see you turn over the water on final approach they'll lift the net and turn on the lights. If there's no answer on the radio abort the landing approach and climb on out. Got it?"

"Got it."

"Good. Go have yourself a party, and then lay up so you'll be fresh," Jackson said. "It's a long flight, followed by a long turn-around and you know how hard it is to shoot a precision landing when you've been flying at high altitude all day."

They were off the freeway and passing through Coconut Grove toward the Atlantic and the hotel. The thought of a party conjured up images from his dream. Was Girl the strawberry? Or was she the white mouse? Too soon to tell. The Mercedes pulled into the back parking lot at the VFW and they stepped out into an afternoon by Dante. St. Jones lost his appetite for lunch and struck out on foot for the hotel. His Adidas were sloshing and his silkie was stuck to him like wallpaper by the time he reached the lobby.

St. Jones was distracted by the heat and oblivious to the monsters and in such a hurry to get to a cold shower in his room that he failed to notice two very important things. He made the elevator just as the door closed and when he got out on his floor he practically sprinted down the corridor and around the corner to his room and began stripping off his sweat soaked clothes. He was standing there naked when he sensed, more than heard something at the door. Turning out the lights, he peeled the tape from the peephole and took a look. It was the Narx Brothers, and they were about to enter his decoy room across the hall with a pass-key and drawn guns. The monsters peed all over the rug.

BOLD

18

In his haste to get out of San Francisco to escape the wrath of the Narx Brothers, St. Jones had failed to think the situation through from their point of view. Given the fact that they knew about the notes and observing that St. Jones had left town, even someone as cognitively challenged as the Narx Brothers could deduce that he had gone to Miami. A phone call to their cousins there at Club Fed and the results were standing less than six feet away on the other side of the door. But the self-flagellation would have to wait for some long, dark night of the soul. In *el mundo real*, St. Jones had a Condition Orange on his hands.

The door banged against the wall as the Narx Brothers burst into the room across the hall. St. Jones put his eye back to the peephole and saw them standing in the middle of the room, yelling and waving their guns in the air. St. Jones remembered Precept 36 and moved away from the doorway. "You're twice as dead if killed by an idiot." You may even reincarnate as a mollusk.

As if on cue St. Jones heard the pop of a .38 Special discharging. The monsters, having nowhere to go, shit where they stood. Curiosity overrode fear and St. Jones put his eye back to the peephole. The Narx Brothers were looking up as fine white dust settled upon them from above, a portrait of fuck-up artists at work. When the smoke alarm went off, they became aware of themselves and looked out the open door directly at St. Jones. He almost shit, until he remembered he was standing behind his own door.

It occurred to the Narx Brothers simultaneously that they had exceeded their authority, somewhat. Holstering their weapons, they furtively glanced through the open door up and down the corridor. Seeing no one, they closed the door behind them and skulked away. St. Jones was still on the right side.

He didn't know whether to flip, flop, or fly. His instinct was to fly, but his mind told him he was probably in the safest place he could be for the moment. So he flopped on the bed and considered his options. The telephone was probably a bad idea. So was a taxi. And it wasn't necessarily good thinking to leave on foot in broad daylight. But he couldn't stay where he was for very long, either.

A knock at the door across the hall froze St. Jones' thoughts and punched his blood pressure up another ten points. He went to the door and peeled back the tape. Her head and shoulders were obscured by a huge, straw, beach hat, but he recognized Girl's exquisite ass, blooming like a golden flower in a blue, French-cut Bikini. He almost flipped. She turned around when he opened the door and he motioned her into the room.

"What are you doing over here, Agent 86?" Girl sniffed the air and stepped into the room, casually grasping his dick like she was shaking hands. "Did we break the bed?" She kissed him on the lips. "That bag you left with me has been burning a hole in my pocket, but every time I do some of it, I think about this and it's making me crazy." Girl squeezed his dick. "Can we party some more?"

St. Jones' religious mother was fond of saying, "God never closes one door without opening another," and after this miracle before him, he was thinking of going back to church. But not just yet. "Anything for you, baby, but have you got some place we can go?"

"Sure baby. Let's go to the safe house. What's going on? I thought I smelled gunpowder in the hall."

"Do you ever watch Roadrunner cartoons?"

"Of course."

"Well, I'm the Roadrunner and the coyote and his evil twin just shot up my room across the hall. Are you still in?"

"Danger makes me wet. Remember?"

"Till the day I die. Did you bring a car?"

"Yeah, it's parked on the street under the big tree."

"I need you to drive into the parking garage downstairs and wait for me at the elevator door with the engine running."

"Okay, baby. Have we got time for a sixty-eight?" She gave him another squeeze.

"What's a sixty-eight?"

"It's like a sixty-nine, only I'll do you now and you do me later."

"You're like the tar baby, Girl. Once I touch you I'm going to get stuck to you all over for a long time."

"Tar Baby, my ass. I'll meet you downstairs in five minutes." She turned toward the door.

"One more thing. Can I borrow your hat?"

She handed him the hat, turned and opened the door. "It's you, St. Jones," she said, closing the door behind her.

St. Jones checked his watch. Since the parking garage was adjacent to the pool level, he put on swimming trunks. He got his things from the slick and packed his bag, draping one of the hotel beach towels over it. He completed his ensemble with Groucho glasses and Girl's beach hat. He checked himself in the mirror. He looked ridiculous. People would be too embarrassed to look at him. All they would remember would be the Groucho glasses and the hat, and the hat would shield him from the security camera in the elevator. St. Jones checked his watch, looked through the peephole and opened the door.

He glanced up and down the corridor and headed for the stairs, walked down two flights and took the elevator to the garage. A couple who rode to the pool level were blushing through their suntans in embarrassment. When he reached the parking level, Girl's blue Camaro was waiting. He tossed his stuff in the back and got in and lay down on the seat with his head on her lap.

"Go baby. Let's get out of here." After they had driven a couple of blocks, St. Jones inhaled deeply through his nose, kissed her belly and sat up. He had her make a series of turns while he watched the traffic behind them. "Better find me a pay-phone before we go much farther."

Girl pulled to the curb at the next corner. First, St. Jones called J&J Travel and informed them that Ray Bridges was no longer at the hotel and would be calling in twice a day, at noon and midnight, for messages from his travel agent. Next, he called the Law Boat in Sausalito and left a message with the answering service saying he would be calling the following day at noon, Miami time. When he stepped out of the phone booth he heard sirens approaching and could see some kind of commotion a couple of intersections behind them.

A clap of thunder announced the on-time arrival of the daily mid-afternoon showers and the air filled with steam as the rain hit the hot pavement. St. Jones jumped into the Camaro and shivered from the shock of the air conditioning.

It was still raining when they reached the safe house. Girl pushed the button on a remote control clipped to the visor and as they turned the corner, St. Jones saw the garage door opening on an attractive single-story gray house with a nicely manicured lawn. They pulled up the drive and into the garage, the door closing behind them.

They got out of the car into 130 degree heat, then went into the kitchen where the AC nearly knocked St. Jones down. As he stood there adjusting to the cold and the relative darkness, his stomach growled and he remembered Bino's advice. "Girl, in all the madness I missed lunch, and considering the mountains we're going to climb, I could use some food."

"Come on in the bedroom and get comfortable, and let me take care of you like you were mine." She led him through the comfortable, well-decorated house to the bedroom they had magically appeared in two nights ago.

St. Jones lay down on the bed and shivered from the cold covers. He was still wearing only a bathing suit, which he shed, and got under the sheets.

After a while, Girl returned carrying a tray. There were

smoked oysters, a tuna salad, sliced oranges, a bowl of shelled pecans, and a loaf of French bread. Also, a pitcher of fresh orange juice and ice cubes and a bottle of Lemon Hart 151 proof rum. Placing the tray on the bed, she removed her Bikini and climbed up. Girl was a bed dweller, too.

After they finished lunch and were getting smashed on the rum and orange juice, Girl got out the bag and served the cocaine and they got busy. Sex was what drugs were all about. In the sixties, it was the quest for truth, and Reich was right. The truth turned out to be sex. The stimulant drugs, the psychedelic drugs and the new Ecstasy-class designer drugs intensified and elevated sex to phenomenal levels. That's why everybody was doing it. It was instant love in a baggie. The pill made casual sex possible, but drugs made it fun. With drugs, you could fall in love every night, over and over again, with a stranger or with your spouse, or both. Drugs did for sex what steroids did for sports.

The last St. Jones noticed, it was late afternoon and the time passed like in the movies, when the hands of the clock go into overdrive and the hours spin by like minutes. When the alarm went off at 11:55, St. Jones crawled back up through his neck and into his head and called an audible. Untangling their bodies, he re-entered his mind long enough to call J&J Travel, while Girl made a couple of half-gram lines on the mirror. There was no message from his travel agent. He set his watch for twelve hours later, and plowed through the cocaine and rolled back into Girl's waiting body and drifted back into the trance.

When his alarm went off just before noon, he stumbled into the shower and ran straight cold water until he thought he could talk straight, then added hot water to get his heart started. His nose was bleeding and his dick felt like his feet did after a long march.

St. Jones called his travel agent and was told to meet his tour guide at the dock at six a.m. Finally, things were moving. Next he called the Law Boat, collect, and Winston came on the line.

"Hello, counselor. What's new in 415?"

"Hello, St. Jones. Well, for openers, we woke up to an earthquake this morning. Five point five. Everybody's a little more awake than usual."

"Sorry I missed all the fun. You know how I love a good shake." St. Jones hated earthquakes. Every time he crossed the Golden Gate Bridge he thought about the Big One. People who live in San Francisco play a game with themselves about the Big One.

"The damnedest thing happened a couple of days ago. Mark Stone was apprehended with a body in the trunk of his car."

"Imagine that. Sounds like a pattern to me."

"I hear he's having a rough time at the Pink Palace. A lot of Mimi's friends are there and Annie's, too. There are even a couple of guys that got themselves busted, just to get in they're with him."

"Well, like Precept 35 says, you eat what you are, and he always was a dick. So, what's new with the Incas?"

"I found the book and decoded the message, but I don't think you're going to like it. All it says is, 'Help I'm being held captive in a cocaine factory.' It doesn't sound like a lot of help."

"This is a case of the medium being the message, Winston. Knowing where she is wouldn't be that useful without knowing how to get in and out of there, and I've managed to do that. I'm leaving in the morning for points South. If all goes well, we should be back in town in a day or two."

"Sounds like things are going well on your end."

"Not too bad, all things considered." St. Jones' mind was licking the lines and crevices of Girl's body with a tongue that seemed to be growing out of his forehead. "The Narx Brothers showed up yesterday and you know how glad I always am to see them."

"The Admiral is very pleased with how things turned out and says to tell you he wants to discuss a partnership when you get back. He promoted himself, by the way. The kicker is that Stone called the firm to represent him. The Admiral thinks it's funny as hell."

"Justice is blond, Winston. I'll call when we're back."

"Be careful, St. Jones. And thanks again."

"Just remember Winston...hundred foot sparks."

St. Jones hung up and thought about these newest developments. He had eighteen hours to pull himself together and come up with a foolproof plan and an airtight alibi.

The slick in the plane was just large enough for Nickie, but it was virtually airtight and she would have to remain in there for around twelve hours without moving. The solution was simple enough. This was a job for oxygen and reds, and a flight extender. And, with Johnson in the plane, he had his airtight alibi.

Fortunately, he had all the pieces, so it became a matter of how to communicate it all to Nickie. He might not get a chance to talk to her, so he would have to write full and clear instructions and she would have to pull off the rest on her own. He doubted that he would be allowed to run loose anyway, and the less contact he had with her the better. When she turned up missing, he didn't want them putting six and nine together. St. Jones needed to get to the airport a few hours ahead of Johnson to sort it all out.

Girl had laid out a couple more giant lines and handed him the rolled up hundred. He snorted the lines and involuntarily shivered, feeling like he'd jammed burning cigarettes up his nose. His eyes teared and he slid the mirror back and Girl did the rest.

"I need to crash around dark and sleep for a while. About two a.m., I need you to drive me somewhere."

"Anything for you, baby. Right now, you just lie back and let me lick you like a popsicle from head to toe, till there's nothing left but the stick."

It was the best idea he'd heard in months. She started slowly sucking his toes and licking his feet with infinite care and concentration, ever so slowly working her way up and down his body, front and back. St. Jones entire being was concentrated on the point where her tongue touched his skin. It was carnal Kriya Yoga. Sometime around sundown, Girl brought it all together with a blow job of such excruciating delicacy that he would have wept if he could have found his eyes, and when she finally let him come, it felt like he'd stuck his dick in a light socket. He screamed into his pillow like a wounded animal and tears welled up in his eyes and he thought that after a lifetime of serious edgework, he might have finally found sin. Anything that felt that good that you lived through, must be wrong. On the other hand, whatever doesn't kill us, makes us stronger. Precept 33.

When St. Jones' alarm went off at midnight, he followed the smell of coffee and other good things to the surface. He opened his eyes to find a tray on the bed with steak and eggs and potatoes and toast and coffee and OJ.

"I called room service while you were asleep." Girl was sitting next to him, smiling.

St. Jones struggled to a sitting position and had a few sips of coffee and looked at the food and then at Girl.

"You ever been to Frisco, Girl?"

"Not yet," she smiled.

"When what I'm doing is over, I want you to come and see me. I want to show you the town." And vice versa, he thought. He knew guys that would jump off the Bridge after seeing her, knowing they'd never have her.

As he ate his breakfast, his blood sugar started to rise and he felt almost euphoric. St. Jones was filled with energy, his body completely relaxed and his mind restored. And he had the anticipation of action with the dawn. Life was good, if fleeting. Of course, he wouldn't be using his dick any time soon, but he didn't need it to fly a plane.

They got out of bed and showered together. St. Jones shaved and dressed and put on Levis and a long sleeved sweatshirt to protect him from the mosquitoes that would swarm when he stepped from the car at the airport on the edge of the Everglades. By the time he was ready, Girl was waiting and they left the house about two a.m.

They listened to music on the way to the airport, each lost in thought. St. Jones was thinking through his plan. Girl was thinking about the past. They turned off the highway into the parking lot at the field and got out.

"I hate this part, St. Jones. I don't know why the hell I'm attracted to cowboys. I've had bad luck in the past. He was a lot like you. I wasn't going to say it, but please be

careful. I really want to see you again."
    He held her and tried to squeeze out the fear.

BOLD

19

St. Jones' watch read five 'til three as he watched the tail lights of the Camaro fade away. There was almost a three-quarter moon and he walked through the gate and across the tarmac to the plane without a flashlight. By the time he got there, every square millimeter of bare flesh was covered with mosquitoes. He checked the security system through the window and unlocked the door and, sweeping the mosquitoes from his hands and face, leapt inside. Quickly closing the door, he turned on the red panel lights and began slapping the ones that managed to get in.

St. Jones began by stacking the padding that covered the tanks to one side. The tanks were constructed in three compartments that ran longitudinal to the aircraft body, to minimize the weight shift from the fuel sloshing around. The upper half of the middle tank was a fake. The top panel, when released electrically by internally mounted screw motors, came off. The seams were hidden by the heliarc welding bead. The inside was lined with half an inch of closed cell foam rubber to keep things from rattling. The tank was thermally stable and airtight except for an equalizing valve.

St. Jones stuck his head inside and carefully sniffed for gasoline. He ran his fingertip under the foam the length of every seam and held it to his nose. Even one drop of gas or oil would become explosive in a high oxygen environment. Next, he wrapped a down-filled jacket around a bottle of oxygen and placed it lengthwise at the front end of the compartment so Nickie could straddle it, and arranged the tubing and mask for easy access. He wanted her to ride feet first in case of a sudden stop. He rolled out a sleeping bag and arranged the flight extender. This is a device that allows you to piss when you need to. For men, there is a fitting like a big rubber and for women, a triangular shaped cup with elastic straps. Either way, it connects to a tube that runs down the leg to a plastic bottle velcroed just above the ankle. Even though she would be lying down, it was better than nothing.

St. Jones moved the athletic bag of equipment that normally rode in the slick to the right seat. Then he lay down inside the tank as best he could, his feet hanging over the edge, and ran every scenario he could imagine. This was risky business, and the compartment resembled a coffin more than anything else. He was glad it wasn't him taking this ride.

Satisfied that he had thought it through, St. Jones got out of the tank and placed the top in position. Reaching under the panel, he operated the switch that secured the lid and then replaced the pads.

St. Jones climbed into the left seat and, opening his

flight case, began to write instructions for Nickie.

Hello again, Nickie. I've seen fire and I've seen rain and baby, I always thought I'd see you again. The business before us is one of those good news/bad news things. The good news is that I think I can get you out of this mess. The bad news is that you have sold yourself into indentured servitude until you've adequately explained why you have reduced my life to a smoldering ruin. And did I mention compensation? As I write this I'm assuming I'm going to see you soon and somehow discreetly pass this note to you. I doubt that we will have an opportunity to cover all this at that time. First of all this is risky business but there is a high probability that it will work. The worst case scenario is that you will go to sleep and not wake up. There are worse ways to go. The decision is yours. Make it with the knowledge that you might not make it through this. On the other hand I've never lost a patient and I have no intention of starting with you.

In the cargo area of my plane underneath three naugahyde covered foam pads are large aluminum fuel tanks. There are three longitudinal sections with thick heliarc welding beads running the length of the tanks and around the edges. The top of the center section is removable and covers an area large enough to lie down in. The heliarc bead covers the seam. Lift it up by the front edge and set it to one side on top of a cushion. Be careful to not leave any telltale scratch marks. Before you get in, rig the flight extender. It's for pissing in. If you've never used one before I'm sure you can figure it out. Lie down with your feet to the front. That way if we make a rough landing it won't jam your neck. Position the oxygen bottle between your legs. I'm sure you can figure out that part, too. The regulator is set at minimum flow. Open the valve a quarter turn and put on the mask before you lie down. Try to delay this until as close to cargo loading as possible. Take as many reds as you can handle about fifteen minutes before you get in. Make certain that you don't have anything on you that will react with pure O2. The tank that you'll be in has an atmospheric equalizing valve that will be open to let the O2 flow. When you're ready to get in the tank arrange the pad on top of the lid and lower them down on top of you. Make sure that the lid is properly seated. I'll seal the tank electrically when I get in the plane.

The rest is up to me. I hope you're not claustrophobic. Try not to think about the fact that you're surrounded by aviation gas underneath a half a ton of cocaine. You should sleep through the whole thing and wake up to see my smiling face demanding a fucking explanation.

The enclosed key is to get in the plane with. Be sure and lock the door once you're inside. That's all that I can think of. I'll see you in Miami. Burn this note.

St. Jones read the note three times until he was certain it was clear. He opened the medical kit and got out four Seconol spansules and folded them tightly into the note along with a key to the plane and put a Band-aid around it and slipped it into his pocket.

St. Jones checked his watch and climbed into the back and stretched out. It was four a.m. and he had time to nap. He set his watch alarm for five-thirty a.m. and lay back and retraced the path Girl's tongue had taken over his body. Yogananda would blush. When the alarm went off, St. Jones didn't want to stop, but nature was calling. He crawled out of the plane to take a piss, keeping himself covered with his hands to avoid being swarmed by mosquitoes.

St. Jones climbed back in and powered up the panel and dialed Miami ATIS Airman's Transcribed Information Service into Navcom 1 for a weather briefing. He dialed in WINZ on the ADF to find out what was going on in the world. His focus had been rather narrow the last few days. He was surprised to learn that a race riot had been going on. According to the radio, two white DEA agents from California ran over a young black kid while pursuing a suspect in a bi-coastal drug ring. It was the grain of sand that finally added up to a ton. The incident sparked a riot during which the two agents were severely beaten. St. Jones was still on the right side.

Headlights turned off the highway and St. Jones could make out the outline of a pickup truck as it parked in the lot. He watched two figures walk through the gate and onto the tarmac and head toward the plane. As they got closer, St. Jones could tell by their silhouettes that it was Johnson and Jackson. When they got to the plane, St. Jones opened the door and they scurried inside, slapping madly at the mosquitoes.

"Morning, St. Jones," Johnson said. "Ready to rock and roll?"

"Put me in, coach. Both you guys riding along today?"

"No, Jackson's just dropping me off. He's going to another airport and fly the beard plane. We'll be waiting for him at the beach house."

"If you boys are set, then I'm outta here," Jackson said. "I'll be talking to you along the way. Good luck."

St. Jones got out with Jackson, and using a flashlight, did a thorough preflight inspection of the aircraft. He saw the truck headlights pull out of the lot toward the highway. Getting into the plane, he ran down the checklist and cranked the engine. They taxied to the runway intersection, did a run-up, and executed a mid-field take-off to the west. As they gained altitude, the sky behind them was glowing with the rapid approach of the dawn. By the time they reached the river, the sun was breaking the line of the horizon.

St. Jones flew the route like a downhill racer and Johnson keyed the code with the mike button as they turned over the river on final. Seconds later, the lights came on and St. Jones pulled the power, setting up his approach. He flared as they reached the edge of the water and then they were on the ground, rolling out under the netting, which seemed even more like a tunnel in the early morning light.

He taxied to the left turn-out and shut down the engine. Joe Bob was waiting for them when they hit the ground.

"Morning, Sergeant," Johnson said. "Breakfast ready?"

"Morning, Captain," Joe Bob said. "Grits and eggs and country sausage and biscuits, just like always."

They walked the trail to the hooch and as they got closer, St. Jones could smell the food. Joe Bob pulled down the ladder and they climbed up and went inside the snakeskin-covered cabin.

"Hi, honey," Joe Bob called out. "You'll never guess who's here."

The table was set for four and Billy was standing with a towel folded over his arm.

"My name is Billy, and I'll be your waiter this morning." He poured coffee and they sat down.

After breakfast, Joe Bob opened the burn box and got out the charts and the SCR-16. "Just peel off the cover on the double-backed tape and stick this anywhere you like, and plug the cord into the cigarette lighter. You said you have an extra antenna port?"

"Yeah, no problem."

"Jackson will call us by radio as soon as he's airborne," Johnson said. "We'll have about ten minutes to get to the plane and crank her up and get into position for take-off. Jackson will call us again when he gets to a way-point that we've worked out. That's when we'll begin our take-off roll. That will position us right under him as he flies over at 2,500 feet at 150 mph."

St. Jones and Joe Bob took the radio, while Johnson waited at the communications desk. St. Jones opened the plane and reached up under the panel and disconnected the antenna from the VHF radiotelephone and attached it to the SCR-16. Peeling off the tape backing, he stuck the radio to the side of the console and plugged the power connector into the cigarette lighter.

"We've already programmed in today's codes." Joe Bob turned on the unit and keyed the microphone.

"What about tomorrow's code?" St. Jones asked.

"It's in the lunch box. Set the code first thing in the morning."

They got out of the plane and walked back to the cabin. Johnson and Billy were sitting at the table having one more cup of coffee. It was the last hot drink they would have until they landed. St. Jones knew that opening a thermos with any hot drink in it at altitude produces an instant cloud chamber in the cockpit along with zero visibility and burned eyes and skin. It could ruin your day. The Reptile Brothers had prepared a lunch box for the flight and a thermos of cold tea.

"You ready to rock and roll, St. Jones?" Johnson asked.

"Almost. I need to rig my F/E. I'm going to go back to the plane. I'll be waiting there."

"Okay," Johnson said, checking his watch. "Jackson will be calling in about ten minutes."

St. Jones walked back to the plane, got inside and opened his flight bag. He put on his slightly used Second Chance vest and his .45 Colt 1911 shoulder rig. He covered the rig with a light nylon jacket from his bag. Then he pulled on the flight extender and snaked the tube down his left pants leg and velcroed the plastic bottle to his calf. Digging into the bag one more time, he came up with an ankle holster and attached it to the outside of his left ankle and inserted his Walther as a left hand draw backup to his right hand draw shoulder rig. He was running down his mental checklist of Mexican standoffs and Asian ambushes, when he saw the boys walking across the runway toward the plane.

Johnson opened the door and jumped into the right seat and turned on the SCR-16. "It's show time. Crank this puppy up and taxi into position. Jackson's on his way."

St. Jones started the engine and taxied to the centerline of the runway. They fastened their seat belts and sat idling, waiting for the signal to roll. The Reptile Brothers were standing just off the runway on the trail and raised the net on Johnson's signal.

"Tome Coca Cola," Jackson's voice came over the radio.

"Let's go," said Johnson.

St. Jones pushed the throttle forward and they began to roll. He held the yoke forward until they cleared the net and eased back and they leapt into the air, climbing out in an ascending 180-degree turn to the left.

"Here he comes," Johnson said, "three o'clock high, straight off your wing tip."

"I've got him." St. Jones estimated Jackson's path and set up an intercept course. He climbed to within a few hundred feet and slowly, carefully, closed the distance, until they were less than fifty feet above Jackson's plane.

"Perfect," Johnson said. "Hold this spacing and climb on out with him to altitude."

Johnson picked up the SCR-16 microphone. "What are we cruising at today?"

"24,000 feet," Jackson said. "Better rig your O2."

Johnson reached behind and retrieved the clear plastic masks attached by tubing to the regulators on the oxygen bottles that hung from the backs of the seats.

The light on the radar transponder began blinking, indicating that they were being interrogated by ground radar. This was the test. There was no unusual radio traffic and nothing from the ground support group. They continued climbing. They went through 13,000 feet crossing the west coast of Florida. They put on their masks and Johnson reached back and opened the oxygen valves.

Half an hour later they were at 24,000 feet, trimmed up and cruising at 245 mph ground speed. It was a beautiful CAVU morning over the Gulf of Mexico. They made the Yucatan Passage west of Cuba by ten o'clock. Around one, the Q's started building over the Caribbean between Honduras and Jamaica and it got bumpy and they had to separate a few hundred feet. They crossed the shore of Colombia west of Cartagena by four o'clock, and by five they said goodbye to Jackson, dropping away from the beard plane in the radar shadow of a high ridge. Johnson picked up the SCR-16 microphone and announced their approach and was answered in Spanish. St. Jones began burning off air speed.

He was a little disoriented from flying at high altitude all day. Up high, there's nothing within miles of you but when you get down low, everything seems too close. He followed Johnson's directions up a canyon that got narrower the farther they went. Coming around a turn to the left, they were surrounded by green. There was no way out but up and St. Jones' instinct was to jam the throttle to the firewall and jerk back on the yoke as hard as he could and try for an Emilman, but in the time it took to think that thought, it was already too late. They were committed.

"There!" Johnson pointed and St. Jones saw the landing strip and set up his glide path with milliseconds to spare. No missed approaches here. The wreckage of several aircraft was visible on the canyon floor and several more planes were crumpled into the canyon wall. He got the taste as he flared, touching down about a plane-length past the threshold. He pulled back on the yoke and jammed the brakes as hard as he dared and then they were at midfield and rolling out on the uphill part of the dirt strip. Two hundred feet from the end St. Jones saw he had it made and eased up on the brakes and rolled to the turnout. He set the brakes and began the shutdown sequence as two guys with Uzis approached the plane. Johnson opened the door and jumped down and greeted the men, who smiled and relaxed when they saw him. St. Jones reached under the panel and operated the switch that unsealed the slick.

He grabbed his bag and stepped down. His legs were stiff and he wobbled when he hit the ground. St. Jones started to lock up the plane but Johnson shook his head, indicating that he should leave it open. Johnson introduced St. Jones to the Uzi Brothers, and declined their offer of a ride in the jeep. Instead, they walked up a dirt road to a clearing in the forest and a small village. Just past the village they came to the cocaine processing compound. They continued another thousand feet along the dirt road until they came to the finca, the main compound. Johnson called out and was answered in Spanish by a voice that soon materialized in the open double doorway.

Don Luiz was fifty-something, tall and poised, with a strong handshake and piercing black eyes. He led them inside to a large comfortable room with a tile floor and a large sunken pool in the middle of the room containing some of the largest koi St. Jones had ever seen. The room had a beamed ceiling and a large fieldstone fire place in the outside wall. The rest of the wall was sliding glass, open to the mountain air. The effect was very pleasant.

"Cervesas, amigos?" Don Luiz offered.

"Por favor." St. Jones' Spanish was rusty, but would return quickly enough.

"How was your flight down?" Don Luiz switched to English.

"Uneventful," Johnson said. "We hit a little weather this afternoon and had to separate a little more than usual, but we were over open ocean at 24,000 feet."

"You would probably like to take a hot bath and rest before dinner," Don Luiz said. "Your usual rooms are ready. Dinner is at ten."

"*Gracias*, Don Luiz," Johnson said, deferentially. "You're a great host, as always."

Johnson led the way up a flight of stairs to the second floor and along a corridor. "You take this room," he gestured. "I'll be in the next one. I'm going to crash for a while. See you at dinner. Nice flying today."

St. Jones' room was spacious and nicely decorated and had its own bath, which he used, and then lay down. The quiet was awesome after a day of engine drone, and he drifted off into the sound of his roaring ears.

BOLD

20

The cold mountain air woke St. Jones about nine o'clock. It was a pleasant change after a few days in Miami. He recalled the altimeter reading 6,500 feet when they landed. He dressed for dinner, putting on Levis, a dark green sweater and Adidas. He was fairly certain the room was bugged, maybe even with video, and it followed that his gear would be searched while he was out of the room. It would be foolish to think they were any less diligent at the command level than they were in the field. Closing the door to the bathroom, he sat on the toilet and turned out the light to rig his ankle holster. The Walther was his ace in the hole. St. Jones' comfort level was in the green and the monsters were calm, but this could become a Commandment Zero situation in a Medallin minute if Don Luiz and his staff were aware of the Mama Coca notes, and had surmised why he was really there. He slipped an extra magazine under the velcro ankle strap.

There was a knock on the door and a man's voice announced dinner in accented English. St. Jones put the note for Nickie in the top of his right hip pocket where he could easily get to it, and turned on the light. He checked himself in the mirror and tried out a couple of smiles. Satisfied with his plan and his preparation, he stepped out the door of his room.

St. Jones scanned the corridor for a good drop and when he came to a planter containing a rubber tree at the top of the stairs, he went for it. Palming the note, he moved in close as though admiring the leaves, and dropped it into the planter. Continuing downstairs to the main area of the house, he entered the dining room to find he was the last to arrive. The table was set for eight with one vacant chair. Don Luiz rose from his seat at the head of the table.

"Señor St. Jones, allow me to introduce my friends. This is my companion, Consuela." The lovely Latin woman smiled and nodded, her eyes brimming with sexual confidence.

"Next to her is my close friend and advisor, Señor Altman."

Altman stood when Don Luiz did, and now bowed slightly at the waist. He looked about seventy, ramrod straight like a military man, and was most probably Herr Altman. South America is infested with second and third generation Nazis, as well as a diminishing number of the original performance cast. "Next to Señior Altman is Nickie, our technical advisor." She smiled and nodded at St. Jones without a flicker of recognition. "Nickie is from America and would probably enjoy talking about home. And, with Señor Johnson is Juanita." Don Luiz's inflection and Juanita's smile explained everything. "Finally, your companion for the evening, Magda." She stood and smiled, extending her hand. Magda had the look. St. Jones hooked fingertips with her and she guided him to the table. After St. Jones was seated, Don Luiz sat down. No flies on his act. Strictly Corinthian leather. He was an aristocrat, with what appeared to be his own personal, high-class whorehouse.

"Paco." Don Luiz nodded at a powerfully built Mestizo Indian who stepped forward and began pouring a white wine around the table. He was gracious enough, but he had the look of Cain in his left eye and a bulge under his right arm. St. Jones checked the Indian's crotch and saw that he dressed to the right, confirming that Paco was left-handed. It was a trick learned at the Purple Porpoise, and vital knowledge if he had to Mambo with Paco. Mestizos are natural born killers and St. Jones figured him to be more than kitchen staff, probably Don Luiz's chief of security. Paco spotted St. Jones' recognition and smiled, slightly. Guys like them could spot each other at the Super Bowl. It was like a secret society, but instead of a ring or a necktie, they recognized each other's eyes and they could feel each other at an animal level.

As the wine and conversation flowed, Magda turned out to be a skilled courtesan, quite knowledgeable about America and things American, but her duty was clear. He was in her custody, and wouldn't be alone until he took off tomorrow morning. St. Jones was under painless transparent house arrest, and it appeared he was going to love every minute.

Dinner was splendid, consisting of *Cabrito* (roasted unborn baby goat), and a variety of perfectly prepared vegetables fresh from the household garden. A second course of wine accompanied the entree, a fruity, medium-dry red. After a dessert of wild berries and fresh cream and strong black coffee, Don Luiz suggested they adjourn to the fireplace. He led them to the room where he had taken St. Jones and Johnson when they arrived that afternoon. The sliding glass doors were closed against the mountain cold, and a fire warmed the room. It was very elegant.

"Those are beautiful koi," St. Jones said to Don Luiz. "As fine as any I've seen in Japan."

"They're Nickie's pets," Don Luiz said. "Aren't they exquisite?"

"They must be very old."

"Nickie," Don Luiz called out. "Come tell Señor St. Jones about your pets." As Nickie approached, Don Luiz excused himself and joined Altman by the fireplace.

"I was asking Don Luiz how old the koi are."

"Those two over there are almost four hundred years old." She pointed to the far end of the pool. "The other four are around three hundred. Not so old as old koi go, but quite old compared to you and me."

"They must know something we don't."

Nickie's eyes flashed and she laughed. They made small talk about the latest movies and rock and roll gossip and political outrages. Paco circulated with the brandy bottle, pouring small increments into empty snifters and eavesdropping on various conversations. After Paco was out of earshot, St. Jones leaned in and kissed Nickie on the cheek and whispered the location of the note in her ear, like an indecent proposal. They laughed together and nodded to one another and after a few more minutes, drifted on to the next person, as everyone mingled their way around the room. The deal was down.

St. Jones eventually mingled full circle back to Magda. A signal passed between her and Don Luiz and he approached them, smiling.

"Señor St. Jones, I've heard interesting things about you and I would like to welcome you to the company. We are much more of a family than other organizations. I believe that the secret to success lies in the manner in which we regard one another. As time passes, I hope to come to know you better."

"*Gracias*, Don Luiz. You're very kind. I must confess that until the moment we met this afternoon, I hadn't heard of you, which speaks well of your organization. I'm impressed with your operation and your hospitality. You're obviously a man of discretion and taste." St. Jones could sling shit with the best of them.

Don Luiz smiled like a man with a deuce showing to a straight flush. "Your aircraft has already been refueled and your oxygen bottles replaced and we will begin loading cargo at first light. I know you've had a tiring day and have another long flight tomorrow, so feel free to slip away with Magda whenever you wish. She is very talented, as you will see. Like the rest of us, she is the best at what she does." St. Jones took his cue and with a smiling Magda in hand, wished everyone *buenos noches* and made his exit.

They walked upstairs to his room. Magda excused herself to the bathroom, and St. Jones sat on the bed and removed his shoes. While his feet were shielded from the room, he peeled the velcro on his ankle rig and slipped it under the mattress. He was swinging his feet up onto the bed when Magda came out of the bathroom, wearing only her bra and panties. She put her things on a chair and crawled up beside him and took a heart-shaped locket from around her neck. She opened it, revealing an opalescent rock of cocaine that easily weighed an eighth of an ounce. To the eye of a *cocalero*, it was of gemstone quality. It had an unusual rose tint, and looked to be the work of a fine chemist working with an uncommon solvent, Nickie and petroleum ether in all probability.

St. Jones had a theory about cocaine. It had come to him once when he was high on acid in Virginia City, Nevada. He was intensely studying a geode, or thunder egg, as the Indians called them, which are blobs of molten lava blown miles into the sky during an explosive volcanic eruption. As they cool ten or fifteen miles up in the sky, they solidify into a 3D mineral photograph of all the forces acting on them at the instant they crystallize. When cut in the right plane and polished, even the positions of the sun and moon and nearby planets can be seen. He knew that crystalline structures were extremely delicate and were thought by some to be mutable by thought, like the crystal skull of the Mayans, with 3D images clearly visible within the crystal. St. Jones thought that cocaine might be a molecular photograph of the influences present at the instant of its crystallization, some quite subtle. He believed that would explain why different batches of cocaine of equal purity produce entirely different mindsets.

Magda took an ashtray from the bedside table and turned it over and went to work on the rock. St. Jones' stomach cut a flip, but what the hell, this was gourmet shit and the rock wasn't that big, and he did get some sleep last night, and his dick wasn't that sore and Don Luiz's words intrigued him deeply. She handed him the ashtray and a two-inch long carved ivory tube she took from her bra. St. Jones shrugged to the gathered monsters and vacuumed up a couple of piles, shuddered, then passed it back to Magda. A few moments later a warm vermilion light filled the interior of his mind and the moment came sharply into focus and he knew that this was the good shit, the stuff they don't send out.

Magda reached into the other side of her bra and produced a joint that he'd been smelling since they came into the room. Lighting it, she dragged deeply and passed it to St. Jones, then casually snorted a couple of piles of coke. He took a deep hit and passed it back and stood up and took off his shirt and pants. Magda smiled and unfastened her bra and took off her panties and let down her long, black hair.

St. Jones loved sex. He was an addict, and got from it what junkies got from heroin: shelter, oblivion, a vacation from being himself, and immense amounts of aching, animal joy. Sexual narcosis. He dealt with his addiction by bingeing. He could abstain for long periods of time by allowing himself to drink deeply when he came to the oasis, and ever since he hit the Grove he had been slaking his thirst. As St. Jones soon discovered, Magda had a powerful thirst of her own, and there was a whole lotta slaking going on. She could do things with her pussy that would frighten even the strongest men. She had a grip that could open a bottle of beer. She explained this ability by saying that her father began trying to fuck her when she was still a child and she had developed her grip to keep him from penetrating her. Don Luiz had been conservative. Magda was truly gifted, but around one a.m. she disengaged and began giving St. Jones a massage calculated to put him to sleep. She was a company girl and she had her orders.

St. Jones offered no resistance, and the next thing he

was aware of, Magda was gently shaking his shoulder, a cup of coffee in her hand. He opened his eyes to see her large, dark eyes smiling at him, sadly. It was first light and she had been crying.

"What's the matter, Magda? You look sad."

"There was a fire last night while you were asleep. Nickie's lab burned and they think she may have been in it. It's still too hot to search, but she can't be found."

Nickie always did know how to make an exit. When St. Jones got out of the shower, Magda was waiting for him at the table with breakfast.

"You have to be at your plane in thirty minutes."

St. Jones checked his watch and finished breakfast and dressed for the day, rigging his flight extender, vest and weapons. He felt pretty good for the shape he was in. Debauchery, like any other sport, requires years of training and St. Jones was an athlete, a contender even.

Magda walked St. Jones through the house to the front entrance where Paco was waiting in a jeep to drive him to the strip.

"Next trip, come early so we can have more time together."

"You're on," St. Jones said, knowing he would never be back, and regretting the hell out of it. "Do you ever get up *norte?*"

"Sometimes, for shopping."

"Look me up and I'll show you the town."

"I've seen the town, but I'll look you up." She ran her tongue lightly around his lips, then kissed them. "*Vaya con Dios,* St. Jones."

He climbed into the jeep with Paco and they began the short drive to the small village and the landing strip beyond.

"Did you enjoy Magda, Señor St. Jones?"

"She's one in a million, Paco." St. Jones shivered in the cold morning air.

"You've had that many women?" Paco asked, with mock awe.

St. Jones laughed. "In my dreams, Paco, but if I live long enough, I'm gonna think about the ones I missed and it's gonna make me crazy."

Paco laughed. "Señor is Spanish in his heart. And Indian in his pants." Something in Paco's laugh confirmed St. Jones' suspicion that he'd been on candid camera.

As they passed through the village, they could see the smoking ruin of Nickie's lab. It was one of a cluster of cinder block buildings with corrugated roofing in the cocaine processing area. The fire was confined to one building. There was the sweet odor of light hydrocarbons in the air and the aroma of barbecued meat, which was either a nice touch or a very bad sign. They followed the dirt road to the end and parked next to the loading truck. Johnson was already there and had supervised the loading. The Uzi Brothers were hovering around the perimeter. The sun was coming over the tops of the trees.

BOLD

21

"Mornin', amigo," Johnson greeted him. "I thought I'd let you sleep in, a little. How's your hammer hanging?" He squeezed his fist closed a couple of times in the air and laughed. "Magda's amazing, ain't she? If you piss her off, she can hurt you with that thing."

"Makes me wonder about Juanita. What's her special talent?"

Johnson laughed. "I won't spoil the surprise. You can have her next trip."

"Where does Don Luiz find these women?" St. Jones was intrigued by Don Luiz's private sexual menagerie.

"He's a collector. He searches out rare women the way some men seek out art, or rare cars or guns. He finds them in Bogota and Cali and Medallin and Cartegena. Who knows? Because he's a collector, they're brought to his attention. He's known to pay big time finder's fees."

St. Jones did a walk-around and wondered about

Consuela, the one Don Luiz kept for himself, the one with the sexy eyes. Had Don Luiz found the Golden Pussy, the one with the tongue? Had St. Jones miscalculated and searched the wrong continent? He'd always had a theory about Lake Titicaca.

"Jackson's already airborne. I've programmed the SCR-16 with today's code. We should be hearing from him in about fifteen minutes. You ready?"

"I could use another cup of coffee and maybe take a leak. It would be a bitch to fill up my bottle before we land."

"I hear that. There's some coffee over there on the truck. And these guys know coffee. In fact, the guy on the left is Juan Valdez himself."

They walked to the back of the loading truck where the crew had a Coleman stove set up next to the scales and poured a cup of the world's best.

"Too bad about Nickie," Johnson said. "She's been with Don Luiz for almost ten years."

"How's he taking it? Were they very close?"

"Hard to tell about Don Luiz and his women. I think they had their time together, early on. But it's a big loss for the company. She designed and oversaw the whole lab operation. She trained a number of cooks over the years, though, and things will go on without her, but she knew it all. She was a Ph.D. chemist and into some genius level shit."

St. Jones finished his coffee and, walking to the edge of the clearing, bent down and unfastened the tubing from the top of the plastic bottle velcroed to his left calf. He stood up and tried to piss, but it was hard to let go like that, with his dick in his pants. Finally he managed, letting it run out of the tubing onto the ground. When he was finished, he bent down again and re-attached the tubing.

"Time to saddle up," Johnson said, looking at his watch.

St. Jones walked back to the plane and climbed aboard and began running down the checklist. He wondered if Nickie was in there. There was no way to know until he opened up the slick in Miami. He flipped the switch under the panel and prayed his plan was good and hoped he hadn't just sealed Nickie in her coffin. If she was in there.

"Crank her up, Amigo." Johnson looked at his watch. "Jackson will be here soon."

"What's the precise weight of the load?"

"Eight hundred and eleven pounds," Johnson answered. "I weigh 189 and you said the plane would carry a thousand pounds net, wet."

St. Jones ran the starting pump and cranked the 400 HP Lycombing engine and while they sat idling, he ran the weight and balance formulas in his head. They were barely within limits calculated for sea level. At 6,500 feet, it could go either way. At least it was cold. The situation called for a flaps-down take off, a short field technique that lowers the take-off speed at the expense of being able to climb. Strictly a bush pilot's technique. Once airborne, the take-off run would be finished, in ground effect, a few feet off the ground, and the plane would climb out once speed was built up. In this situation, there would be no ground effect, but he had about eight hundred feet of space to get it under control. He added forty degrees of flaps.

The Uzi Brothers had looped a rope through the tail tie-down eyelet and tied it to the back bumper of the loading truck parked about twenty feet behind the plane. When St. Jones and Johnson got their cue from Jackson on the

SCR-16, St. Jones ran the engine up to 110 per cent and the Uzi Brothers chopped the rope loop with a machete, catapulting them down the sloping portion of the runway.

When they hit the level section of the strip, the gear sagged and the wings drooped and their assholes puckered and the monsters were screaming bloody murder. St. Jones kept one eye on the airspeed indicator as they approached the end of the runway, and he didn't like what he saw. They were outside the envelope as they approached the precipice and then they were hurtling into space. He fought the monsters for control of the yoke as they tried to pull up. Instead, he pushed it forward slightly and somebody, he wasn't quite sure who, screamed, "Ohhhhh shit," as they plunged toward the canyon floor. The airspeed went into the green about 300 feet from forever and he began hauling back on the yoke. They were pulling over four G's as they came within fifty feet of the path of wreckage and lost souls strewn along the canyon floor below. They were heavy and barely flying, but they were in balance. It would be okay after they burned off some fuel. St. Jones had the taste and was exhilarated. He had experienced an Adrenalini Yogi's equivalent of satori.

"I thought we were buyers back there, St. Jones. That was balls to the wall flying, man. I'm putting you in for a fucking medal, Silver Wheelbarrow with Cluster. I don't know how you held that yoke forward that fucking long. Every instinct in me was screaming to pull up." But St. Jones knew that if he had attempted to pull out of the dive any sooner the control surfaces would not have had enough airspeed to function and they would have lost their one opportunity for survival.

St. Jones could see the beard plane about 2,000 feet

above them and a mile ahead, and began taking off flaps, ten degrees at a time. Their rate of climb sucked and Johnson got on the radio and asked Jackson to throttle back so they could catch up before they hit radar surveillance. They put on oxygen masks going through 14,000 feet, and St. Jones thought about Nickie, sealed in the tank, out cold, under a half a ton of cocaine. Probably. It would be ten hours before he would know if she made it. If she was in there. Of course, if she didn't make it, he had a great idea of what to do with the body. To keep his mind off her, he re-ran the take-off, over and over again, savoring the rush like a memorable fuck.

They could see the Florida coast a hundred miles out. St. Jones began a 300 feet per minute descent, matching the beard plane. As they approached the ADIZ Air Defense Identification Zone, they heard Jackson contact Miami Approach and announce his intentions, thereby averting an escort of F-14s out of McDill. They cleared the coast going through 7,000 feet. The magic trick was working again. They were less than fifty feet over the beard plane, on an approach into Miami that took them over the beach house. The rabbit was almost out of the hat. They were at 3,000 feet when they entered the radar free zone and the light on the transponder stopped flashing. Johnson had programmed the VOR's and when they reached the intersection of two particular radials, he signaled St. Jones to break away from the beard plane. Executing a descending 180-degree turn, he set up a half-mile approach to the threshold of the covered landing strip.

As they cleared the last of the cypress trees and dropped down over the water, St. Jones put down the gear and held the nose high to burn off speed, carrying 1,500 rpm of power to control their descent. Johnson had been on the radio with the Reptile Brothers on the ground and St. Jones watched the camo net rise up and the threshold lights come on. At the water's edge he dumped the power and flared going under the net. They touched down on the steel grate runway and he hauled back on the yoke and stood on the brakes, watching the wall of green coming up fast. This was the heaviest he had landed there and he only had about a hundred feet left when he got it stopped.

While the Reptile Brothers unloaded the plane, St. Jones and Johnson dumped their flight extenders and drank a cup of coffee in the cabin. It was almost dark when they climbed back on board and took off for Miami. St. Jones fought off thoughts of Nickie.

When they landed at the Tamiami Trail strip, Jackson was waiting for them in the pickup truck. They invited St. Jones to dinner at the VFW, but he declined, saying that the plane had been there too long, and that he was going to move it to another airport. He told them he had a date later and said he would see them tomorrow for lunch. He was silently going crazy inside, knowing that Nickie could be dying at that very moment, but he couldn't appear impatient. They sauntered to the truck, slapped hands up and down all around, and St. Jones casually stood and watched them pull out of the lot.

BOLD

22

As soon as they were on the highway, St. Jones sprinted back to the plane. He jumped inside, praying he would find Nickie alive. Operating the switch that unsealed the tank, he pulled up the pads and scrambled into the back and lifted the metal panel and slid it to the side. Nickie was in there but she wasn't moving. He pulled the oxygen mask off and shined a flashlight on her face. Her lips were blue. He checked her fingernails and they were also blue. Holding the mask to his ear, he didn't hear the characteristic hiss. He checked for a pulse and at first couldn't find one, but when he lightened his touch he felt it, slow and weak under the corner of her jaw. St. Jones grabbed an oxygen mask from the back of the seat and held it over her mouth and nose and opened the valve on the O2 bottle. He held her eye open and shined the light on it. The pupil pinned. A good sign.

"Nickie! Nickie!" He shouted. "Wake up, baby!" St. Jones slapped her cheek sharply. She moaned and stirred.

"Breathe deep, Nickie. You're gonna be okay." She had made it, but not by much. Another ten minutes and she'd have been gone. But she was alive and back in the USA and St. Jones wasn't feeling that bad, himself. He had beaten the Reaper twice in one day, fair and square.

"Bra...bra." Nickie was trying to say something. "In my bra," she mumbled.

St. Jones shined the light on her breasts, thoroughly searching the right side. They seemed larger than he remembered. "Other side," she said after a little too long. He reached inside the left side and found a 10cc glass vile. "You found it too fast," she slurred. "I wanted you to search for a while longer. I feel uneven." Same old Nickie. "Gimme a hit of that shit." She was slurring her words. "I'm okay, but if you slap me again I'm gonna set your pubes on fire while you're asleep and burn your dick at the stake." Phenobarbitol talking.

Curling his first finger around the end of his thumb, he dumped some coke onto his thumbnail and held it under her left nostril. She sniffed it up and he dumped out some more for the other side. Then he did himself. It was the same coke as the night before, and St. Jones felt his fatigue fly away like a big, black buzzard. After a few minutes of breathing pure oxygen, Nickie began trying to get up, and he gave her a hand getting out of the tank. Grabbing a small leather grip, she climbed up front into the right seat. St. Jones gathered the hardware he had on him and in the plane and rolled it up in the bedroll and put it in the tank, sliding the lid into position. He replaced the foam pad and climbed into the left seat and operated the switch, resealing the tank.

"How are you feeling, Nickie?"

"I could use a drink and some food, for openers."

"Sounds good to me. And then you owe me a cogent explanation of why you heated up my life like a fucking lava flow."

"You sound like you're getting old, St. Jones."

"That's the general idea isn't it?"

"Pretty soon you'll be sitting around talkin' about the man you used to be."

St. Jones thought about that for a minute. Precept 77 allowed a way out: Grace is knowing when to give up voluntarily, what will eventually be taken from you by force. "I guess you're right, Nickie. It's not like anybody gets out alive."

"Don't bet on it."

"What does that mean?"

"It's too long a story to tell on an empty stomach. Feed me and fuck me and I'll tell you everything."

"This better be good, Nickie." St. Jones turned on the ignition and ran the pump a few seconds and cranked the engine. "We can eat at the Fort Lauderdale airport. There's a hotel there, too." He taxied to mid-field and took off to the east, towards the lights of Miami.

They landed at Fort Lauderdale about twenty minutes later and taxied to transient parking. St. Jones called the fuel truck on ground control frequency and they walked to the restaurant, which had an entrance onto the tarmac. They took a booth in a secluded corner and ordered a couple of triple Stolychnayas and the Pompano special.

"So tell me baby, I'm dying to know. What was so fucking urgent that you had to nuke my life? I've got Angels knocking on my door in the middle of the night and narcs following me all over the country."

"Does forever young do anything for you, St. Jones? You know...eternal life?"

"Oh shit, you've been bitten by a Christian."

"Hey, St. Jones. You wanted a story. I got a story for you. You remember my old man, Sandoz? Well, we went down to Bogota back in '72 cause it was happening and everybody was doing it and there was money to be made. We'd been there a couple of weeks and were out in the country one day. We'd taken a few hits of acid and were running around naked in the countryside, when Sandoz decided he could fly like Castaneda and took a dive off a 300 foot cliff. It was the most graceful thing I ever saw. He actually thought he was flying. When he hit the ground, he probably kept on flying right into the light. But I was still there and in deep shit. There I was, a young *gringa* who spoke no Spanish and had no witnesses, very high on acid with a husband lying dead at the bottom of a cliff. I went to the village for help. The *polizia* came and took me away and charged me with murder.

"I'd been in jail about a month, when one day I had a visitor. It was Don Luiz on one of his sex safaris. Someone in the polizia had informed him there was a *bonita gringa* in jail and he'd come to check me out. He liked what he saw okay, but when he found out I was a chemist, he bought me out of jail and into his custody on the spot. In those days the Colombians didn't know shit about cooking cocaine. They were using white gas for solvent. I was the first real chemist they ever had, and all I knew was what was in that book you gave me. See, it was all your fault, in a way. It was that book you gave me that got me into this and it was that book that got me outta there. It's funny how things fit together when you can look at them going away instead of coming at you. Anyway, I got really good at it fast, cause that's my thing, you know.

"So Don Luiz takes me to the country and we worked out a deal. I cook for them and they treat me like a lady and get me anything I want and deposit my end in the Caymans. It was a sweet deal. I'm living in a beautiful home in the mountains of Colombia with princess status and they're getting me everything I want, which is a lot of very expensive laboratory equipment and instruments. I didn't spend ten years at Berkeley just for the party. There was some stuff I really wanted to do and through a very strange chain of events, I wound up where I needed to be, to do what I wanted to do. But I'm still wanted for murder and I don't have a passport and it's hard to leave when you can't find the door.

"Okay. Enough about that." Nickie shifted gears. "Now comes the good part. Remember those koi in the pool?"

"Yeah. They were beautiful."

"I had them shipped from Japan. They're very old. That's the thing about koi. They live a long time, a very long time. In fact, nobody knows how long they live. There are some in Japan that are known to be more than five hundred years old. There are rumored to be some that are over a thousand. It seems that they may live forever if nothing kills them."

Nickie was warming up to her subject. "As you know, my doctorate is in molecular biology, but the things I wanted to do aren't allowed in the U.S. Cross species human gene splicing is a very big no-no. No *chimeras* allowed."

St. Jones was starting to get chicken-skin. "Nickie, you're not gonna tell me what I think you're gonna tell me, are you?"

"Oh, but I am, St. Jones." Nickie's eyes were on high beams now. "I've come up with the cure for the number one killer of mankind: natural causes. I've developed a death vaccine."

BOLD

23

"Does it work?" St. Jones had heard some bizarre stories along the trail and this one was a whopper. He was going to take some convincing.

"Hell, I don't know," Nickie said. "Give me a fucking break. It's the forever bug. It takes a while to test it. The only way to find out for sure is to wait a hundred years and see who's still standing. But bet on it, St. Jones. The science is good."

"This is a hell of a thing, Nickie. This is bigger than the bomb. Something like this could destabilize the whole game, the entire social order. We have to be extremely careful, whether it works or not. Do you know what would happen if certain interests even thought we had a you-know-what? They would torture us to death just to make sure they got it all."

"I'm way ahead of you, St. Jones. That's why I had to send out the Mama Coca notes. I had to get out of there before they figured out what I had done. Imagine what would happen if Don Luiz and Altman got their hands on this. Altman is Nazi royalty, you know, and was the source of the original research."

"Oh my god, Nickie. What have you gotten yourself into? What have you gotten me into? Colombian drug lords weren't enough? You had to get involved with the Nazis. Surely you've heard about them. It was in all the papers."

"Don't patronize me, you prick. And don't call me Shirley. I didn't have a choice. That's why I had to torch the lab and that's why they've found my body in the ashes by now."

"How'd you manage that?"

"A woman was brought in from the bush to see if I could help her. She'd been snake bitten. She died in my lab. She had no family and no one claimed the body. She was about my size and weight, so I froze the body in liquid nitrogen and faked a burial. That was a year ago. I've been planning this for a while."

"You've been playing me like a flute from the start."

"Nice image, St. Jones," Nickie smirked. "Face it, when it comes to this kind of job, you're the man. Insertions and extractions. Isn't that what it's called? Ins and outs. Very sexy. I've heard about some of your exploits even in Colombia. Besides, I always thought I'd see you again."

"Strange that you should say that, Nickie."

"Johnson was a nice touch. The perfect alibi. How'd you manage that?"

"It wasn't easy. But then, that's why you pay me the big money."

"How much did you make on that run, anyway?"

"Two-fifty, large."

"You did okay."

"Only because I lived through it. And this isn't over. I've got a feeling this is going to get expensive."

"Poor baby. You just need some of Mama Coca's red hot pussy to take your mind off of things." Nickie reached under the table and gave St. Jones a squeeze. "Let's get out of here and get a room."

"If you think you can just promise me eternal life and lead me around by my dick, I'm your boy." He stood up. "Wait here."

St. Jones paid the check and walked into the adjoining lobby of the hotel and checked in under a *nom de voyage*. Going back to the restaurant, he gave Nickie the room key and then walked over to the FBO office and paid his fuel bill. When he got to the room, Nickie had laid out some lines on the table. He greedily plowed through the powder. This was the shit that was illegal.

"Let's hit the shower and wash this day away." Nickie stood up and stretched and began peeling off her clothes.

The years had been more than kind to her. Nickie had been a tall, slender young woman with a bubble butt and high, firm breasts and shoulder length blonde hair. She had gained a few pounds since the old days, but it went to all the right places. Her ass had bloomed into a showpiece and her breasts were fuller and still rode high and her hair was down to her waist.

When St. Jones took off his shirt, Nickie saw the bruise. "That's an ugly bruise. How did you get it?"

"Don't ask."

Nickie laughed. "That big dick of yours is going to get you killed, St. Jones." Women just seemed to know these things.

The shower was a good idea. They both stunk of dried

sweat and spent adrenaline. They tried to run the hot water out, but it was a class hotel and it just kept coming. They finally gave up and dried off and lay on the bed, steam rising from their bodies in the refrigerated air.

"So what's the plan, St. Jones? It seems I've placed myself in your hands, and vice versa," she said, fondling him. "Jesus. I forgot how big this thing gets. Will you take the case?"

"What's in it for me?"

"Eternal life and all the pussy you can eat." Nickie grabbed his dick with both hands and using it like a saddle horn, swung over and mounted St. Jones' face like the cowgirl that she was and rode off at a gallop.

St. Jones took a taxi to Dupont Plaza, walked through the main complex and out the other side, and caught another taxi to Coconut Grove. He got out at the hotel and walked the four blocks to the VFW, arriving about 1:30 p.m. The cold and dark were bliss after the blinding Miami mid-day. The boys were at their usual booth. Jefferson was there, too. Some of the monsters were still lurking under the covers with Nickie at the hotel, but those that were with St. Jones were subdued.

He was ravenous after the night's exertion and ordered another special. The boys had already finished lunch and were drinking coffee. While St. Jones ate, Johnson told the story of the take-off the day before in Colombia. He concluded by nominating St. Jones for the coveted Silver Wheelbarrow with Cluster, the wheelbarrow signifying the size of his balls. It was the dope pilots' highest award. He would be decorated at the next company party and his story would become part of the dope runners' oral history of heroic deeds. If they only knew.

Jefferson reached under the table and came up with a gym bag and placed it on the seat between them. It would have been a breach of etiquette to count the money, but St. Jones would have bet more than what was there, that the count was right. The vial and spoon came out and made its way around the table, signifying a done deal.

"Just one question, guys. What is the significance of Tome Coca Cola?"

"Well, you know how Latin America is covered with *Tome Coca Cola*–Drink Coca Cola–signs. It became the battle cry of the Cuban revolution. They would scream *Tome Coca Cola* when they charged into battle. We sort of carried on the tradition."

That raised more questions than it answered but St. Jones decided that he knew all he wanted to about that one. He said his good-byes and walked outside into the daily afternoon thundershowers. Sprinting across the street to the beach, he savored the rain and the reprieve it brought from the thermal mugging he had dreaded. He found a Cuban cabbie finishing lunch at the hamburger stand.

The Narx Brothers, who no longer looked just alike, were sitting in their car on the street fronting the hotel. They were just out of the hospital and were trying to figure out what to do next, and would have bought a clue if they only knew how. They couldn't believe their eyes when they saw St. Jones run across the street. Even the coyote gets lucky, sometimes. They were radiating malice as they pulled into traffic behind the taxi, which was fortunate for St. Jones. A real hunter never thinks directly about his prey. At an animal level they can sense it. The monsters started acting weird and looking out the back window of the taxi, and in spite of having his own pack of invisible dogs, St. Jones had developed a sense after a while. He had a creepy feeling that came from having followed his own share of people. In this case, it was unanimous.

The cabbie took the MacArthur Causeway to Miami Beach and dropped St. Jones at Fifth and Collins. He went into Wolfie's and used the payphone to call Girl. He told her he was back and okay and would be in touch when it was over. He walked to the other side of the park and caught another cab to the Fort Lauderdale Yacht Harbor, where he caught a third taxi to the hotel. By the time St. Jones got to the room, he was flashing bright yellow around the periphery of his vision. Nickie was just finishing breakfast in bed.

"Time to get up, baby. We gotta get out of here. I hear footsteps. We gotta get in the wind." St. Jones picked up the phone and extended their stay another night.

A veteran of the fast getaway, Nickie saved her questions for later and was ready in under three minutes. They sauntered through the lobby into the restaurant and out onto the tarmac. St. Jones opened up the plane and climbed into the left seat and quickly began running down the checklist while Nickie arranged herself in the right seat. He cranked the engine and got on the radio to ground control for taxi clearance. Rolling to the hold line at the active runway, he switched to tower frequency and was immediately cleared for take-off. He taxied to the centerline and pushed the throttle forward and they were out of there. St. Jones had no way of knowing that the Narx Brothers were walking up to the front desk of the hotel as the T-210 cleared the end of the runway. Chalk one up for the monsters.

St. Jones decided to stay over land to avoid ADIZ and under 18,000 feet so he wouldn't have to file an IFR flight plan, thereby staying out of the military and FAA data bases. The oxygen supply was low, which put a 14,000 feet ceiling on their options. He flew north up to the Florida panhandle at 12,500 feet. and turned to a more westerly course at Tallahassee, flying into the setting sun.

They crossed the Texas border two hours later. Nickie had been asleep since Alabama, giving St. Jones time to sort through various options. He had the fragments of a plan. It was about eight o'clock and he figured he had about two more hours of flying left in him without having to resort to the spinach. St. Jones thought that people were introduced to the idea of drugs by Popeye the sailor man when they were kids. When things got tight and he was being overwhelmed by Bluto or some giant octopus, Popeye would whip out a can of spinach and suck it through his pipe and get a full-blown rush and explode with superhuman strength.

After a while, a pilot gets to know a continent like a cabbie knows his town. In his mind, St. Jones drew an arc five hundred miles to the west, considered Midland and Odessa, but decided on Fort Stockton. It was an uncontrolled airport with virtually no traffic, and it had a nice little Holiday Inn close by that would send a station wagon when called. It had a good cafe and it was almost exactly halfway across America.

St. Jones preferred flying at night. In the daytime, other planes were hard to see. At night, he could spot other aircraft thirty miles away, and cities and towns were visible for a hundred miles and more. West of Austin, they began to move through a weather front, encountering a thick line of towering Q's (cumulonimbus clouds). A three-quarter moon back-lit the ten-mile-high monsters and lightning danced between them like the spears of battling Titans. St. Jones respectfully threaded his way among the marching giants.

Ten miles out of Fort Stockton he brought up the runway lights with his radio to locate the airport. The lights would remain on for fifteen minutes, giving him time to land. He began a 500 foot per minute descent and made left traffic to get a look at the lighted windsock at midfield. There appeared to be a fifteen knot wind out of the northwest, so he flew the pattern once and approached to the west into a quartering headwind. Nickie woke up as they touched down.

"Where are we?"

"Deep in the heart of Texas."

"Ever get the feeling you're going around in circles?"

St. Jones saw headlights approaching and figured it to be the FBO (Fixed Base Operator). He reached across Nickie and opened the door. "Step out Nickie, so I can talk to the man."

"Evenin', sir, ma'am," the man said, leaving the headlights on as he got out of the truck. "Will you be needin' fuel this evening?"

"Yes, sir," St. Jones replied. "Sir" will get you a long way in Texas. "We need fuel and a ride to the Holiday Inn. We'd like to tie down here tonight."

"Go ahead and tie her down and lock up and come over to the trailer with me. Y'all can call the hotel while I bring the fuel truck over and top her off."

They were gone with the dawn and over New Mexico

by eight o'clock. It was a CAVU morning but they were flying into a forty-knot headwind that was slowing them down and eating fuel. It was a thousand miles to their destination, which would have been a four-hour flight, but with the headwind it was looking like five and change, plus lunch somewhere and a wild ride over the Sierra.

"So what's the plan, St. Jones? Where are you taking us?"

"There's an isolated little hot springs hotel on the western slope of the Sierra with a 2,500 foot paved runway. It belongs to some old friends. They're extremely discreet. We're going there to hide out and think this through. And right now, I want you to tell me about the forever bug. Everything! How you did it, how you make it, how it works. This is the time and place to talk."

"Okay, St. Jones. Well, first let's take a look at the aging process. From a biological point of view, every day past about nineteen is superfluous. Up to that time we are genetically driven from conception to manifest ourselves. When we run out of that information, each cell replicates itself over and over again. But each time, tiny inexactitudes are introduced that make each successive generation of cells slightly different from the last. Over time it adds up and we age, but only because we run out of forward information and the replications are inexact. It isn't fated. That's where the koi come in. Koi possess a factor that keeps the replications accurate and relatively un-mutated, and working with research notes from earlier work, I managed to isolate that factor. Getting it into another organism was a separate problem, involving splicing this factor onto a benign virus, which by its nature penetrates to the nucleus of every cell in the body and the new genetic information takes over, effectively stopping the aging process at whatever stage it's in. It's a virus, a bug, and can even be passed on from one person to another under certain circumstances."

"It sounds weird enough. How did you get the original research notes?"

"After I'd been at the finca for a couple of years, Altman realized the extent of my training and probably realized he wasn't getting any younger. One night he came to the lab and gave me a suitcase containing the notes from research done by the Nazis on immortality. I picked up where they left off. They were on the right track. They just didn't have the microscopes or the number crunching capability that we have now. Altman arranged computer time in Germany."

"What's to keep them from picking up where you left off?"

"All of my math that went outside was processed with an algorithm only I know. And then, of course, there was the fire."

"Have you taken it yet?"

"Yes, of course."

"Anybody else?"

"A few lab rats and a couple of monkeys."

"What happened?"

"Until the fire the rats had reached the equivalent of three hundred human years old. It was too soon to tell about the monkeys. But they were normal in every way."

"You said it could be passed on. How?"

"By blood. Also sexually, from male to female. It passes in the direction of the fluids. But it's probably only contagious the first week or two after inoculation. I don't really know."

"How much have you got?"

"A thermos full, probably ten thousand doses."

That was enough to change the course of human history. They were quiet for a while as St. Jones absorbed the information and considered its implications. He was getting scared and the more he thought about it, the more he understood the wisdom of his fear. This was the big one. What would you do for eternal life? What had people already done in the pursuit of eternal life? What would people do if they found out you had eternal life? All those questions and any others he could think of had disturbing answers. Whoever possessed the forever bug could stage a revolution by attrition that no one would ever know about. It would be like a Trojan Horse across time. They would simply quietly outlive the opposition and take over. Precept 39: If you sit by the river long enough, you will see the bodies of all your enemies float by.

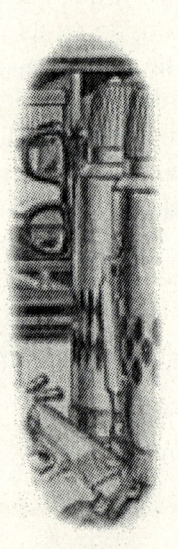

BOLD

24

They landed at Grand Canyon Village on the south rim and had lunch and took on fuel. After a pit stop to dump their flight extenders and a few minutes of walking to stretch out the kinks, they took off to the west.

"Can we fly in the canyon?"

"Sure. Everybody does. That's the problem. They're thick as flies in there."

"Can we do it?"

"Sure baby. Anything for you."

St. Jones got on the tower frequency and asked the procedure. He was given two frequencies, one for east bound and one for west bound traffic in the canyon, and told to stay to the right and call out his position often. They flew out over the canyon and began to burn off altitude. Soon they were level with the rim and then began to descend into the canyon. He leveled off about five hundred feet below the rim and held that altitude as they followed the north wall. He wondered how many millions of years he was looking at displayed in geological cross section, like a biopsy of time.

"Nickie, forever is a long damn time, baby."

They followed the canyon to Lake Mead and flew up and across Nevada to Reno. There was a strong westerly flow over the Sierra and flying Donner Pass was like shooting an invisible Category 5 rapids going up stream.

It was late afternoon when they turned north along the western slope of the mountain range. Less than an hour later, they were lining up on a landing strip that looked like a half mile of two-lane blacktop highway in the middle of absolutely nowhere. They used about a third of the runway and turned around and taxied back to the east end, pulled onto a turnout and shut down. St. Jones was tying the plane down when a pickup truck from the lodge drove up.

"I thought that was a hopped up 210 I heard. How the hell are you, governor?" The man looked exactly like the guy who said, "Badges? I don't got to show you no stinking badges," in *Treasure of the Sierra Madre*. The fact that he spoke with a British accent and had the style of a very hip English butler made him unforgettable. "What brings you to the secret mountain laboratory?"

"I wasn't too sure you'd be glad to see me, Leo."

"Why? Just because you fucked me ol' lady? Hey gov, you saved my life. I was so twisted after Thailand, that bloody nothing was getting through. It was bitter medicine, what you did, but I'm well now. Feel my nose. Just don't do it again."

St. Jones hadn't been in an altruistic mood when he'd done the dirty deed. They were just too high and it was too late and she was too easy. It was too bad. And of course she had to tell Leo. But it worked. Leo had become so enraged that he found a reason to live. It was what he needed. Leo had a rough time in prison. There weren't many round-eyes and the Thais are very tough people. Even Rambo couldn't have broken him out. St. Jones checked. And the Thais had wanted major six-figure money for Leo, more than could be raised, since he was captured with 400k of his and his associates' money. But there's more than one way to buy a Thai.

St. Jones had always been well paid for his services, but he reserved the right to call in a favor in the future. When he learned that the top narc of Thailand was a tennis fanatic with a Kojac hairdo, St. Jones arranged lessons for him with his idol, a former U.S. Open winner. The pro owed St. Jones big time for solving a problem in Hong Kong, and that debt had been Leo's ticket to freedom.

"Leo, say 'hello' to Nickie. She's dead."

"My condolences. A lot of dead people come here. I regret not meeting you while you were alive. Maybe I could've gotten even with His Lordship, here. But alas, you're dead and I'm not feeling that good myself."

"Can we finish this someplace warm? I'm freezing my tits off."

The sun was going down and the temperature was dropping fast.

"Sorry, Nickie. We can't have that." Leo inspected the tits in question. "Let's get in the truck and go up to the lodge. We've got a fire going in the bar. Whenever you're ready, you can hit the hot springs in the woods or go for a swim in the pool at the lodge. It's 106 degrees and filled from the springs."

"I think I'm gonna like this place."

They climbed in the truck and drove the quarter mile gravel road up to the lodge.

"Your old room happens to be vacant. In fact, just about the whole joint is bloody vacant. I think you know just about everybody here."

The truck pulled around the circular drive to the entrance of the lodge. The place was beautiful. It was three stories, finished in split cedar shakes and constructed of huge eighteen and twenty-four-inch timbers, probably cut from the site. It looked like it had been designed by Bernard Maybeck during his massive period.

St. Jones and Nickie sat down at the bar while Leo took the Remy bottle off the shelf and set up three snifters. "So what brings you here, St. Jones? Having a convention of your ex-ol' ladies?" Leo had a certain amount of residual bitterness, regardless of what he said.

"Now Leo, don't bite the hand that freed you."

"Do all your friends like you as much as Leo?" Nickie asked.

"Oh, some of us love him to death. How many times have you been shot, St. Jones?"

"Lately?" His stomach twitched. "Well, it's like Precept 18 says, friends come and go, but enemies tend to accumulate. It's the nature of the business. I'm utterly ruthless on behalf of my clients. Need I remind either one of you?"

Leo looked at Nickie. "You, too?"

"Fresh," she shrugged.

"How fresh?"

"Straight from the oven."

"So this isn't just some tide-pool romance?"

They shook their heads in unison. "Me and Nickie go way back, but right now we have hellhounds on our trail. It would be bad medicine if anyone knew we were here."

Leo poured more Remy and walked around the bar. "I'll be back in a minute." He left the room.

"Where's he going?"

"To kill the phone and post a guard down the road."

"Sounds like you've done this before."

"A time or two."

"All this danger is making me horny."

"Air makes you horny."

"That, too."

Leo came back into the bar. "The phone's out of order. Let me know if you need to make a call."

"Are there many guests in the hotel?"

"A few, but we'll be down to family by tomorrow noon. Are you staying long?"

St. Jones bent over and opened the gym bag and came up with a bundle of bills rubber banded together. A small piece of paper on top had 10K written on it in pencil. "I'd like to rent the place for a week, maybe longer. Here's a deposit."

Leo bowed sharply at the waist. "What time will El Patron be requiring my wife?"

"Just a little more Remy will suffice, Leo."

Precept 76 states that dope money is found money. When you live outside the law, it's very important to be generous as well as honest. Over time, people you know will be taken into the little room and told that they will never see wives or husbands or children or whatever again if they don't give up somebody. It's important that at that moment they remember you fondly and can find no reason to sacrifice you.

Nickie reached into her bra and came out with the magic vial. She selected a cocktail straw from a glassful on the bar and dipped it into the powder, held it to her nose and sniffed. After doing the other side, she passed it to St. Jones, who passed it to Leo.

"You really must stop in more often, Governor."

"Don't worry, Leo. If things go wrong, I'll be living here. It's important that no one see us. Or know that we've been here. We'll slip up the back stairs and have dinner in our room."

"Sahib's wish is my command." Leo rubbed the money against his cheek like a stuffed animal. "What rare delicacy can I provide?"

"Anything will be fine." St. Jones picked up the Remy bottle and stood up.

"Can Bwana tell me what's going on?"

"If I told you, I'd have to kill you, Leo." St. Jones had always wanted to say that. "All I can say is that it's been a ten-thousand-mile adrenaline rush."

"You're hooked, St. Jones."

"I know, Leo. If it just wasn't for the damned side effect."

"What's that?"

"The shit keeps wearing off."

After a good dinner and a hot soak and a long, slow screw, Nickie drifted off to sleep, leaving St. Jones to contemplate eternity, the enormity of which was beginning to settle in on him. He was in over his head and knew it. The Dirty Harry Imperative came to mind: A man's got to know his limitations. Precept 33.

St. Jones needed the council of men who had the vision to see over the horizon of time and play out the consequences of every move for centuries to come. He knew men like that, but it was an act of faith dealing with people vastly more intelligent than you, especially in a high stakes game. He would have to decide if each one of them was worthy. Once he brought them in, there would be no refusing them. They would demand the bug as compensation for their participation.

On the surface, the forever bug seemed like a miracle, the answer to the prayers of everyone. But what if people stopped dying, but they kept on being born? Bad idea. At some point we'd be standing on top of each other and the lifestyle wouldn't exactly be Sharper Image. Parking was already tight.

So, he pondered, who gets to live forever? On what basis is the selection made? Who makes that decision? What about those who are left out? If someone is known to be an immortal, what's to stop the angry villagers from stoning them to death out of envy? What happens when someone obviously isn't aging, while all around them are? Does one move abroad periodically to avoid discovery, like Count St. Germain? Did it even work? Would it even matter soon? And what if it did work?

The most frightening thought St. Jones lived with was the fear that man can conceive of eternal life, but isn't equipped to live it. From an investigator's perspective, the only really plausible explanation he had found to explain the species, was that we are space mongrels, the offspring of ETs and LIPs (Local Indigenous Personnel), space men and earth women. He knew it sounded weird and he kept it to himself, but it was Occam's razor again. The simplest explanation consistent with all the facts was almost always the correct one. Man's star fathers were virtual immortals, which accounts for his higher aspirations and desire to reach the stars. But man's ancestral earth mothers descended from reptiles, and he is cursed to freely love and murder, and to conceive of eternal life but be condemned to the death of the flesh. "We can see it, but we can't be it," he feared. And if the Buddhists and the Hindus were right and the law of Karma true, what would the forever bug really do to us? St. Jones was humming the Third Eye Blues as he drifted into troubled sleep.

The accumulated fatigue of the last week made sleep easy and the cold mountain air made it sweet. It was nearly noon when they woke. St. Jones crawled out of bed and stirred the embers in the fireplace and added a couple of pieces of split wood.

There was a tapping at the door. "Are you guys up in there?" Leo stage whispered.

St. Jones walked to the door and opened it. "Just barely, no pun intended."

Leo's eyes glanced downward and quickly back up. "Oh Jesus. I wish I hadn't seen that. I feel inadequate enough as it is. How big does that thing get, anyway?"

"Not as big as mine," Nickie smirked, getting out of bed and walking to the fireplace. "No matter how big his gets, mine's still bigger." She bent down and blew the embers into flame.

"She's right, Leo. I've been taking very careful measurements. Hers is bigger." St. Jones held his thumb and first finger together in front of his eye. "By that much."

"Thank you both for sharing that with me and possibly warping me for life. I just came up to tell you that we're down to family. The last guest left ten minutes ago."

"Thanks, Leo. We'll be down for breakfast in a little while, soon as we get dressed."

Leo gave Nickie's naked body a long, slow slurp with his eyes. "I've seen you with some strange ones, St. Jones, but I've never seen you with a bad one." Leo sighed deeply. "Life's not fair," he said, as he closed the door.

"And then you die," St. Jones said to back of the door.

"Not anymore."

"I keep forgetting."

"Maybe it would help if you took it. It would be a shame to come so close and miss. What is it you fly-boys call it? Screwing the pooch?"

"When you put it that way, who could pass it up? Are you sure there are no side effects?"

"No, I'm not sure. But think of all the things you've taken without a clue as to side effects. At least this time the prize is worth the risk. I took it almost a year ago and I haven't even had a cold."

"Well, what the hell. You only go around once."

Nickie made an exasperated sound and walked into the bathroom. She came back with her mystery bag and sat on the bed. "Come sit over here."

"Are you gonna stick a needle in my butt?"

"I can do that, if you like." She filled a disposable insulin syringe. "Roll over."

St. Jones complied and barely felt the needle.

She slapped him on his bare butt. "Live long and prosper." Nickie held up her left hand in the Vulcan salute. "I'm glad you took it, St. Jones. I was afraid I might have to live a long time alone with this wonderful, terrible secret." Nickie put the syringe on the bedside table and rolled St. Jones over on his back. "You can't soak in the hot baths for a couple of days. The water's so hot it would act like artificial fever and it might kill the bug. Other than that, I recommend lots of sex. With me. Think of it as giving me booster shots." Nickie began fondling him. "Just don't fuck anybody that you don't want to have around for a very long time."

They were late for breakfast.

BOLD

25

After breakfast, Leo drove St. Jones and Nickie to the plane and they took off for San Francisco. After making a course for Sebastopol, St. Jones explained to Nickie what he planned to do, and why. He presented it in terms of Precept 33, the Dirty Harry Imperative. It was too big a decision for the two of them to make alone, in light of the fact that they had access to some seriously superior, high frequency minds. But in order to reach these men, he needed an address book from the Russian Hill studio. It contained numbers too sensitive to list in the Rolodex. The book was hidden in the broiler section of the kitchen stove. It could be destroyed more or less instantly by simply turning on the oven. They landed outside Sebastopol at three o'clock.

After hangaring the aircraft, St. Jones and Nickie drove south on Highway 101 in the van. Traffic was light heading into the city and they made good time, turning onto Taylor going up Russian Hill about 4:30. Driving past St.

Jones' building at Green, they turned left on the next street. He activated the electric door opener as they approached, and pulled into the garage.

The ambient thought field level is very high in the city and the signal to noise ratio is low, which makes for a great deal of psychic static. Only very late at night is it possible to think clearly in the city. That's probably why St. Jones failed to notice that the monsters had fled.. However, there was no use having a pack of invisible dogs if you didn't pay attention to them. A precept if there ever was one. St. Jones also failed to see Lyla as she sprinted across the street and ducked under the door just before it closed. But the monsters remembered her well and split when they first sensed her presence, just like the last time.

The problem in dealing with a crazy person as an adversary is that they're psychic, especially when it comes to you. Also, they have the madman's advantage. There's no way to figure for sure what they're going to do. And because they're incandescing with psychic energy, you can't hold a candle to them. St. Jones had a formidable opponent.

Lyla made her way in the dark garage to the driver's side of the van. As St. Jones opened the door, he realized the monsters were gone, but the interior light was already on and that was all Lyla needed. She opened fire. St. Jones grabbed the seat lever and slammed the seat all the way back behind the door-post, the thickest part of a vehicle body. Lyla kept firing until the gun was empty, but St. Jones had no way of knowing that, because after the first two shots a sledge hammer hit his head and he was tumbling down the vortex to oblivion. He hated when that happened.

St. Jones' first recognizable sensation was pain, followed by motion, then nausea, then really bad pain. He tried to open his eyes but couldn't seem to remember the right way to do it. He tried to move his body and got some scattered response but he didn't have a quorum. It was like a joke that only the band laughed at. It wasn't encouraging. He decided to just lie there for a while. He could feel motion and hear the sound of the engine and surmised that they were on their way somewhere in the back of the van.

St. Jones finally found the right combination for his eyelids and managed to ratchet them open. He didn't like what he saw. There was a lot of blood and he knew some of it had to be connected to his headache. Nickie was lying next to him and she didn't look good. Her eyes were open but St. Jones had seen that look before. He knew she was dead without even checking her pulse. It was just like Precept 65 said; the hero never gets killed, it's always his best friend.

St. Jones went from zero to total rage in one heartbeat. Struggling into a crouch, he lunged for the back of the driver's seat. He wasn't sure who was driving as he reached around the headrest, but when he grabbed the throat of the driver, he recognized the hair. He had Lyla by the neck and he was going kill her this time. If only he'd done it when he first knew he was going to have to, Nickie would be alive. The irony was overwhelming. A good woman who may have changed the course of history, killed by an evil woman who stole the life she had.

The first shot was so loud it got quiet and he barely heard the rest of them. Lyla had her gun out again and was trying to shoot St. Jones, but she couldn't see him.

She was firing backwards over her head, blowing out windows and punching holes in the roof and the sides of the van. They swerved radically from side to side as Lyla tried to drive and shoot at the same time she was being strangled. In the confusion she stomped on the brake and the next instant there was a tremendous crash as they were rear-ended, followed a split second later by a bigger crash as they slammed into the back of the car in front of them and St. Jones was tumbling down that damned vortex again.

He had to swim against the current to find his way back to the surface, and the mother of all headaches was waiting for him when he got there. He found himself lying on the console between the seats with his head jammed against the dashboard, and there were people looking in the windows. Somehow St. Jones knew, even in his condition, that Nickie's bag was the highest priority, and he frantically searched, but it was gone. And so, of course, was Lyla.

It wasn't until he got out of the van that he discovered the extent of the chaos. They were near the north tower on the Golden Gate Bridge at rush hour and there was wreckage everywhere, all the way to the middle of the span. As he climbed out of the van, people backed up. When he saw his reflection in a car window, he understood. His entire head was solid red with blood. He looked like a match. At least he wouldn't be recognized.

St. Jones took off running north toward Marin. When he reached the scenic lookout at the end of the bridge there was a vacant taxi about to pull out. The driver had dropped off his fare, who had walked out onto the bridge. Apparently the cabbie thought St. Jones was another one of San Francisco's colorful masked men and allowed him to get into the taxi, but when he realized it was blood and not makeup, he freaked. St. Jones tossed a wadded up hundred dollar bill over the seat and it had an immediate calming effect, but he knew the cabbie would be questioned about the incident on the bridge, once he found out what had happened. St. Jones had him drive to the ferry landing in Sausalito, the closest point of public transportation. That would complicate the search.

After the cab left, St. Jones walked across the parking lot to the gay bar downstairs at the Sausalito Hotel. He needed to get off the street and clean up and it was the one bar in town he wasn't known in. There was scattered shrieking at the sight of him. Attempting a lisp, he told the bartender that he'd just been rolled, and asked if he could clean up. The bartender was sympathetic and showed St. Jones to a real bathroom at the top of the stairs.

St. Jones' hair was matted with blood and as he began to wash away the gore, he discovered he had actual holes in his head. The entry wound was on the left side an inch above the ear, and it was big. The bullet had flatten to the size of a quarter and slowed down passing through the door post, and then burrowed under his scalp, coming out at the top of his head. If his head hadn't been tilted so far to the right in an instinctive effort to get away from the source of the danger, it would have penetrated his skull. The wound was so ugly it was understandable why Lyla thought he was dead. He covered the damage with his hair and washed the blood off his flight jacket with a wet towel. He looked like hell and felt like he looked, but it wasn't going to get any better, so he went back downstairs to the bar.

Everyone wanted to buy him a drink. He accepted a

Remy, which he knew he shouldn't, and drank it much too fast. The bartender put the lost and found box on the bar and gave St. Jones his pick of the lot. He chose a dark crew neck sweater large enough fit over the one he was wearing, removed his jacket and put it on. He took a navy watch cap to cover his head. He held a wad of folded paper towels to the wounds and pulled on the cap to hold it in place.

St. Jones was in pain and feeling deeply weird. He was sweating on the left side of his body but normal on the right, and knew he had a concussion at the very least. Every so often, he would get a flashback of Nickie's sightless eyes and involuntarily moan. But he couldn't deal with it then. He would mourn when he could, but he had his work cut out for him. He had to get off the street and call Dr. Deep.

It was dark outside when St. Jones left the bar. He put on the Groucho glasses and began walking toward Gate 3. He reached the parking lot in about fifteen minutes and headed out the pier to Randy's boat. His head hurt so bad he couldn't have gone much farther. His equilibrium was getting worse and he almost fell into the water getting down the gangplank.

Randy was sitting at the galley table. One look, and he knew St. Jones was VSF. Besides the blood running down his neck behind his left ear, St. Jones' searchlight eyes were down to a few candlepower.

"What happened, man? You look severely Draculated."

"I've been shot." St. Jones took off the glasses. "Can I lay up here and would you get Dr. Deep for me?"

"Sure, man. Of course. Who shot you?"

"Lyla." St. Jones thought about Nickie and moaned.

"I told you that bitch was gonna kill you if you didn't kill her first. Go lie down in the foc's'le and I'll call Doc. Stay awake. You know the drill."

BOLD

26

St. Jones lay there, doing what he'd done since he was a little boy at times like that and consoled himself with the thought that in a little while, this moment would be in the past. But the pain he felt over Nickie was inconsolable. It had only been three days more or less since she had come back into his life, but the reconnection had been so strong that their fates seemed intertwined. Relationships sometimes take on the intensity of the situation they begin in, and this one seemed like it could go on forever. St. Jones was beginning to realize that he had always loved Nickie, ever since the old days, and that she had joined the growing number of people that he wouldn't be seeing again. He would have drunk himself unconscious, but he knew it would kill him in his present condition. This was a job for smack if there ever was one, but that would kill him, too. Maybe later, when he needed a vacation from the grief, but right now he had important business among the living.

It wasn't often that a man got a chance to play a hand in the game of the Gods, and it was vital that the good guys won this one.

Dr. Deep was at his home on the Sausalito hillside, and was at Randy's boat in fifteen minutes. Doc was a career ER doctor. He wasn't really interested in getting to know his patients and had no bedside manner whatsoever. He had been a meatball surgeon in Vietnam and later in Afghanistan. It was the only kind of medicine he wanted to practice. He was in it for the rush. When Doc went to work, he played "Beat the Reaper," over and over again every day. He was a Black Belt Adrenalini Yogi and a member in good standing of the Order of the Bold Stroke, the Sly Pass, and the Ace in the Hole. He was the right man for the job.

"I keep telling you about this time and space thing, St. Jones, but you don't seem to be getting the hang of it. You just can't be there at the same time as the hot metal." The doctor ran deep. "You can be damned close, right up to less than a millisecond or a millimeter, but not at the same time." Doc turned his attention to St. Jones' solar plexus. "I've seen that kind of bruise before. You must have been wearing a vest." He poked at the bruise until he got a reaction. "This living legend shit is gonna getcha killed, St. Jones. You need to write Precept 4 a thousand times on the blackboard. Remember? 'One should not be where one does not belong.' Say it out loud with me, St. Jones."

"Come on Doc, give me a break. My head is killing me."

"That's the way it works. You kill the head and the body dies. Were you in that van on the bridge that I saw on TV?"

"What van?" Randy asked.

"The one with the dead woman?"

"What dead woman? Come on, guys. Deal me in."

"There was a fifty car pile-up on the Golden Gate Bridge, and at the center of it was a shot-up van with a dead woman in the back. Two people were observed leaving the scene: a woman who caught a ride south, and a man who ran north. They said the man appeared to be injured. Was that you, St. Jones? Are they gonna trace that van to you?"

"No, they're not." Since it would be a bad idea to register a surveillance van in his own name, St. Jones had registered it to the Han Zup Holding Company, one of his cut-outs. But they might find his prints. He had a sheepskin steering wheel cover for just that reason, but he hadn't had time to WD-40 the interior. "I was walking down the street minding my own business." St. Jones winced at Doc's probing. "That's my story and I'm sticking to it."

While they were talking, Doctor Deep had been thoroughly examining St. Jones from the top of his head to the bottom of his feet. He was poking the bottom of St. Jones right foot with a sharp instrument, checking neurological response.

"Ouch. Is that necessary?"

Doc went back to St. Jones' eyes and shined a pen light into each of them. "I should take some pictures of your head, but I don't suppose I'm going to get you to go to a hospital."

"That's a bad idea, Doc."

"That's what I thought. It's really too soon to tell, but chances are if you were going to die, you would have when you were running off the bridge. Whoops, I forgot. You were walking down the street, minding your own business.

"Randy, I'm going to write some prescriptions in your name for our boy, here. Find the closest thing you can to a nurse and have her watch him constantly, and wake him up every hour or so and check him. If there's any change, call me. I'm working the graveyard shift tonight. I'll come back in the morning when I get off duty. Pull down your pants and roll over, St. Jones. I'm going to give you a couple of shots."

"Something for the pain, I hope." St. Jones complied, pulling down his pants and rolling over, anxious for relief.

"You know I can't do that. You've got a concussion." Doc saw the dick. "Jesus, St. Jones. Can I have that thing when you die? It would look great in a jar on my desk. A real conversation piece." Doc gave St. Jones an injection in his right butt cheek.

"Knowing you, doc, you'd sew it on the end of yours."

"What would be so bad about that? Think about it, St. Jones. You would be immortal, in a way. You could go on fucking, even after you're dead." Doc struck again with the needle on the other side. "I'm offering you immortality. I've got an organ donor card here in my bag."

"Where'd you go to school, Doc?" St. Jones rolled back over and pulled up his pants. "The Dominican Republic?"

Doc feigned outrage. "I demand to know who told you that."

"What's the prognosis?"

"Well, I've got good news and bad news."

"Give me the bad news first." St. Jones braced himself for the worst.

"The bad news is that you've got a depressed skull

fracture and a very serious concussion. If your brain swells anymore we'll have to take you in and open up your skull or you'll die. To put it in a nutshell, you're VSF, St. Jones. Very Severely Fucked. You've been shot in the head for Christ's sake. You belong in ICU You could die."

"You're just saying that to cheer me up, Doc." That's about the way St. Jones had figured it, but it was a shock to hear it from a doctor. "So what's the good news?"

"The good news is, I finally fucked the new ER nurse last night." Doctor Deep cackled and stood up carefully, so as not to bang his head on the low overhead. "And, St. Jones, if you find yourself in a long, dark tunnel with an intensely bright white light at the end, mention my name. They'll give you a deal. I've sent them a lot of business."

St. Jones had no way of knowing for sure if the Afro-haired, naked black woman that hovered over him in space was real.

"Did God look like Angela Davis?" he wondered. "Or is this what brain damage is like?"

"Talk to me, baby," she said, gently shaking him. "How's your head?"

"It hurts like a motherfucker," he said. "Are you, aaaa, real, or what?"

"Oh yeah, baby. I'm the real deal. My name's Lascivious X and I'm your personal nurse." Lascivious X had been an RN before she became a call girl to put herself through medical school. "Let's check you out." Lascivious X began by shining a light in each eye and then wrapping a blood pressure cuff around his arm. She pumped it up and held a stethoscope to his forearm, all the while straddling his naked body with her own. But for once, he just didn't care. St. Jones' head hurt so bad, it was the only part of his body he could locate with his eyes closed.

"Here, man. Doc said for you to take these." Lascivious X handed him some pills and a bottle of Calistoga.

He took his medicine and tried to sleep, but he cycled between pain and grief and guilt. To escape, St. Jones concentrated deeply on the pain and was surprised to discover that if he just got into it far enough, it didn't hurt. A fire cannot burn itself and a knife cannot cut itself and a pain couldn't hurt itself. Either he was channeling Basho, or St. Jones was delirious.

It was six days before he was open for business again. When he woke up, St. Jones had only one thing on his mind, and that was to find Lyla and the thermos bottle containing the forever bug. St. Jones was obsessed. He got up, went into the head, and looked in the mirror. He wasn't completely certain who it was, but he shaved him anyway. While he showered and dressed, Lascivious X fixed breakfast. By the time he finished eating, St. Jones had a plan.

BOLD

27

There's one emotion that's stronger than love, more powerful than hate, and able to leap ivory towers in a single bound. It feels better than a speedball, more exciting than adrenaline and more seductive than the Goddess herself. It's the premise of every Kung Fu movie and Western ever made and the motive behind easily ninety-nine percent of the first and second degree homicides on the planet throughout history. St. Jones was consumed with the most potent of all emotions. He was inflamed with God Almighty's Righteous Fucking Rage. There is nothing that feels better than to have reptilian rage flowing through your veins with the certain knowledge that God is on your side.

In the movies the hero is given the gift of righteous rage to absolve him from any guilt or responsibility for the trail of death and karmic debris he leaves in his wake. After all, the bad guys have kicked his woman, fucked his dog, and pissed on his blue suede shoes. A guy can only take so much, and righteous rage gets him one free ride on the wheel of necessity.

St. Jones wanted to kill Lyla more than he'd ever wanted to kill anyone before. In fact, he'd never wanted to kill anybody before. He considered it one of his flaws. It had always been forced upon him by the moment, a Commandment Zero situation, but it was never personal. But this was, and there was the added dimension of the guilt he felt for not having killed Lyla when he first knew he was going to have to, before she killed Nickie. He could forgive Lyla for shooting him. Twice, even. After all, she was crazy and he was an asshole. But not Nickie. He couldn't forgive Lyla for Nickie. This was a case of extreme prejudice. For Nickie, Lyla had to die. There was also the matter of the forever bug.

St. Jones sent Lascivious X to the payphone at the head of the pier to summon ChuChu, enforcer extraordinaire. It cost St. Jones the price of a blow job but Lascivious X was a working girl, and even though he wasn't using the equipment, he was taking up her time and time is money, honey. She didn't charge for what she did, just how long it took. She'd make a good doctor.

After Lascivious X called ChuChu, St. Jones had asked her to walk over to the Law Boat, which was the equivalent of about three city blocks away, and discreetly bring Winston back with her, without revealing that St. Jones was waiting there. Winston thought Lascivious X was going to fuck him right up until they arrived at the boat and he saw St. Jones. After Winston got over the shock of not getting laid, he noticed the bandage around St. Jones' head.

"Oh god, it really was you in that van, wasn't it?"

"Yeah, Winston. It was." St. Jones didn't think things

could get much worse, but he was wrong. Winston brought the dreaded news that the police found his prints on the inside of the van.

For the price of a straight fuck, Lascivious X ran another errand to Big G Supermarket and got dinner. During her absence, St. Jones told Winston the whole story, except the part about the forever bug. The stakes were just too high and the knowledge too heavy to begin generating loose ends. Once he told somebody about the forever bug, he either had to deal them in, or deal them out. Besides, can you imagine a lawyer with eternal life? No one would be safe.

St. Jones asked Winston to get him a clean car and park it at the restaurant and leave the keys with the bartender for Lascivious X. As Winston was leaving, St. Jones asked him to brief Birmingham about everything except the fact that he was about a thousand feet away. After Winston left, St. Jones lay down for a while to rest and think his plan through one more time before ChuChu arrived.

An hour later he felt the boat rock, and a moment later ChuChu poked his head into the foc's'le.

"Well finally. My own private dick has called me to his boudoir. Love the MASH drag. Does this mean you're finally ready to play doctor?"

"Not tonight ChuChu, but if I ever feel the urge, you're the one, baby. I hear you're the hottest."

"You got that right honey, and I hear you're the biggest. The girls tell me everything, you know." ChuChu beamed with pride.

"Jesus," St. Jones said to himself. They do tell him everything. Or, maybe not. ChuChu could have learned these things because of a special talent he had, the very talent that made ChuChu the right man for this job. Besides being the most feared enforcer in town, ChuChu could read lips. His older brother was born deaf and ChuChu had learned the skill as a child.

"ChuChu, I need you to stick to somebody like a hair on a grilled cheese sandwich, until she goes to a payphone to meet a schedule. It could take days. The call will be incoming. Take along a pair of binoculars and a cassette recorder so you can dictate as you read her lips." St. Jones peeled ten Frankies off his working roll. "Rent a van and take a friend. In fact, take two, so one of you can always be watching." St. Jones wrote the name and address on one of the hundred dollar bills. ChuChu kissed the money and touched it to his forehead and was on his way.

ChuChu was the ultimate operative. He was so bizarre no one ever thought that he might be the watcher, and he was so outrageously gay that he was the most feared enforcer in the West. When ChuChu started acting like he knew you in a special way, your social rep was pretty well shot unless you hung out south of Market. He was born rich and gay and was never in the closet for a minute and he was utterly fearless. He served papers on Jimmy the Weasel in Las Vegas after every tough guy on the West Coast passed on it, including St. Jones.

St. Jones knew Lyla would stay in touch with Leah. When he first met Lola, before she became Lyla, she was already involved with Leah. Sometimes Lola would disappear for days at a time and go to Leah. Other times Lola brought Leah home and they would party together. Lola didn't care if St. Jones fucked Leah as long as she was there, too. St. Jones never knew for sure if they intended for Leah to get pregnant or if it just happened, but they seemed pleased about it. But they never let him see the kid. In fact, St. Jones' very existence reminded them that it wasn't just theirs, which made it hard for them to maintain the myth that they lived. It was like "Who's Afraid of Virginia Woolf," except the kid was real. It was another reason why Lyla wanted to kill St. Jones. The big reason. If she killed him she would assume his power and Lyla and Leah's *folie a deux* would be complete. Life in San Francisco can be very complex.

St. Jones knew there was no use checking Lyla's credit card activity or accessing Leah's long distance phone records or searching the airline computers. Lyla knew all the usual methods that St. Jones would employ in a skip trace. But Lyla didn't know about ChuChu's unique ability. A good operative will always keep an ace in the hole, and follow Precept 73: Never tell anyone everything.

St. Jones knew Lyla would call Leah. And, he figured that Leah probably had a way of reaching Lyla in an emergency. One of his most effective methods of locating someone was to tap the phone of a person who knew where the subject was, and pressure them enough to cause them to make a phone call, or even physically lead St. Jones to the subject. But Lyla had seen St. Jones use this technique, and had undoubtedly cautioned Leah about it.

St. Jones went back to bed and slept straight though to morning, when Lascivious X woke him to give him his medication. Two days later, a little after eleven o'clock at night, St. Jones felt someone step onto the boat. He knew it was ChuChu. A moment later he knocked on the foc's'le bulkhead.

"Knock, knock. It's the little engine that could."

"Tell me you got good news for me, ChuChu." St. Jones struggled up into a sitting position. "Where is she?"

"I don't know. What I could get is on the tape." ChuChu handed St. Jones a small cassette recorder.

"You look like hell, ChuChu."

"That's going to cost you extra, St. Jones, cause I know it's true. You made me miss a lot of beauty sleep and it's a bitch eat bitch world out there, honey."

St. Jones pulled out the roll and peeled off ten hundreds. "This is for the job, and this is for the beauty sleep," he said, peeling off ten more.

"You got class, St. Jones. You know how to make a girl feel pretty." ChuChu stood up. "I haven't slept in three days so if that's it, then I'm going home."

"Sweet dreams, ChuChu."

St. Jones got out of his bunk and went into the galley and sat at the table and listened to the cassette recording of ChuChu's reading of Leah's half of the conversation. St. Jones could tell that Lyla did most of the talking by the length of the pauses. Leah talked about the kid and the fact that St. Jones was wanted by the police, and she talked about how much she missed Lyla. That was it. There was nothing else. It was a Precept 72 situation: Some days you get the elevator, and other days you get the shaft. St. Jones went back to his bunk and drifted off into frustrated sleep.

When St. Jones woke up, the monsters were acting jumpy and he had the feeling he'd been where he was too long. He also had the vague sensation that he had missed something. Lascivious X heard him get up and when he came out of the head, she had coffee waiting for him.

"Seen any strangers around, lately?"

"Yeah, now that you mention it, I have seen a couple

of guys around the last few days. They look like brothers."

"I've been here too long, LX." He had shortened it to LX, which sounded like Alex. "I need to find a new place for a few days. Someplace secure."

"I guess you could stay at my place. It's nice to have a guy around that's not trying to get a freebie off me all the time. That girl that died, she was your sweetie, wasn't she?"

"Yeah, I guess you could say that." St. Jones wasn't used to thinking of it that way. "Where do you live?"

"Between Gate 3 and town. You're gonna love it, St. Jones. It's you. It's even got a phone."

It had been raining when St. Jones woke up and now it began to really come down. Rain is good cover to move around in when you're trying not to be seen. Other people are occupied with trying to stay dry, and it's just about the only acceptable reason to run around in broad daylight with a hood covering your head. They gathered up their stuff in garbage bags and put on the slickers they found in the hanging locker by the hatch. They locked up the boat and took off in the driving rain. It was a twenty-minute walk.

The road dwindled to nothing amid a two-story pile of scrap metal, junk, and rubble that had been accumulating since WWII. It stretched for hundreds of yards. LX led St. Jones through the bushes into a tunnel in the rubble and wreckage. About thirty feet in, they came to an intact bus completely buried under the debris. It was an old municipal bus that had been sold for salvage. It had been converted into a comfortable hooch with an enclosed bedroom and bath at the back of the bus and a living room and kitchen in the front. It was nicely furnished and had all the comforts of home.

"One of the guys that works over at the salvage office ran a garden hose and an extension cord and a phone line over from the office. Old man Arquez doesn't know, but I take good care of the kid. I can use the phone from six in the afternoon to six in the morning, and weekends. No long distance calls, okay?"

St. Jones liked the idea of a built in cut-out. He liked the whole setup. "You're right LX. I like it. It's even got a view." He reached into his inside jacket pocket and came out with the roll and peeled off ten hundred-dollar bills. "Let me know when this wears off." This was better than the other way, paying for the time it takes to perform specific sexual acts. "Do people stop by?"

"Nobody drops by."

"Is there another way out of here?"

"Out the back door is a crawl space where the utilities come in. It comes out behind some bushes next to the building." LX began building a fire in a stove made from a 55-gallon steel drum. "Why don't you get out of those wet clothes and get in bed. You're a long way from well, pal. I'll make some tea."

St. Jones drank some tea and took his medicine and drifted off to sleep and slept until the following morning. LX was right. He was a long way from being well. Getting shot in the head wasn't as easy as it looked.

BOLD

28

St. Jones woke with the same nagging sensation that he was forgetting something, and as soon as he had coffee, he called ChuChu. It was the weekend and he could use the phone all day. There was no way to tell if it was day or night in the bus, but his watch read nine something.

The phone rang twelve times before he answered. "This better be good." ChuChu was in a bitchy mood.

"Morning, ChuChu. Sorry to wake you. I know it's early, but I forgot to ask you something the other night. Where was the pay phone that she used, and did you happen to get the number?"

"It was a booth at Upper Grant and Union. Hang on and I'll get the number." ChuChu put down the phone but St. Jones already knew what it was. Lyla was using the list. St. Jones' list.

"The number of the booth was 5551525."

"What time did she get the call?"
"Within a minute of 10 p.m."
"Thanks, ChuChu."

The list was of phone booth numbers scattered around the north end of the city. St. Jones had compiled it to make secure phone calls to associates when he was out of town. In her haste to get away, Lyla resorted to the list and since she felt safe using it, she must be moving around using payphones. It also meant that St. Jones could determine what number she would call next, and that was all he needed. Lyla had fucked up.

St. Jones needed a piece of equipment from his office. It was reasonable to assume that the Narx Brothers had the Law Boat under surveillance. He gave LX the keys and the security code and described the unit to her and where it was kept. He told her to take a garbage bag to disguise the unit's appearance and keep it dry, and to drive around for a while and make certain that no one followed her.

St. Jones found the list in his wallet. It was typed on a cut-down index card. The phone booth ChuChu had followed Leah to was eighth on the list, which meant she had started at the bottom with number ten and called three times so far. The incident on the bridge had happened nine or tens day ago, he wasn't precisely certain. That meant after the first call she was calling every three days. She would call the seventh number on the list the next night. It was a payphone in front of Alioto's at Fisherman's Wharf. St. Jones visualized the place and called the number, letting it ring until one of the crab sellers answered, verifying that the number was still good.

LX had gone to the Big G earlier to buy groceries. St.

Jones told her he would cook dinner and she thought that was a great idea. St. Jones loved to cook. He had eaten so many thousands of meals in restaurants that he relished any opportunity to cook. St. Jones had just finished prepping to cook almost anything Italian, when LX staggered onto the bus with the equipment. He gave her the choice of entree and she chose Bolognese, which he prepared while LX schlepped the car back to the Gate 5 lot and walked back in the rain.

LX took off her pea coat and shook the water out of her giant 'fro and sat down at the table he had prepared. "What's in the box I've been lugging around?"

"I'll show you after dinner." He poured the wine.

"I saw those guys I told you about. They were sitting in a white van in the lot at the head of the Law Boat pier."

"Did they follow you?"

"No, they just sat there when I left. I took a drive, anyway." She took a sip of wine and tasted the food. "Goddamn, St. Jones, this shit's illegal. Where'd you learn to cook like this?" She ate with gusto.

After dinner St. Jones opened the test set and clipped the leads to the phone line at the wiring block. He started out tapping phones the old fashioned way, climbing poles. As his studies of the telephone system progressed, he inevitably discovered the telco signaling test-set. With this device he could access the entire phone system and do anything an operator or a long-lines switcher could do, and he could do it from anywhere.

One of the more interesting features of the phone system is that every telephone in the world is tapped, from the inside. When you've been trying to reach a number for hours and you finally call the operator to see if the phone is out of order, they utilize that feature. It's called the verification loop. Every phone number has one, and it can be accessed with a signaling test set from anywhere. No more climbing poles and sneaking around the back of apartment buildings. He could even retrieve billing information.

He accessed the Ma Bell computer and got the verification loop code for the payphone at Alioto's and brought it up on a common line circuit. He checked his watch. It was after seven. He didn't think Lyla would call before 10 p.m. but he would monitor the rest of the night. Since he was killing time, he accessed Leah's long distance billing, but it was like he thought. No activity at all. They passed the evening playing gin and listening to dope deals and hot propositions and several calls that troubled them deeply. There was some weird shit going down in the city.

At a minute before ten an incoming call rang the payphone and St. Jones seated himself in front of the test set and put on his headphones. He recognized Leah's voice when she answered, and then he heard Lyla and broke out in a sweat, his pulse picking up a few beats. His body was afraid of her. While he listened to their conversation he began a trace and discovered that the call was coming from area code 503. Lyla was in Oregon. He hacked away at the number and came up with a 555 prefix. He was getting close. Lyla was talking about having seen Ry Cooder the night before, and then she abruptly said goodbye and hung up. She must have remembered how long it took him to trace a call. It was too bad about Lyla. Of all the graduates of the St. Jones Finishing Academy for Young Female Operatives, Lyla was by far the most talented. If the three-lettered spooks ever got hold of her they'd know just what to do.

St. Jones accessed the Portland telco database and cross-referenced the three-digit prefix into a location. The exchange was the Sellwood-Moreland district of Portland on the east side of the Willamette River.

St. Jones called the city desk of the Portland Oregonian on a common line circuit and asked if Ry Cooder was playing in town. There was no guarantee that they would have that information but it's amazing what you can learn that way. This time he was lucky. Ry Cooder had played at Reed College the night before. It wasn't much, but for St. Jones it was enough. He knew tricks that Lyla had never seen. Like how to find a stranger in a strange town with nothing to go on but righteous rage. He looked at Lascivious X and could see that no explanation was needed, so he gathered his gear and headed for the Gate 5 parking lot.

St. Jones pulled into the hangar next to the Cessna a little before midnight and went to work. The plane couldn't see the light of day until he changed the numbers again.

He landed at Hillsboro airport outside of Portland at dawn. The car rental booth didn't open until eight o'clock but the cafe opened at six, so St. Jones ordered a full breakfast and set about locating Lyla. St. Jones had been a full time tracker at one time and had been in this situation before, knowing that a subject was in a city but not knowing anything else, and he had developed a technique. Virtually all American cities have a key to them that can't be seen on a map but can be found in any local newspaper or by looking in the phone directory under Theaters. The key to cities are the movie theaters. When Loew's and others began building movie theaters across the nation in the twenties, they built them in the major neighborhoods as well as the central districts. Over the decades these neighborhood theaters have survived and are at the hub of small villages scattered within cities, with restaurants and bars and laundromats and markets and merchants. Therefore it is possible to break a city of a million people down into maybe a dozen small towns. Frequently the search can be narrowed even more by a knowledge of the subject's inclinations, and with one fragment of information, the search can be narrowed even more.

By the time the car rental counter opened, St. Jones had it narrowed down to five districts with a couple of strong possibilities. He drove toward Portland in an invisible Dodge Diplomat.

It was the morning rush hour and a bad time to search. St. Jones wanted to hit the first district around five-thirty or six o'clock when people were on the street for dinner. He saw a decent motel in Beaverton and decided to get off the street and lay up until late afternoon.

St. Jones slept until three, got up and showered and was on the road by four o'clock. It was rush hour, so he stayed off the freeways and re-familiarized himself with the city. He was using the Dodge like a dowsing rod, drifting from district to district, waiting for the front of the car to dip. It was at John's Landing, across the Willamette River from the Sellwood-Moreland district, that he felt the hot breath of the Muse of Pursuit on his cheek. When against odds a parking place opened up in front of him, he took it as an omen and pulled to the curb.

St. Jones had made a study of the omen. He had realized that every significant event in his life had been preceded by an omen that he failed to recognize at the time. He spent a lot of time reflecting on this, trying to remember something about the quality of those moments that would help him recognize them in the future. They were temporal precursors, like ripples in the ocean of time, spreading outward from an event in every direction, into the past and the future and even sideways into eternity.

St. Jones was irresistibly drawn to a fern bar at the corner he had just passed. It was the kind of place that he and Lola would have gone. The sun was down and the place was getting busy and he just managed to get a deuce by the restrooms before the place filled up, but he had a view of the entrance and the bar. He had been studying the menu about a minute when, over the top of it, he saw Lyla striding through the bar headed straight for his table. He braced his feet and got ready to spring. She was almost on top of him before she saw him.

"St. Jones!" She was beaming and seemed delighted to see him. "What a surprise. What are you doing here?" She leaned over and kissed him. "I haven't seen you in ages." She sat down across from him. "What are you doing here in Portland?"

The performance was beyond Lyla's theatrical ability. It was Lola, the good one, the one he liked, the one that liked him, the one he'd gotten involved with. He hadn't prepared himself for this eventuality. It hadn't even occurred to him. He had assumed that Lyla had completely dominated Lola and was calling the shots, so to speak. "I guess we're star-crossed, baby. What are you doing in Portland?"

"I asked you first," she said, playfully.

"Oh, you know me, always looking for a good restaurant." St. Jones scanned her eyes for a sign. "Speaking of food, have you had dinner?"

"No, that's what brought me out. May I join you?"

"Are you kidding? I'd fly half way around the world just to have dinner with you." He thought she must get hungry, always eating for two. "Are you alone?" It was his little joke.

"Yes." She smiled, giving him her "fuck me quick" look. "Are you?"

"Deeply." St. Jones knew where this was headed. He could smell the hormones. Lola was one of the all time hot fucks and so was Lyla. St. Jones had fucked both of them, separately and together. This could get kinky.

The specialty of the house was razor clams, which were delicious and the symbolism wasn't lost on St. Jones, but after two bottles of Chardonnay, Lola was looking good and Lyla was nowhere around. It was like the old days out on the road. They traveled well together, which was why Lola was out tonight. She liked the old days out on the trail.

She went into her purse and came out with a 10cc vial almost full of white powder. She dipped a small silver spoon into the vial and held it to her nose with such casualness that no one could have seen her do it. She did it again, like a sleight of hand trick, and passed it across the table palm down. Now it was his turn to commit a felony in full view of fifty people. It was a game they used to play. He bent forward like he was telling her a secret and passed the spoon under his nose with a ninja like move, laughed out loud and did it again.

"Bravo." Lola clapped her hands together and laughed and he could see her as a child and remembered why he got as close to her as he did. "Houdini lives. You're still the best."

He felt her knees against his and she was looking at him with her high beams on, and he was caught like a deer on a dark mountain road. At that moment a familiar warm vermilion light flooded the cockpit in his head and he shed his fatigue like climbing through a storm front. It was Nickie's coke. St. Jones would know it anywhere. If Lyla had that, then she also had the forever bug. St. Jones knew what he had to do.

"Why don't we go to your place, baby?"

BOLD

29

    This was easily the most dangerous thing St. Jones had ever done. He was headed to bed with a woman who had tried to kill him more times than he could remember. She'd shot him twice this month alone. How ironic that the hottest fuck of his life shared the same amazing body with a homicidal maniac intent on killing him. It was mythological. The monsters were flipping out and wanted no part of it, but St. Jones had no choice. He had to play it out. He knew that Lyla had Nickie's thermos, but he wasn't sure that Lola even knew about it.

    She had rented a place in the neighborhood about four blocks away and they decided to walk. He took a route past his car to see if she recognized it. If she had spotted him before he came into the restaurant, then he was in fact, playing her game. He had to be careful. Lyla was smart and utterly ruthless. He saw nothing in her eyes or body language that indicated she knew it was his car.

But it could have been Lyla that spotted him on the street, and Lola that walked into the bar. They stopped at a market and bought a bottle of Zinfandel and went on to her place. It was a furnished garage apartment set back from the street behind the main house. It began to rain as they arrived.

St. Jones opened the wine and poured two glasses while Lola began building a fire. At least he hoped it was Lola. It was a subtle change, but he had always been able to tell before. But it happened fast. The first time he saw her switch, they were crossing a street. When they stepped off the curb she was Lola, and by the time they got to the other side, she was Lyla. It happened suddenly, just before the median. He felt safe enough at that moment, though. Lola was catting for a fuck and he thought Lyla might be, too. One for the road. He didn't think Lola would let Lyla make a move on him until after the sex. They sat on the couch in front of the fire, sipping their wine, the very picture of civility, but he knew Lyla would try to kill him before the night was over.

She got the vial from her purse and dumped out a pile of Nickie's powder on the glass tabletop. "I've missed you, St. Jones." She got out a compact and, removing a razor blade, began making lines.

He kept his eye on the blade. "I've missed you too, baby." He didn't want to call her by the wrong name. "We were good together."

"Especially in bed." She snorted a couple of lines with a straw from her compact and passed it to St. Jones. "Where'd we go wrong, St. Jones?"

"I don't know, baby." His pulse picked up a couple of beats. He didn't like bending down over the table while she had the razor blade in her hand. "Everybody's free up to the neck." Precept 95.

She laughed. "You always did have a way with words."

She put the blade back in her compact and slipped it in her purse. The sound of serious rain filled the room. Oregon rain. He knew she was thinking the same thing he was. It would mask the sound.

Lola had been gently tweaking her left nipple through her sweater and now reached over and began stroking St. Jones with her fingernails. She took a sip of wine and slid between his knees and began unbuttoning his Levis, putting St. Jones into a state of high anxiety. He gently but firmly took her head between his hands in a caressing manner, checking her hair for weapons, ready to snap her neck if she tried to bite his dick off. It was the kind of thing Lyla would do, and St. Jones had a lot to lose. He was walking a tight rope between pleasure and fear, loving every minute and fearing every second.

After a while she got up and took off her sweater and walked around the room turning off lights. Then she took off her Levis and stood warming herself in front of the fireplace. The sight was inspiring, especially for an ass man like St. Jones. He stood and began to undress, wondering where Lyla had stashed the gun. She might try using a knife because of the neighbors–he'd foolishly taught her how–but she had really taken a liking to that gun of hers. He needed to stay close to her, so he'd have a chance if she went for it.

He went to the fireplace and reached around her, cupping her breasts in his hands. The last time he'd seen her, he'd been reaching around her from behind, trying to strangle her, and she had been trying to shoot him. She put her hands on the mantel and thrust her ass back against him. She was wet. Scanning the mantel for weapons, he guided himself in. He liked this arrangement, and not just for the view. She was in the regulation position for searching and handcuffing. He gripped her pelvis and sank himself in her to the hilt.

"I want you to deep fuck me, St. Jones." She adjusted her feet and arched her back. "Fuck me like it was forever."

He didn't like the sound of that, but the sight of himself sliding in and out of her perfect ass back-lit by the fire was something he would remember in the next life. Bad choice of words considering the nature of the game and the stakes involved. This was high stakes poker. He smiled at the pun.

After a while, his thighs began to burn and Lola's knees were shaking, and he knew they would have to change position soon and he would lose his advantage. But soon he wouldn't be able to stand. "Let's move to the floor."

"Ooooh, good," she panted. "Fuck me from the front so I can see, too." She was so hot her voice was quavering. She picked up the vial and spooned the coke directly to her nose, rocks and all. She arranged herself on the rug in front of the fireplace while he double hit himself on both sides. He knelt between her legs, and hooking his elbows under her knees, lifted her legs in the air. The position also gave him a tactical advantage.

She guided him in. "Ooooh God," she said, as he penetrated her. "Oooooo God, yes."

Raising up on his knees, he leaned forward on his hands and began to slowly deep stroke her. If she wanted to see it, he would show it to her. As Nickie's coke began to surge through them, Lola's eyes lost horizontal hold and she began whipping her head from side to side, moaning continuously. He knew she would come soon if he kept up the pace and he was starting to feel it creeping up, too. The danger would begin when the pleasure ended. He had two excellent reasons to drag it out as long as possible.

He needed a rest and rolled onto his back taking her to the top in the move. He would let her do the work for a while. And did she ever. She went after it like a jungle cat on a fresh kill, growling deep in her throat, her tits swinging wildly, her nails digging into his chest as she slammed herself against him. He could feel blood running from his pecs but he didn't stop her because the pain was helping him maintain control of himself, as well as keep track of her hands. She was flailing away with such ferocity that he was afraid she would damage herself, but he remembered Nickie and hoped Lyla would kill herself on it.

She was speaking in tongues now, spazzing out and beginning to lose coordination, so he rolled back on top and began pounding her with a vengeance. A sound started low in her throat and, gaining pitch, turned into a rising wail and finally a blood-curdling scream that he stifled with his hand. She arched her ass off the floor and slammed herself against him again and again, as she dug her nails into his back. He could feel blood trickling down his sides and rage flared in him. It would never be easier to kill her than at that moment and he looked at her throat and felt his hands tremble at the thought of it, but he didn't know where the thermos was. As soon as Lyla showed up, he would ask her, and he knew she wasn't far away, but until then, he had to keep his priorities straight. He had to play it out. This was the way to Lyla. He took his hand off her mouth before he succumbed to temptation. She gasped for breath, and blood mixed with sweat dripped onto her from the rivulets running down his sides.

"Fuck me in the ass," she gasped. She was so hot she was blithering. "Fuck me in the ass. Please, oh please, fuck me in the ass." She practically bucked him off. He had seen this before. It was Lyla, wanting to come out. Grabbing the vial, she dumped it all on the table and snorted right off the glass top and came up with white all over her nose. "Please fuck me in the ass. Please, please, please," she begged.

"Okay baby, just hang on." He bent over the table and plowed through the pile like a pig, while she climbed up on the couch.

She kneeled on the cushions and leaned against the back of the couch, presenting her ass to him. He gathered as much saliva as he could manage, and smeared it on the head of his dick, then dipped his wet fingertips into the pile of coke on the table and rubbed what stuck to them onto himself. He nuzzled it against her ass and gently began working it in. She gasped and groaned and slowly worked her pelvis, and he watched himself disappear a few millimeters at a time. The sight was so sexy, St. Jones was afraid he was going to blow it right there. But that would be unacceptable. Not only would he be passing on the forever bug, but he might knock her up, and everybody knows that's where lawyers come from.

St. Jones knew that this was where Lyla lived, and that this would bring her forward, and her body was already beginning to feel different, like another woman. He had never figured out how the linkage had been established, but he had seen it many times before. When she wanted it this way, it was Lyla wanting to get laid. And when she got laid, she stayed. After she came, he knew she would attack him, because as much as she loved it, Lyla hated St. Jones for making her come, which wouldn't be long for either one of them.

He knew it was Lyla he was fucking now, but he couldn't help it. He was going to come in spite of himself. He could feel it getting close, and when she sensed him letting up slightly, she pumped even harder. It would be a victory for her to make him come first. But he thought of Nickie, and began slamming away at Lyla, fucking to kill. She began screaming and he shoved her face into the cushion and continued ramming away. She was bucking like a mustang and he heard the scream of a wild animal in her throat as her asshole gripped his dick again and again and again, and then, like a punch rising all the way up from the floor, St. Jones came with murder in his heart.

Her hand moved so fast he never saw the ice pick, but he felt her body torque with the strike and he instinctively moved just enough to take the blow in his right thigh. She had planned to drive it through his scrotum, and when his hands dropped, the next strike would be straight up under the jaw, up through the tongue and pallet and into the brain, just like he taught her. What could he have been thinking? He grabbed her wrist before she could strike again, and reaching around with his left arm, caught her neck between his forearm and biceps and began clamping down in the sleeper hold. A warm numbness was spreading through his thigh. He still had Lyla impaled on his dick like a bayonet. He knew if he let her go she would have her gun in seconds. It was a Greek stand off.

"Okay Lyla, here's the deal." He was whispering to keep from screaming. "I'm going to put you to sleep in a minute. Whether or not you wake up again is up to you. What I want is the bag you took, contents intact, and I want you to stop trying to kill me. What I'm willing to do is let you live tonight, and I won't testify against you for the murder, and I'll even throw in fifty large so you can go work on your tan." He thought he'd try a little of everything.

She stopped struggling at the mention of money and thought for a minute. "I don't have it with me," she rasped. It was Lyla's voice, deeper, more driven.

"Where is it?" He was still breathing hard.

"San Francisco."

St. Jones thought for a minute. "I'll meet you at midnight tomorrow night at the Playpen." They had used the Playpen many times. He knew she still had a key. He tightened his press around her neck. "What's it gonna be, Lyla?"

"Okay," she gasped through the choke hold.

"Sweet dreams, baby." He tightened his arm against her carotid artery and she began to struggle fiercely, but ten seconds later she went limp in his arms. He maintained the hold a few more seconds, until he felt her asshole relax and her warm piss running down his legs. Another ten seconds and she'd be dead, maybe even five. He fought the temptation to end it then and there, and released the hold, taking the ice pick from her limp hand. He pulled out of her abruptly and stepped back, letting her slump over the back of the couch. He pushed her over onto the cushions, then went into the bathroom to wash off the blood and the piss and the shit. He knew she would be out for a while. He bandaged his thigh and poured peroxide onto his chest and back and then went back to the couch and put on his clothes. St. Jones gazed at her with a mixture of lust and loathing.

That had been absolutely the kinkiest fuck of his life, a moment presided over by Kali. Sex and death were truly linked, just like the Hindus said. He searched his jacket for the codeine. Lyla and codeine just seemed to go together, too. Covering her with an afghan, he put a log on the fire and limped out the door into the pouring rain.

He parked the Dodge Diplomat at the rent-a-car parking, wiped down the steering wheel and handles, and limped in the pouring rain through the gate to transient parking and climbed into the cockpit. He was soaked. His mind was roaring from the coke and the sex and violence, and his leg had passed from warm numbness into bone deep pain. Lyla had rammed the ice pick into him to the hilt.

St. Jones marveled at the irony. So did the monsters who were huddled in the plane waiting for him.

He filed an Instrument Flight Rules flight plan over the radio and changed into dry clothes while he waited, idling on the tarmac. When clearance came, he lied about the visibility and took off in a blinding rain. It was an uncontrolled airport after 10 p.m. His weather briefing had said icing at 7,000 feet and tops at 24,000 feet, and when he reached 25,000 feet, he could see stars. He was on the ground at Sebastopol by 3 a.m. and back at the magic bus by four. He limped in and woke up LX and had her move the car back to the Gate 5 lot. When she returned, she dressed his wounds.

"Goddamn, St. Jones," LX said as he undressed. "Was anybody killed?"

"Only me."

"If you live, you gotta take me for a ride on that thing one of these nights." LX was bandaging the claw marks. "I gotta find out for myself what makes a woman do something like this."

"I promise, LX, but not tonight. It's in a bad mood, and I'm not feeling that good myself."

"You're a lucky mothafucker, St. Jones." She was cleaning the wound in his right thigh. "That ice-pick missed the femoral artery by about a millimeter. You gotta take good care of this. If it gets infected, it could cost you your leg or even kill you." She got up and went to the fridge, returning with an ampule and a syringe and an alcohol pad.

"What's that?" he asked, suspiciously. "Don't give me any pain killers or anything that will fuck me up. I gotta play in the big game tomorrow night."

"It's only antibiotics, baby," she said. "And considering the condition your sad ass is in, I'd like to get a little money down on the other team." She rolled him on his stomach and gave him a shot.

They smoked a couple of joints and curled up together under the covers and went to sleep around dawn. He slept for twelve hours.

LX was sitting on the bed looking at him when he opened his eyes. "You look like shit, baby."

"Did they teach you that at medical school?" He couldn't feel his leg until he tried to move it, and then he wished he hadn't.

"I think you ought to phone this one in, baby." Lascivious X looked at St. Jones like he was circling the drain.

BOLD

30

The rain that had been falling in Portland the night before began to come down on Sausalito. The monsters knew St. Jones was going to meet Lyla and would have no part of it and stayed behind with Lascivious X. They preferred the company of women. St. Jones arrived about 11 p.m. and found a parking spot that gave him a view of the head of Gate 1 pier. He had taught Lyla to always show up early and watch. About 11:30 p.m. he saw her Volkswagen pull into the lot. She waited until almost midnight before getting out of the car and walked swiftly across the lot with her head bent down against the rain, headed for the Playpen.

St. Jones waited until she was out of sight before he got out of his car and began to limp out on the pier. He had taken enough codeine to take the edge off the pain but not enough, he hoped, to slow him down too much. The Dexie hearts would make up the difference.

St. Jones pulled his watch cap down over his ears and crouched in the cold rain, watching the Playpen. He knew only one of them was going to walk back up the pier. If it was him, he figured he would go get Randy and do it again, just like with Screaming Mimi. There was no point in wasting a perfectly good body. There was an endless supply of fucking assholes out there, waiting for service. Satisfied that Lyla didn't have an accomplice lurking in the darkness, he edged out of the shadows and carefully shuffled down the gangplank, which was almost level. It was just past high tide. The rain was coming down hard now and he was operating mostly by feel.

It hit him so hard and fast, St. Jones never saw it coming, but as he was propelled backwards over the rail and into the freezing water of the bay, he caught a glimpse of the huge creature silhouetted against the sky. He was black, over six feet tall, with fangs and terrible breath, and St. Jones had seen him before. It was Murphy, Birmingham's Great Dane. His favorite trick was to rear up on his hind legs to his full height of over six feet and put his paws on your shoulders and lick your face. Birmingham was very proud of this trick. But that was no longer important. St. Jones was on the Farallon Express, headed out of the bay at eight knots, in forty-five degree water, in the middle of the night, at the height of a storm, and VSF going in. It didn't look good.

He remembered a drawing Gilbert Shelton had done on the wall of a coffeehouse in Austin of two guys falling through space toward the patchwork quilt of the ground thousands of feet below, apparently thrown from an airplane. Not only did they not have parachutes but their hands and feet were bound, and they were wrapped in chains and had bombs with burning fuses strapped to them and were covered with dynamite and one guy is saying to the other, "Here's my plan."

That's the thing about man. He doesn't know when to quit. Sisyphus knew that no matter how many times he rolled the boulder up that mountain, it was bound by the immutable laws of gravity and karma to roll down the other side. It was an analog of life, by the day, by the year, and by the lifetime. And yet, in the certain knowledge of this, he goes ahead and does it anyway, again and again and again. It's the only true distinction of the species. That, and he's the only creature in the kingdom that will commit hands-on suicide. It's the ultimate in bipolar behavior. It's his way of telling God, "You can't fire me. I fucking quit!" Man is either the missing link that he's searching for, or he's the link that missed.

St. Jones watched the lights on shore getting farther away. He pulled his knees up to his chest and clasped his arms around his legs to conserve his body heat. It would give him a few more minutes of life. A case in point. A few more minutes of pain and fear and loathing. What a dirty fucking trick. It just didn't seem right that it should end like this, with St. Jones just drifting away into the night, without a trace, knocked into the water by a dog named fucking Murphy, and Lyla, warm and dry with a lifetime supply of lifetime supplies. On the other hand, it did have a certain resonance. It would seem that one shouldn't fuck with Mother Nature. Nickie had, and died an ironic death. St. Jones had, and was breaking new ground in irony by the minute. Maybe that's what kills you when you can live forever. Irony.

Karma was all starting to make sense, now. He was

like an astronaut in zero gravity, and every action he made caused an opposite and equal reaction. When he set something in motion, it set him in motion, too, and in zero gravity desire alone was enough to set the thinker and the thought moving. He knew he was dying. He was understanding too many things. Soon his life would begin passing before his eyes and the things that he couldn't let slide would take him to the circumstances of his next life. It was like the Hotel California. You can check out anytime you like, but you can never leave. Precept 74.

It would seem like we could make more progress if we could just remember why we were doing this. Why did we have to swim the River Lethe and forget everything at birth? What was the point? Or, was that the point? Are we all figments of God's imagination with every force of nature aligned to keep us from this knowledge? If we all recognized our true nature, would the world stop?

"I'm three, three times seven, and that makes twenty-one, and it ain't nobody's is-ness but my own," he sang out loud to the rain. He was thinking like a born again Hindu and thought he could hear the beating of wings. He didn't even hurt anymore. In fact, he couldn't feel his body at all. Hypothermia wasn't such a bad way to go, really. He was just on the verge of understanding the unifying principle underlying everything, the one word that explained it all, when he banged his butt on a rock. Opening his eyes, he let go of his legs and, stretching them out, discovered he was in water only three feet deep.

His eyes had become used to the dark and there was a certain amount of ambient light that came from the lights of San Francisco across the bay illuminating the low clouds and rain. He struggled onto feet he couldn't feel, and staggered out of the water to the edge of a small rocky beach covered with driftwood and debris. He listened to the foghorns, each of which had a unique pitch and pattern, and realized he was still inside the Golden Gate. He figured he was at the bottom of the cliff along the north side of the Golden Gate passage, below the old road from Sausalito to Fort Barry. He had been caught in an eddy current that probably only existed for a short time each tide. A little earlier or later and he would have swirled right past the beach on his way out to sea. The cliff behind the narrow beach went straight up for three hundred feet and he was only slightly better off than before, but he would take it. Anything to roll that stone up the mountain one more time.

When he saw the flash and heard the pop he knew what it was, but his mind refused delivery on the obvious. When he landed on his butt, three lemons came up on the screen, and he knew the only possible answer. The dog that had knocked St. Jones into the bay had knocked Lyla in first, when she opened the door to the Playpen. At that instant, St. Jones became enlightened. He experienced Satori. He saw the whole fucking elephant. He had seen the hand of God moving, and He cheats at cards.

But St. Jones wouldn't have long to enjoy this new found spiritual understanding if he didn't manifest a defense in the gross physical plane. This was obviously why God made guns and if he didn't get to his fast, he was going to be leaving his meat suit at the crime scene. As he struggled with the zipper on his flight jacket, he discovered that the impact of the bullet that knocked him down had broken his left collarbone through his vest.

The next shot passed so close to his head, he could

feel the heat from the bullet. Lyla was gifted at violence. She was almost on top of him when his hand found the grip of the .45 and he drew toward her charging body, firing just as she did. He saw Lyla change direction from the impact of the 230-grain slug just as his eyes slammed shut from the muzzle flash and powder blast of her Magnum. He was momentarily blinded but he kept firing until the slide locked open, screaming at the top of his lungs in fear and rage.

When he could see again, St. Jones crawled over to Lyla on his hands and knees. He had hit her several times and she was a mess. He searched the area for the thermos, but wasn't surprised when he didn't find it. She probably let go of it when Murphy knocked her into the water. He grabbed Lyla by the hair and dragged her down to the water and launched her onto a back wave, and watched her swirl away from shore as the current picked her up and she was on her way out the Golden Gate to the Pacific Ocean. Precept 41: No corpse, no cops.

St. Jones field-stripped the Colt, replacing the barrel with a spare that he carried in his shoulder rig. One of the many splendid features of the Colt 1911-A. He loaded a fresh magazine and holstered the weapon and, wincing in pain, threw the used barrel as far as he could into the bay. As he walked up the beach, he found Lyla's gun and was about to throw it into the water, when he realized that he shouldn't close out that option. It was the gun that killed Nickie. St. Jones held the weapon by the checkered grip with two fingers and slipped it into the inside pocket of his jacket.

His legs were filled with pins and needles and his feet burned like he was walking on fire as blood began flowing in them again, and along with sensation came pain. St. Jones' leg hurt to the bone and his head felt like a monkey drum, spinning and pounding at the same time. He searched around in the debris on the beach and found most of a sheet of plywood and some plastic film.

St. Jones made a lean-to with the plywood and, wrapping himself in the plastic, crawled under. Soon, he began to shake uncontrollably and thought he would break his teeth, but after a while the seizure subsided, leaving him warm and feeling euphoric and he fell into a profoundly deep, dreamless, exhausted sleep. The rain was intense, but he was oblivious to it as it washed away every trace of what had happened on the beach.

When St. Jones woke, it was getting light and raining even harder. He hurt from the top of his head to the tips of his toes. Besides hypothermia and his trauma injuries, he was suffering from hydrostatic shock. Since the body is mostly water, it's like a water balloon and when you thump it hard enough, like with a bullet, the shock wave travels throughout every cell in the body. It can kill you.

He crawled on his hands and knees to the Sausalito end of the beach and struggled through the underbrush onto a very steep, densely-wooded slope. Stumbling through the trees, he ran into a rope that almost brought him down. It was waist high and tied from tree to tree, going up the sixty-degree slope. It had been put there by fishermen to gain access to the beach and it was his salvation. He could never have made it without it, even without the rain, which had turned the hillside into a mud field. Each time he tried to use his left arm, he felt like he was being stabbed in the shoulder, and while his right leg was structurally sound, the pain was breathtaking. He thought he had some other damage, too. He had pain he couldn't match up with the injuries that he knew about. But he had one good arm and one good leg and one awesome desire to get up that slope.

St. Jones thought about Sisyphus as he struggled up the incline, and felt like a true brother of the rolling stone by the time he reached the roadside, maxed out from exhaustion and pain, covered head to toe in mud. But the rain was coming down with biblical intensity and he was freshly washed in only a minute or two.

It was full daylight now but there was no traffic on the little-used road and he began lurching toward Sausalito, like Frankenstein fleeing the angry villagers. After a while a restaurant supply delivery truck headed from the Fort Barry Yacht Club to Sausalito took mercy on a poor wretch beside the road in a storm and St. Jones was at the Gate 1 parking lot in fifteen minutes.

BOLD

31

If St. Jones' theory was right, Lyla could have dropped the bag on the deck of the Playpen as she was knocked overboard. In spite of his condition, he knew he had to check it out. He started down the pier dragging his right leg, marveling at the intensity of the rain. Noah would have been impressed. As he neared the boat, he remembered Murphy and began to laugh in spite of the pain. He didn't know whether to shoot the fucking dog or take him out for a steak dinner, but no matter what, St. Jones wasn't going in the water again. He would sink like an anvil.

He carefully shuffled down the gangplank, which was much steeper now, keeping an eye out for Murphy. St. Jones searched the deck for the bag or anything like it, but found nothing. He tried the door and found it locked, which he thought curious. The dog wasn't that smart. Searching his jeans, St. Jones was surprised he still had his keys. He unlocked the door and, stepping to the side, opened it.

Nothing. Thinking the dog must be asleep on the waterbed, he lurched inside and closed the door. St. Jones checked every room, but Murphy was gone.

St. Jones went into the bathroom and undressed and took a long hot shower and thought about the puzzle. He decided Birmingham must have left Murphy on the boat the night before, while he went out to dinner. Birmingham did that sometimes when his wife came into town with the dog. That would explain the locked door. The dog had only been there a few hours, at high tide, on the one night in all of eternity that he and Lyla would choose the Playpen for a showdown.

After his body temperature was restored to near normal, he wrapped a towel around himself and went into the kitchen to put on hot water for coffee. That's when he saw it, sitting on the counter. He would know it anywhere. It was Nickie's bag. The one she brought from Colombia. The one with the thermos. The one Lyla took. It was wet like it had been sitting out in the rain. Lyla must have dropped it when Murphy hit her, and Birmingham found it when he came to get the dog, and left it on the counter when he locked up. Occam's Razor.

When St. Jones opened the bag he found two thermoses. Unscrewing the top of one, he found the mouth of the bottle to be stretched with latex rubber and secured to the neck with mono-filament nylon. The seal appeared to be intact and he figured it to be the Forever Bug. He replaced the outer lid and opened the second bottle. It was almost full of Nickie's finest. She was a class act, and he would think of her every day for the rest of his life, and quite fondly while the coke lasted. He found some rice in the kitchen and added a handful to the thermos to act as a desiccant and screwed the lid on tight.

In a zippered inside pocket, he found an aluminum 35mm film-can with a yellow top. He figured it was Nickie's lab notes. The film was probably undeveloped, as a security measure. He would check it later in a dark room. St. Jones wrung out his soaked clothes and put them back on and headed back up the pier in the rain. He drove to Lascivious X's, and dragging one leg, with one arm hanging limp, staggered into the Magic Bus.

"See, I told you you'd get killed."

"You should see the other guy."

"You should see yourself, baby. Is it over?"

"Yeah, mostly." St. Jones went into the bathroom and began stripping out of his wet clothes.

"You look like hell, St. Jones."

"I can still smell the sulfur, baby." He lay down on the bed and covered up. "I nearly died from hypothermia, LX. It's not a bad way to go. I've also got a broken collarbone and probably some other stuff. I'm generally VSF. Hand me my wallet."

"Fuck your wallet, St. Jones." She got on the bed and pulled back the cover and went to work on him, treating and bandaging his various injuries. She discovered a broken rib and torn cartilage from another bullet he never felt. It must have been that last flash he saw. "You need your own fucking ambulance, St. Jones. I've known you less than two weeks and you been shot, stabbed, and shot a couple of more times. And then there's all those claw marks. Is it always like this?"

"LX, someday I'm gonna wake up from this nightmare and it'll all seem like a bad dream." He was afraid he was already awake, but it sounded good. "There's something important I need for you to do. In the inside pocket of my jacket is a gun. Dry it off with a hair drier and be careful not to get your prints on it. Use two fingers on the checkered part of the grip and put it in an old, used brown paper grocery bag. I need you to get that bag into the back of that white van."

"The two guys that look like brothers, right?"

"That's them. If you can get that taken care of, I'll take care of you big time."

"Take it off your mind, baby." Lascivious X gave St. Jones a couple of shots in the butt. One was antibiotics and the other was a Morphine/Seconal cocktail. In a few minutes the heavens opened and allowed him to slip away, leaving behind his pain and sorrow and guilt. He slept for 24 hours. When he woke, LX was cuddled against his back and the monsters were snuggled around them, and the brown paper bag was in the back of the white van. He didn't ask her how she did it.

The next day, Lascivious X brought Winston to the Magic Bus. Over lunch, St. Jones gave Winston instructions to form a trust for Leah's kid. He also gave him Nickie's full name and asked him to do a public records search. He was looking for family that might be heirs. St. Jones figured he and Nickie were still partners. He also had Winston set up an education trust for LX. He thought he would need a personal physician someday. Like Dr. Watson, but with inside plumbing.

He saved the best for last. "Winston, the gun that killed Nickie is in a wadded up brown paper bag in the back of the Narx Brothers' van." He handed Winston a shopping bag with his bulletproof vest. "This vest is full of matching bullets and LX took a Polaroid of my wounds, which match the vest. It's in the bag, too. Lyla's prints are on the weapon. What if you float the story with Inspector Falcone that the Narx Brothers were the ones who shot Nickie and me? I never saw the shooter, you know, and the Narx Brothers had motive, they were in town at the time, and they don't know it, but they're in possession of the murder weapon. In the process of proving that they didn't do it, they'll have to prove that I didn't do it either."

"That's very sexy, St. Jones. I like it. I can work with that. We've got more on them than they've got on you."

The crisp Sierra air agreed with St. Jones, and the hot baths were slowly repairing the damage he had sustained. Lascivious X had driven him to the secret mountain laboratory on his Harley, spent a couple of days satisfying her curiosity, and caught a ride back to the waterfront. She didn't know it, but St. Jones had given her the gift that keeps on giving. He'd have to tell her someday, if it turned out to be true.

Before they left Sausalito, LX had gone to the Russian Hill studio and retrieved St. Jones' little black book of magic numbers. He had given it a lot of thought and knew that what he did next would have far reaching consequences. After a very careful review of the options, he arranged a meeting with three wealthy Berkeley Ph.D.s who lived in extreme seclusion. St. Jones had known them for many years. They were part of a network of benevolent psychedelic illuminati. In the sixties they had come into possession of the fabled Yugoslavian ET (ergotamine tartrate) and had manufactured tens of millions of doses of real LSD and become deeply wealthy and extremely high. They saw themselves as cosmic undercover agents, working for Mr.

Big. Who knows? Based on their past exploits, St. Jones believed they were bold enough to deal with what was at stake, and that their hearts were in the right place. And, they had the money.

They met at a gold rush era hotel seventy-five miles from the lodge. St. Jones followed them on his Harley the last fifty miles of their route to make certain no one else was following them. Over lunch he told them the story, presented the thermos, Nickie's notes, and his deal, which was simple; one million to a Hong Kong corporate account, access to the product, and ten points after it went into profits. Put your money on the table and drive it off the lot. They talked amongst themselves for fifteen minutes and made the transfer of funds from the payphone in the lobby. St. Jones verified the transfer from the phone in the men's room fifteen minutes later. They left with the goods, their eyes burning with purpose. He hoped he had done the right thing.

St. Jones stayed on at the secret mountain laboratory. In fact, he bought it. It was the right thing to do. That way, Leo could do what he did best without the pressure of having to balance the books. Things would go on just as they were. It was the monsters' idea, really. They liked the mountains and the hot springs a lot.

St. Jones spent his days walking the trails and thinking, and his nights soaking in the baths, thinking. He had a lot to think about. His old life had ended the night the Angel Michael came to his door. St. Jones had since acquired great wealth, and if Nickie was right, a vastly extended life, but his epiphany in the bay and subsequent satori on the beach had rendered the usual life pursuits largely meaningless.

A few days after Girl arrived to become his chief of staff, they were in the bar one night listening to Leo rant about a recent outrageous injustice, when it occurred to St. Jones that people shouldn't be allowed to get away with shit like that. He might just have to straighten it out. Anonymously, of course. That was the nature of "The Work." Anonymous, third party, pro bono revenge. It was very satisfying work, and there was no end to the number of fucking assholes out there, waiting for service. Now that he owned the lodge, maybe he would convene a meeting of the Order of the Bold Stroke, the Sly Pass, and the Ace in the Hole. Who knows where that might lead? It was like Precept 88 said: Your being attracts your life.

Mr. Shannon is a former San Francisco private investigator whose clients included politicians, entertainment figures and government agencies. He has over twenty-five years experience as a pilot, flying charters of opportunity in Asia and Latin America. He lives in a far away place with a strange sounding name.

Discretion being what it is, he writes under a pseudonym.

The Alchemy of Love

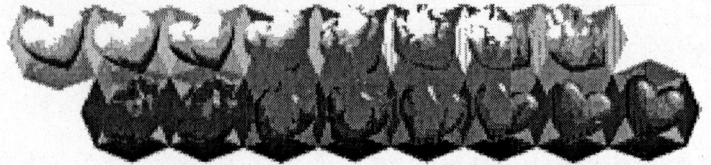

A collaborative endeavor between
author **Elizabeth Engstrom**
and artist **Alan M. Clark**

This critically-acclaimed volume fictionalizes the idealization of romantic love and how it translates to the reality of human experience. A volume of eight pieces of fiction and eight paintings, Engstrom "literates" four of Clark's disturbing and surreal works of art, while Clark illustrates four of Engstrom's dark and haunting stories.

ISBN 0-9666272-2-9

Available only in a hard-cover, signed, limited edition of 500 copies for $49.95 plus $5.00 s&h on orders of any size.*

Make checks payable to TripleTree Publishing. Mastercard and Visa orders may be faxed to 541-484-5358. Please include credit card Number, expiration date, and signature.

*Foreign s&h rates vary. Dealer inquiries welcome.

TripleTree Publishing ✻ P.O. Box 5684, Eugene OR 97405
(541) 338-3184 ✻ TripleTree@aol.com

The SLY Pass

Follow the continuing adventures of Revelations St. Jones as he gets away with more than any private dick has a right to.

Volume two in a series of three.
Set for publication Fall, 2000.

Reserve your copy today
via phone, fax or e-mail.

TripleTree Publishing ✻ P.O. Box 5684, Eugene OR 97405
(541) 338-3184 ✻ TripleTree@aol.com